Mr. Fred L. Fagin
P.O. Box 132
Coopers Mills, ME 04341

PRETTY DEAD

A JACK McMORROW MYSTERY

Other books by Gerry Boyle

Jack McMorrow Mystery Series
Deadline
Bloodline
Lifeline
Potshot
Borderline
Cover Story
Home Body
Once Burned

PRETTY DEAD

A JACK McMORROW MYSTERY

GERRY BOYLE

ISLANDPORT PRESS

This is a work of fiction. Names, characters, places, and incidents either are the product of the author's imagination or are used fictitiously. Any resemblance to actual events or persons, living or dead, is entirely coincidental.

PRETTY DEAD
First Islandport edition / December 2016

ISBN: 978-1- 944762-04-9
Library of Congress Control Number: 2016931852

Islandport Press
P.O. Box 10
Yarmouth, Maine 04096
www.islandportpress.com
books@islandportpress.com

Publisher: Dean Lunt
Cover Design: Teresa Lagrange, Islandport Press
Cover image courtesy of iStock / Sigarru

Printed in the USA

PRETTY DEAD

A JACK McMORROW MYSTERY

GERRY BOYLE

ISLANDPORT PRESS

PRETTY DEAD
First Islandport edition / December 2016

All Rights Reserved.

Copyright © 2003 by Gerry Boyle

ISBN: 978-1- 944762-04-9
Library of Congress Control Number: 2016931852

Islandport Press
P.O. Box 10
Yarmouth, Maine 04096
www.islandportpress.com
books@islandportpress.com

Publisher: Dean Lunt
Cover Design: Teresa Lagrange, Islandport Press
Cover image courtesy of iStock / Sigarru

Printed in the USA

For Vic, as always

ACKNOWLEDGMENTS

Several people generously assisted at various stages of the creation of *Pretty Dead*. They include Walter "Mitty" Robinson, who knows where the real skeletons are buried in Boston; Chip Gavin and Andrea Krasker Gavin, who showed me the town; Jim Scott, who provided culinary guidance; and Mary Grow, who reads closely in China Village, Maine.

INTRODUCTION

His home is just fifteen miles inland, but Jack McMorrow doesn't spend much time on the Maine coast. Tourists, summer folk, Mainers hustling to make a living off them—it just isn't McMorrow's scene. He'd rather go west from his hideaway in Prosperity to explore the small towns and hollowed-out mill cities where his stories spring up and life is laid bare.

Pretty Dead is the exception.

Actually, it's Roxanne who brings Jack to the coast. David and Maddie Connelly, summer residents of Blue Harbor and members of a dynastic Boston political family, have been accused of abusing their daughter. Roxanne is pulled in to investigate for the State. Jack tags along, and soon it's both of their backs that need watching.

The idea for *Pretty Dead* came one summer as I sat in a rented house hard on east Penobscot Bay. We tromped the rocky coastline, collected mussels for dinner, cooked them in white wine. Every day a procession of stately boats motored and sailed past, and I began to wonder. What if McMorrow were tossed into this world? What would he think of the yachting world? What would the whale-belted, pastel-shirted, Topsider-wearing crowd in Blue Harbor think of him?

That's how these books begin. What would happen if McMorrow were dropped into this town, the scene of this crime? How would he relate to this place, situation, cast of characters? Who would he protect and defend? Who would he target for his own brand of justice? Who would be hurt in the process, caught in the crossfire or taken down as people scramble to save themselves?

Often the characters who become victims in my novels are the ones I'm most fond of. That's the case here, though I can't tell you much more without ruining the story. As I reread Pretty Dead to prepare for writing this introduction, I came upon scenes that made me smile:

McMorrow doing interviews in Boston's North End, one with a young woman named Monica, "wide-eyed and wary, drawn into a big sweatshirt like a turtle." McMorrow being threatened by a couple of Boston thugs, Mick and Vincent. Mick wants Jack to write about his life in prison. He's got the first paragraph all written. He recites: "Mick hasn't slept in a year. Not like you sleep, in your soft bed in your nice, safe house. Mick dozes like a fucking watchdog. A sound that ain't right and, bam, he's wide awake before you can stick a shiv in his back. And remember. In prison, that ain't no figure of speech."

There's a lot of Boston in *Pretty Dead*, including Maddie Connelly, who married into her husband's wealthy and accomplished family for better or worse. Her life is a fairy tale that quickly and secretly becomes very grim. The facade, the perfect life portrayed in the society columns, is very thin indeed.

Reviewers of many of my books compared my writing to that of Robert B. Parker. While I admire Parker's work and his seminal detective, our territories are very different. I couldn't see the similarity of writing styles—until I reread *Pretty Dead* this time and heard echoes of Spenser and Susan Silverman.

I pictured handsome David Connelly chatting up some cute kid, convincing her that she was special, that the attraction they felt for each other was something extraordinary.

> *"He's got to be a hell of a liar," I said.*
> *"A prerequisite for philanderers," Roxanne said.*
> *I turned to her.*
> *"Keep your knickers on."*
> *"I'll do my best," she said.*

Pretty Dead is more urban than some of the McMorrow novels (only Cover Story has more big city), but it's also exceptional for the power of the players. Money can't always buy you happiness, but it sure can bring some serious weapons to bear. That's the case with the Connelly family and the hangers-on who surround them. After all, a hired gun is still a gun. A villain can become more deadly if they are able to keep their hands clean. Who would McMorrow rather tangle with: a wrench-swinging small-town thug or a ruthless millionaire from Boston? I don't know, but maybe the answer is in the pages of this book.

So what's *Pretty Dead* about? I'm going to take a cue from the late Robert B. and keep it short. It's about ambition and the ways it can turn deadly.

I hope you enjoy.

—Gerry Boyle

December 2016

PROLOGUE

They drove in silence, away from the glittering Maine coast, on a day when the summer air was cool and the sky was like a bright blue tarp torn with clouds. There was no particular route, no plan, just to drive generally west until the right place presented itself. So they left Route 1 and drove on a narrower road that climbed ridges, skirted rock faces fringed with spruce. The foliage was many shades of green, and as they turned onto narrower and narrower roads, left and right, right and left, golden light flooded the openings between the trees like sunlight streaming through stained glass.

It was a beautiful dappled glow and the car slipped through it. And then the road became a path, then twin furrows through the grass. The furrows faded and the brush—burdocks and goldenrod and sumac—scraped the side of the car as the path turned and climbed, then started to pitch downward. It seemed the car might not make it back up.

The car stopped. The motor was shut off and for a moment there was only the sound of the wind and birds, chickadees flitting through the woods.

But this wasn't the place, still too open, so the trek continued on foot, along the remnant of the path and then into an opening that led through a grove of blackened pin cherry and then into denser stands of poplar and birch. Thirty yards into the birch there was a small sunny clearing filled with asters, a place to consider. But still it felt too open and it seemed worth going farther, into the trees to a cool dark space where the ground was soft and littered with last year's leaves. This seemed right.

So it was back to the car, where she waited, stretched across the backseat, her hair gleaming in the sun.

The shovel was in the trunk.

1

—ɷ—

It was a Tuesday morning in August, very early. The birds were chattering in the fading dawn and Roxanne was folded into me, my arm under her breasts, my chest pressed against the warm smoothness of her back.

"Oh, God," she said as the pager chirped on the bedside table.

"Shoot that thing," I mumbled.

Roxanne peeled away from me and reached for the pager, disarming it like a hand grenade. She peered at the numbers and sighed wearily and slipped from the bed. I watched her as she walked naked and beautiful to the wardrobe and I remembered the previous night, the reckless, rollicking abandon.

"Come back," I said.

"I will," she said, pulling on one of my chamois shirts and wrapping it around her. She crossed the loft and slipped down the stairs. I heard her cell phone beep and then her voice.

"Yes . . . Well, I wasn't planning on it. I was supposed to be off. Oh, yeah. . . . What? . . . Who? . . . You're kidding . . . Today? . . . Oh, God . . . It's going to be . . . Yeah, very bad. . . . Okay . . . Give it to me now."

I heard paper rustling. She was writing.

"No, I'll go. I'll call you. Yeah, I'll need it."

Roxanne hung up. I heard her feet on the stairs and I held the quilt open for her. She slipped under and I covered her up and wrapped myself around her again.

"So much for your day," I said.

"Yeah, well."

I sighed.

"Bad one?" I said.

"Mmmm."

"Where?"

"The coast."

"What happened?"

"Oh, a little girl's been talking to a church worker. Five-year-old said she gets locked in the closet in the pitch dark as some kind of punishment. And she's got squeeze marks. Bruises like the marks of fingers."

"Where?"

"Arms, shoulder blades."

"For that they call you at five in the morning?"

"That's not the bad part."

"No?"

"They're rich," Roxanne said.

"And rich people get up early?"

"This is Blue Harbor rich."

"So?"

"And that's not the worst of it."

"What is?"

"I can't tell you," Roxanne said.

"Okay."

I nuzzled into her, ready to go back to sleep. Or not. She had a beautiful back, hips, thighs. I ran my hand across them.

"But it's bad," she said.

"I'm sorry. Why you?"

"They want somebody senior. Assessment worker who's been talking to this church person is totally green. And these people are going to flip out."

"Unleash the lawyers?"

"Oh, Jack, if only you knew."

"Knew what?"

"I can't tell you."

I didn't say anything.

"You've really got to promise this time," Roxanne said.

"Okay."

"You can't say a word."

"Okay."

"To anybody. Not Myra. This ends up in the *Times* or anywhere else and I'm done."

"Okay."

"They'd have my job."

"Who?"

"The Connellys."

"As in—"

"As in *the* Connellys. The Boston Connellys. This is David and Maddie. They're at their place in Blue Harbor."

The implications flashed through my mind. Big bucks. White-shoe Boston law firms. Serious, serious political clout.

"They're gonna try to bury this," I said.

"Yup," Roxanne said.

"Will His Excellency the commissioner back you?"

"I hope so."

"I predict they'll twist his arm right out of the socket."

"Yup."

"So what do you do?"

"Meet the worker at eleven."

"Want some company?"

"No. You know you can't come."

"Just for the ride. Drop me in town. I could nose around."

"I don't know."

"For other stories, I mean."

Roxanne didn't answer, just intertwined her legs with mine. And then there was that moment I'd seen before, when she would begin to gather herself up for the work she did, steeling herself for what was to come. I could feel it, the hardening of her resolve, and I held her closer, gently kissed the back of her neck.

"I'm not going to be intimidated," Roxanne said.

"No."

"Because what if it's true? The poor little kid, locked in a closet in the pitch dark."

"Lots of company. All the other Connelly skeletons," I said.

"But this is worse than some rich cokehead chasing the maid around."

"Yeah, it is."

And then she was quiet for a minute, and as I held her she said, "All right."

"All right, what?"

"All right, I'd like some company."

"You got it," I said.

"You know they'll fight back," Roxanne said, worry seeping into her voice.

"Like cornered animals, I'm sure."

"Cornered animals with millions of dollars and tons of clout."

"The worst kind," I said.

2

We left at nine, Roxanne wearing her game face and slacks and a blazer.

Driving east on the back roads from Prosperity toward Belfast, we passed small, lonely houses set into the edge of the woods like shelters along a trail. They were tired and unlikely places, rooted along the two-lane road like straggly weeds. Rusting cars and trucks sat in the brush-ringed yards, disused but not discarded, and nothing was thrown away. Good times were regarded suspiciously here and, for that reason, everything was saved in case the mill closed, the shop laid off, the bad leg got worse. In this part of Maine, good fortune was watched closely, like a dog that could turn.

Roxanne was pensive, staring out the window at nothing. As we approached the coast, the houses got newer and bigger, the lawns more carefully etched. Money seeped up from the ocean like the tide, tourist money, money spent by retirees from places to the south. They flocked along the shore like ducks, some staying year-round, others sweeping in with summer, winging their way south in the fall.

I turned onto Route 1, where roadside signs waved frantically to tourists like beggar kids greeting cruise ships, Victorian bed-and-breakfasts named for sea captains beckoned like hookers. Crossing the Penobscot River at Verona, we skirted the paper mill town of Bucksport and continued up the coast, into rock-scrub blueberry country and then down a peninsula, past ranch houses and old farms. A few miles later we glided down into elm-shaded Blue Harbor, where the village houses were historic, the oceanfront estates were priceless, and all the money was made elsewhere.

"It really is pretty, isn't it?" Roxanne said.

"Like a country club, except it's a whole town."

"With a long waiting list," she said.

"Old money," I said.

"Connelly money isn't that old."

"But Connellys had money *and* power. If you have enough of both, even Wasps make exceptions."

"I don't," Roxanne said as the Explorer ground to a stop.

The plan was to meet the other DHS worker, Tara, in the parking lot of the Blue Harbor Grocery, a quaint store and cafe ringed with Mercedes and geraniums. Tara had said she drove an older white Subaru with a UMaine sticker, which in Blue Harbor would tag her as a gawker or a waitress. We parked and refreshed our recollections of Connelly lore.

There was David's great-grandfather, Patrick Connelly, fresh from famine-weary Ireland, gobbling up Boston like it was a fat, ripe plum. Smart, savvy, and tough, he amassed money and power through what might have been called racketeering—lotteries, bootlegging, construction-labor kickbacks—if he hadn't been so good at it. Steal a little and they throw you in jail, Bob Dylan said. Steal a lot and they make you king. Patrick Connelly was crowned; his son, Joe, added a layer of respectability, moving into real estate development and hardball politics, which went hand in hand in the growing city. By the time he was done, Joe Connelly had enough money and political savvy to send one son to the State House and another to the US Senate. And the next generation of Connellys, the generation Roxanne was about to meet, didn't have to do anything at all.

"At least that's my take on it," I said.

"So they just play," Roxanne said.

"It's hard work," I said. "Climbing in the Himalayas one day, going to a black-tie thing in Boston the next. Giving away money through, what is it?"

"The Sky Blue Foundation."

"His money. I don't think she had any."

"No, but she has the looks," Roxanne said. "And style."

"They have a cute kid. You see them in the paper, the perfect family. I wonder how long it was?"

"What?"

"Before he started screwing around."

"Don't believe everything you hear," she said.

"Remember the stuff about the college intern?"

"She was Harvard, right?"

"Well, of course," I said.

We were quiet for a minute. I pictured handsome David Connelly chatting up some cute kid, convincing her that she was special, that the attraction they felt for each other was something extraordinary.

"He's got to be a hell of a liar," I said.

"A prerequisite for philanderers," Roxanne said.

I turned to her.

"Keep your knickers on."

"I'll do my best," she said.

3

At two minutes past eleven, the Subaru rolled up with a clatter. Tara, a small solid woman with big hair and bangs, looked around for the Explorer and then got out and walked over. She was younger up close, in black jeans and sneakers, and she looked nervous, like a freshman at the senior prom, unsure she'd worn the right dress. She hadn't. In another incarnation she carried wood on her back.

"They'll send her around back with the rest of the deliveries," I said.

"Let 'em try it," Roxanne said.

She gave a discreet wave and Tara approached. Roxanne got out of the car and Tara shook her hand, then looked at me.

"Oh," she said. "I thought you were from Central Office."

"No, just the chauffeur."

"This is my friend, Jack. He's got some business down here. He'll meet me after we're done."

"What business are you in?" Tara said.

"This and that," I said.

"Jack's a reporter. He may do a travel article on this area," Roxanne said. "You know, which bed-and-breakfasts have the best muffins and all that."

I looked at her. The best muffins?

She smiled.

"I'll call you," she said.

"I'll be around."

"Do you think they'll let us see the girl?" Tara said, then looked at me and said, "Whoops."

I smiled at her and put the car in gear. "Sometimes it isn't what they tell you," I heard Roxanne say as I backed out of the lot. "It's what they don't. That's what I want you . . ."

When there was a break in the traffic—a slow procession of Suburbans, Volvos, a Porsche, and a Jaguar—I backed out. I drove up the main street, an eye on the rearview mirror. The Subaru pulled out and drove through the village the other way. I hesitated for a moment, then swung into an art gallery lot and turned around. As I moved back into traffic, I saw the white car turn left. I sped up and followed. I took the left, which led up the hill and out of town. A hundred yards up on the right was a white clapboard church, gleaming in the sun. The Subaru was parked at the side entrance. I pulled into a bookstore lot and sat.

This must have been the church where the kid spilled the beans. Roxanne and Tara would interview the church person. How long would that take? A half-hour? An hour? They'd have to ask exactly what the girl said, what she was like with the other kids, with adults. When did they first notice the marks? Did she tell anyone else?

I waited. Roxanne wouldn't like this, but what else was I supposed to do? Let her head off to some estate in the middle of nowhere to tell a couple of rich, arrogant parents they were being investigated for child abuse? I was just watching her—

They came out, striding like they were all business, and got in the car. I backed to the rear of the bookstore lot and peered over the hood of a Range Rover. A golden retriever panted at me from the backseat but didn't bark, this being Blue Harbor. The Subaru went by and I counted to ten and followed.

We went back down the hill to the center of the village. They took a right, drove under the elms, and took a left by the Blue Harbor library. I was five hundred yards behind and I followed. When I took the left, they were out of sight.

The road followed the shoreline, with the harbor to my left beyond the houses. For a quarter-mile or so, it was an extension of the village, the houses tucked together, separated by hedges and ivy-covered walls and fences. Then the road rose and banked away from the water and the drives were marked by stone walls and gates, the houses glimpsed through the trees and rhododendrons, the waters of Penobscot Bay glittering in the distance. If they turned through one of these gates I could lose them, so I sped up—and saw the Subaru turn to the left and disappear.

I slowed and peered down the drive as I passed. There was a glimpse of their car and then it was gone. I stopped at the next drive and turned around. Stopped short of the Connelly entrance and pulled against the hedges.

The place was marked by a number: 415. There was a gray-shingled gatehouse behind dense hedges, an empty boat trailer parked beside it. The driveway was paved with crushed white shells. There was no one in sight. I sat for a minute, then pulled back out and made a U-turn and drove back to the road to what appeared to be the edge of the Connelly estate. The line of demarcation was a point where the hedges were replaced by a stolid row of cedars, like soldiers on guard duty. The grounds of this next place were more open, and in the distance I could see the house, a white colonial with carriage houses and barns. The ground-floor windows were covered with what looked like plywood painted dark green to match the shutters.

I parked the Explorer across the road and walked up the drive.

I figured the owners had decided to sail the boat to Ireland or ski in the Andes. Or maybe they'd died and the kids were fighting over the place. No matter. Where the cedars thinned I could see the Connellys' drive, then a glimpse of a gray slate roof. Just short of the first carriage house I checked the road and slipped into the trees.

I stayed behind the cedars and the banks of shaggy rhododendrons that edged the Connelly property, and I walked slowly but deliberately. Beyond the white house the trees and shrubbery opened up and on the Connelly side there was some sort of woven cedar fence. The fence extended to the end of the lawn, where steep ledges dropped to the shore of this finger of the bay, an expanse of blue-green water studded with spruce-bristled islands.

At the end of the fence I peered around. On the Connelly side a long dock spanned the rocks and ended on a float. There was an inflatable dinghy overturned on the float; a forty-foot yacht that looked a little like a lobster boat and a smaller, open boat, a Boston Whaler, were moored to orange buoys. The tide was out and the water was lapping the barnacle-covered rocks. I poked my head around and saw the main house, a massive, shingled "cottage" with turrets and fieldstone chimneys and a screened porch on the side. Perennial gardens spilled toward the shore like brightly colored waves.

The Subaru was parked to the left, toward the rear of the house. Tara appeared at the car, opened the door and reached in for something, and then moved back toward the house and out of view.

In the stillness I heard gulls, an osprey, a catbird in the shrubs, then even the birds were quiet.

I moved behind the fence toward the house, stopped at the end and listened. Peered through the cracks. The Subaru was parked by a black Suburban and a dark green Volvo wagon. The Suburban had Massachusetts plates and semaphore-flag stickers on the back window. Very yachty. A black BMW 750 was parked in a separate three-bay garage. The side door to the house was closed.

I leaned against the fence and watched and listened. On the bay, all was tranquil. Inside it was hard to tell. The place was probably soundproof as a tomb.

A half-hour passed. I alternated between watching the house and the glittering bay. In the distance there was a windjammer with rose-colored sails, smaller sailboats showing like scattered tissues. Close by there was the looming rumble of a big marine engine, and then a lobster boat came around the next point, one guy at the helm, another in the stern. They moved from one brightly painted buoy to the next like lumbering bees buzzing from flower to flower. I watched the lobstermen, wondering if wealthy summer people paid them just to provide local color.

And I heard a snap.

"Can I help you?" David Connelly asked.

4

I recognized him from the newspapers, but in person he was bigger, better looking. He was wearing khaki shorts and a faded blue T-shirt that said BARBADOS Y.C., and his legs and arms were tanned and muscled.

"Just watching the boats," I said.

"Technically, this is private property," he said.

"No kidding. I thought it was Acadia National Park."

I smiled and he gave a little snort and grinned and watched the lobstermen. The guy at the helm waved and Connolly waved back.

"I'm with Roxanne Masterson," I said.

"I figured. What, you have the house under surveillance?"

"No, I drove her down here and it seemed a shame to miss the view."

"Work for the State?"

"No," I said. "We're—"

I paused.

"Together?" Connolly said.

"Yeah."

"Really. Kind of an unpleasant job she has."

"It's for a good cause," I said.

"That's very true, but I wouldn't want to do it."

"Good thing somebody does."

"A very good thing."

He held out his hand.

"I'm David."

"Jack McMorrow."

I took his hand and we shook. He held my gaze and I noticed that his eyes were mesmerizingly blue, an unnatural color, like somebody had colored them with crayons. His smile was a little crooked and it gave him a bemused, philosophical expression, like he'd seen a lot and had taken it all in stride.

We turned back to the water.

"The sea," he said, gazing out at the glittering expanse. "You live on the coast?"

"No, inland. Deep in the woods. I like it, but this is beautiful."

"The great equalizer. The sea puts everything in perspective, don't you think? It's where I go when I need to get my head screwed on straight."

"Your boats?" I said, nodding toward the pair on the moorings.

"My refuge. The big one is called *Escape*. It's a Hinckley Talaria."

I looked at him blankly.

"If you're into boats, that means something," Connelly said. "I'll take it out in anything. Maddie gets a little queasy in real heavy weather, but I love it. I'll take it across, around Mount Desert and way Down East. Away from the day-trippers, you know? You get up there and there are stretches of coast that look like they did when the first Europeans came sailing down from the north four hundred years ago. They really do. I like to find a stretch like that and anchor and—"

He glanced at me and smiled.

"Sorry. Get me going on boats and I can ramble."

"It's okay. It's interesting," I said, and it was. I gave him a closer look. This wasn't the David Connelly from the tabloids. Where was the party boy?

"So what do you do, Jack, if you don't work for the State?"

"I cut wood some of the time," I said.

"You mean, in the woods? Cutting down trees? Like a lumberjack?"

"Yeah."

"Now there's something I've never done. Dangerous?"

"Only if you begin to think it isn't."

"A lot of things are like that," Connelly said. "Like these lobster guys. The risk actually increases the more comfortable you become with it. And then you're out there and it's winter and you're talking, thinking about something else, your kids, your wife, your bills, and a rope catches your arm, your ankle—"

"And over you go," I said.

"Vigilance is hard to keep up," he said.

"True."

"So what do you do when you're not cutting wood?"

Crunch time. I considered how to answer. I could say I was a writer, seem less threatening. But there was something straightforward about him that said I should just tell the truth.

"I'm a reporter. A stringer for the *New York Times.*"

Connelly looked at me and tried not to show anything but couldn't do it.

"Jesus," he said.

We both looked toward the lobster boat, pivoting as it maneu-vered close to a trap buoy. For a moment or two neither of us spoke and then I said, "But I'm not working."

He didn't answer at first, instead gave a brief, discouraged sigh.

"Reporters are always working, aren't they?"

"I don't write about Roxanne's business."

"Pass things along to somebody else?"

"Nope."

"Ever?"

"No."

"But you know what this is about?"

"I know what Roxanne does."

"My daughter has bruises. We didn't notice them at first. Makes you feel like kind of an idiot. This woman at the church play group, she saw them when Maeve got her shirt all wet and they took it off to dry it. By law they have to report this stuff, I guess. Would have been nice if they just told us, but I understand."

"It's a good law," I said. "Actually, I'm surprised she had the—"

"The nerve? This lady's by the book."

"Even with you?"

David paused, looked away.

"Yeah, well. I guess she did."

Then turned back to me.

"But you know this wasn't from being hit or anything. More from being squeezed on the shoulders. We had an au pair from Ireland, we use a lot of Irish kids. Roots, you know? And they've all been just great. But this one, Devlin, had a mean streak. Probably the way she was raised. We fired her and sent her home."

"Huh," I said.

"That's it."

"Then I'm sure Roxanne will take care of it."

"Now we've gotta find this kid, so she can back us up," Connelly said.

"You don't know where she is?"

"Sent her to Shannon, so I guess she'd be back home in West Cork, but who knows? She's nineteen and single and we gave her a thousand dollars' cash. Sort of a severance. She could have gone to Dublin or London or goddamn France for all we know."

"I'm sure it'll work out."

"It has to. And Ms. Masterson, she seems very reasonable."

"She is."

"Seems to have common sense."

"She does."

"She asked me to leave her alone with Maddie. That's my wife."

"I know."

He hesitated, watched the lobstermen move to the next trap. "But as a member of the press, you must know that sometimes this family is treated a little differently," Connelly said.

"Better or worse?"

"Some of both."

"So it averages out?" I said.

Connelly smiled.

"Some days are better than others," he said.

"And this one isn't too good, is it?"

"A social worker in the house and the *New York Times* in the bushes," Connelly said. He laughed, said, "Oh, my word," and shook his head.

I found myself feeling bad for the guy, like I should give him a pat on his broad shoulders. Despite all his money, looks, and clout, his life, for the moment, was a bit of a mess. But suddenly he turned to me, the blue eyes blazing, the crooked grin back.

"Come on in," he said.

"No, I really shouldn't—"

"Really. You need to meet everybody. I need you to know that we're not some child beaters. Maeve is at her cousins' house in Northeast Harbor so she's not here. But you'll see we're normal, nice people. Hey, I'll get you a cup of coffee. How 'bout something to eat?"

He took me by the arm and started to guide me around the cedars. I took a couple of steps and stopped, said, "That's nice of you, but this is Roxanne's thing. I really can't get involved."

"But you are involved, Jack," Connelly said, showing he could see the heart of the matter. "Like it or not, you know some of the story and you need to get the full picture. You need to know that we're like any other parents."

He got me moving again, an arm on my shoulder. The lobster boat had gone beyond the next rocky point and there was a quietness in its wake that seemed to draw us closer together. We rounded the row of cedars and started across the lawn. Connelly still had his hand on my shoulder, like we were old friends, and I wondered if this was the same sort of easy intimacy he conveyed to women.

"You've got to understand, Jack, and I know you will," he said, his smile only half-softening his words. "Our child comes first. Nobody hurts our daughter."

5

There were five of them, three in their thirties or forties, two much younger women who looked like they might have been somebody's college-age daughters. The older trio was two men and a woman. The guys were tanned and fit, legs crossed, sunglasses hanging on their chests from cords; the woman was white-blonde and very big-city. The younger two were slouched in their chairs and one was dark and very attractive. They were all sitting around a vast living room that opened onto the porch that overlooked the lawn and the bay. Laid at their feet like tribute were canvas tote bags packed for some sort of outing.

Connelly introduced me as Jack, a friend of Ms. Masterson's. They looked at him for their cue, and when he smiled and put his hand on my shoulder, they smiled, too. If he'd jumped me, they would have piled on.

"Jack's from—where in Maine?" David said.

"Prosperity," I said.

"Oh, how quaint," the blonde woman said. "Is there really such a place?"

"Very much so," I said. "Has been for a hundred and fifty years."

"Is it prosperous?" a guy with tortoiseshell glasses said. "Or did the founding fathers just have a keen sense of irony?"

They chuckled smugly.

"I think they were hopeful," I said, prickling.

"This is Tim Dalton," Connelly said. "Helps run Sky Blue, among other things."

Dalton was wearing a green polo shirt with a logo I didn't recognize. He was small and muscular, like a soccer player, knotted quads showing below his shorts. He sprang from the big leather chair and held out his hand in an earnest, manly way.

"Jack writes for the *New York Times*," Connelly said.

"Oh, really," Dalton said.

He and the others looked to Connelly for their next cue.

"But today is his day off," he said.

They nodded in relief.

"New Yorker?" Dalton said.

"A lifetime ago," I said, and I could tell I'd moved up a couple of notches in his estimation, not being a native Mainer. Tara would be assigned to a lower caste.

"McMorrow," he said. "Sure, I've seen your byline. You write the northern New England stuff. I have friends at the *Times*. People I knew at Harvard."

He dropped a couple of names. I was acquainted with them. Me and Dalton, we were simpatico.

"Jack, this is Kathleen Kind," Connelly said. "Kathleen is a number cruncher."

"And that's not all she crunches, if the numbers don't add up," Dalton said, and the guys chuckled. Kathleen dropped the *Wall Street Journal* to her lap and gave a little wave from one of the couches. She was stiffly pretty, blonde hair trimmed just below her ears, jeans and a tight black T-shirt, black-rimmed glasses that perched on the end of her precisely pointed nose. She looked over the glasses at me like she was appraising me for Sotheby's. Then she said, "Hi there, Jack," in a knowing way, like we'd met at a party but I didn't remember.

The other guy was Sandy something, maybe six-two and lanky. Shorts and Topsiders and a blue denim shirt, the sleeves carefully turned up. Oakley sunglasses on top of his head. He looked like a ski bum, off season. He saluted, said, "Welcome aboard," and gave me an easy grin.

"Sandy's our man in Maine," Connelly said. "Looks after things for us, the boats especially, and does it very well. Sandy's a sailor. If you ever decide to put together a crew for a transatlantic, he's your first mate."

"He can take the stern in the canoe," I said.

"Been there, done that," Sandy said. "You do white water?"

"No," I said. "Mostly I drift around marshes and look at birds."

"Lots of bids on the bay," he said, ever helpful, like a true courtesan, a guy whose social skills had been honed in his service to the very wealthy. "I'll take you out."

We turned to the two younger women, sitting in a window seat. Ten years ago they were in grade school. Now they were perched with their knees up to their chins, wearing shorts and tops with spaghetti straps. One was very pretty, one was not. The not-so-pretty one was wearing soccer sandals that had the Adidas logo across the top, and her toenails were painted dark blue. There was a gold ring on her left little toe.

"This is Monica Vitale," Connelly said, less easily than with the others, like he'd had to think about it. She had a mop of black hair that she pulled back and tucked into an elastic scrunchy, and when she raised her arms behind her head to fuss with her hair, she showed a gold stud in her bared navel. She looked bored, like the bus was late, and at first she didn't respond. When her hair was arranged she finally said, "Hi," and I did, too. Connelly said she worked for Sky Blue, one of the behind-the-scenes people who kept the place running. I began to get the picture that this was some sort of office outing.

"And this is Angel Moretti, last but not least," Connelly said.

She looked up at me. She had deep dark eyes, skin so fine it seemed to have no texture at all, a faint rosiness in her cheeks, and a thick shock of dark hair hanging loose. The rest of her was perfectly proportioned, and I felt that heart skip that men get, that tongue-tied moment. But then I said hello and she said, "Very nice to meet you," like a little kid, but there was something in her expression that said she knew the effect she had, and it was her magic weapon: She may have been twenty, but she made rich men swoon.

She smiled at me, and then turned her attention to Connelly. Her smile changed into something more knowing, and there was a boldness in her gaze, like they were accomplices and she didn't care who knew. Connelly flinched and looked away.

"David," she said, her voice faintly provocative like her big, unblinking eyes. "Do you think we'll get out on the water?"

He looked back at her and smiled, but it was the kind of smile that fends someone off.

"I hope so," he said. "Just hang tight."

"Sandy said I could, what did you call it, 'Take the helm'?"

She looked at Sandy and he seemed to squirm.

"In open water, of course," he said.

"Preferably halfway to Portugal," Connelly said, and Angel faked a pout and said, "David, don't you trust me?"

I looked around at the group. Dalton was staring at Angel like she was a Siren and he was shipwrecked. Kathleen had her smile fixed but her stare was icy. Monica looked more obviously annoyed. Angel's sandal dropped to the carpet and she fished for it with her bare foot.

"We were all headed out on the bay when"—Connelly paused, forcing a smile as he turned to me—

"when plans changed."

As if on cue, a door rattled somewhere deeper in the house. I heard footsteps and then Roxanne's voice and the voice of another woman, and Connelly said, "Sounds like they're done. Come on and meet Maddie."

They all smiled and nodded and Connelly headed out of the room. I followed. We walked down a corridor lined with photographs of Connellys on big boats, on horses, on tops of mountains. At the end of the corridor we took a right and moved into a paneled study. Roxanne was standing in the middle of the room; there was another woman with her. They both turned. The other woman smiled, but in a weary way. Roxanne smiled, too, masking her surprise.

"Maddie," Connelly said. "Somebody I want you to meet. This is Jack. He's Ms. Masterson's friend. I went for a walk and ran into him and told him he should come in and see that the Connellys don't have horns and fangs."

He caught himself, looked at Roxanne.

"Not to belittle what you do," Connelly said, backpedaling. "That wasn't intended the way it sounded. I'm glad you're looking out for

Maeve. And other kids. I really am. I mean, at the foundation it's a priority, protecting children. Nurturing them."

"It's okay," Roxanne said.

"I just wanted Jack to know we're not monsters."

"No one is saying you are, Mr. Connelly," Roxanne said.

"David, please. And I understand. But you know what people think when they hear 'child abuse.' And this family, well, things tend to get—"

He paused, turned back to his wife.

"Maddie, this is Jack McMorrow."

Maddie Connelly smiled a bit wanly and said, "Hi, there." She held out her hand and I took it in mine. It was small but her handshake was very firm and her gaze was direct. She was attractive but in an arresting, intriguing sort of way, not like bowl-you-over Angel. Her blonde-streaked hair was cut practically short, and she had a dash of freckles across the tops of her cheeks. It was a squarish but very pretty face, and she'd probably seemed tomboyish until one day some guy looked across the boat, the ski slope, the tennis court, and thought, *My god. She's sort of beautiful.*

But today she looked weary and red-eyed.

"I don't want to intrude," I said. "I really didn't intend to come in or—"

"This really is confidential," Roxanne said. "Don't feel you have to share this with—"

"Oh, we won't," David Connelly said. "But I just felt that Jack should get the whole picture. I told him about the au pair and what happened and how we sent her home. I didn't want him to get the wrong idea."

"But David," Maddie began, trying to remain gracious, but now a little puzzled.

"We were outside looking at the bay, and Jack was telling me what he does," David said. "Jack cuts wood. You know, in the woods, with a chain saw? But that's not all. He's one of those Renaissance Mainers."

He paused and looked at his wife.

"When he's not cutting wood, Jack's a newspaper reporter, honey. He writes for the *Times*."

Maddie Connelly's face went gray. She actually caught her breath, then tried to smile, but it was pained. I could see her searching for the right thing to say, but finally she gave up.

"You're shitting me," she said.

6

Roxanne went out to tell Tara she might as well head back to the office, that I'd stopped to pick her up and we'd go back home together. When Roxanne returned to the study, I was still trying to convince Maddie Connelly that every word she'd uttered in Roxanne's presence wouldn't appear in the *Times* the next morning.

"But how can you not, if you know something?" Maddie said, leaning against the end of a couch.

"Reporters don't print everything they hear," I said.

"And this involves me," Roxanne said. "Jack wouldn't hurt me."

"But he knows why you would come here. It's what you do."

Roxanne didn't answer.

"And then David confirmed it," Maddie said to me.

"That was unexpected," I said. "But it doesn't change anything. I don't even think it's news. Maine has hundreds of reports like this every month. This one just happened to be—"

"Us," Maddie said.

I glanced at the wall behind her. There were more photographs: Connellys shaking hands with Bill Clinton, Connellys outside the White House.

"They can't help that," David said. "They have to look into these things. What if Devlin were still here and it was still going on? Or what if it was us doing it?"

"But they don't usually bring the media, do they?" Maddie said. "Is it just a coincidence that the case involving this family gets a reporter from the *New York Times* tagging along?"

"Yes," I said. "I came along for the ride, see if there was anything in town that might lead to a story."

"Well, you hit the jackpot, didn't you?" Maddie said, arms folded across her chest.

"No," I said. "I didn't intend to talk to David. I didn't intend to get involved at all. I just ran out of places to go and I was waiting for Roxanne. Got out of the car to stretch my legs and look at the water and—"

"But you'd talk about it when she got home, right? 'How'd it go in Blue Harbor? What'd they have to say for themselves?' "

"We generally don't discuss my cases," Roxanne said.

"But this is different?"

"Not really."

"And it won't amount to anything," David said. "We told you what happened. You can talk to Maeve—"

"David," Maddie said.

"She'll have to," he said. "She can't just take our word for all of this."

"I don't want Maeve upset. I don't want her to think this is a bigger deal than it is."

"I'll do my best to not upset her," Roxanne said.

"And that will be the end of it?" Maddie said.

"In all likelihood, from what I've heard, yes," Roxanne said. "But I can't promise at this point."

Maddie looked to David and their eyes met and held and some sort of invisible, almost telepathic communication went on, the kind you see in couples who are very close.

"Okay," David said.

"Then let's get her home," Maddie said. "I'll call. She'll be here in an hour."

"Then I have more questions for you," Roxanne said.

"I'll stay," David said. I looked to Roxanne and moved to the door, and I had my hand on it when he said, "Jack, you go. You'll love it out there. But could you tell Sandy he'd better go without me? Tell him to just take them around so they can see Cadillac Mountain, but probably skip Somes Sound. Getting too late if they're going to make dinner in town."

A cruise around Mount Desert Island? Cadillac Mountain from the water? A chance to get out of Roxanne's way.

So I left them, Maddie sitting on the couch, David moving to take his place beside her, Roxanne taking a legal pad from her bag. I closed the door behind me and, when I turned into the hallway, almost walked into the pretty girl, Angel. She was standing in front of the photographs as though the house were a museum and she'd rented headphones.

"Hey," she said.

"Hello," I said.

"Look at this. Look at that boat."

It was an immense racing sailboat, like something from an old America's Cup. It was under sail, heeled over with one rail practically in the waves.

"You think they owned that?" Angel said, a trace of North End Boston in her accent.

"I don't know," I said.

"Must be worth a large fortune," she said, and she stepped to the next photo.

"Who's this old guy?" she said.

Another boat picture, this time Connellys in the cockpit, David Connelly at a wheel the size of a hula hoop, an older man beside him.

"That's Walter Cronkite," I said.

"Wasn't he some news announcer?" Angel said.

"Yeah."

"You know him?"

I shook my head.

"You interview a lot of famous and influential people?"

"Some," I said. "Not as much anymore. I work mostly Maine and New Hampshire now."

"Who have you interviewed who's famous?"

She had moved to the next set of photos and was peering at them as though she were looking for lost relatives.

"I don't know," I said. "Jimmy Carter. Rudy Giuliani, but he wasn't famous then. David Dinkins and Ed Koch."

"Never heard of the last two."

"New York mayors. How 'bout Bruce Springsteen?" I said.

Angel turned to me, big eyes wide. She reached out and put her hand on my upper arm and held it there. She was one of those women who like men the way some people like chocolate.

"Really? What was he like?"

"Very nice," I said. "A very regular guy."

"I don't want famous people to be regular," Angel said. "I want them to be mysterious and different. I can meet all the regular people I want."

The hand fell away.

"Where are you from, Angel?"

"Boston. My whole life. I love the city."

"Some people in Boston would say the Connellys are famous, and they seem pretty regular."

"Oh, I don't know," Angel said. "They're nice, but they carry a lot with them."

"The family baggage?"

"The history. I mean, just being a Connelly. Having everybody looking at you like you're some sort of royalty."

"They are, in a way. American royalty."

"You know somebody else told me that?"

"Who?"

"Barbara Walters. I went to this benefit dinner with David and Maddie, at the Ritz. She sat at our table, Barbara Walters, and she said to me, once she knew what I did, 'What is it like working with royalty?' I said, 'They try so hard not to show it.' Too hard, I think."

"Too hard?"

"Yeah. Like this thing with their little girl; I would have tossed those people right out and called my lawyer. I mean, this woman with the hair? And she comes in here bossing people around? I mean, who the hell does she think she's talking to?"

"To just another parent who might be mistreating a kid," I said.

"Oh, who are you kidding, Jack?" she said, turning to me and cocking her head. "This family isn't 'just another' anything."

"Then what are they?"

"They're amazing people who do amazing things. Yesterday we gave this outfit five hundred thousand to train foster parents who take crack babies. Just like that. Last year David and Sandy flew to

South Africa and picked up this huge sailboat and sailed around the end of Africa, that point. It has a name."

"The Cape of Good Hope."

"Whatever. But they just do it."

"Like the Nike ad?"

"Yeah. There's no blabbing on about things."

"You like that?"

She turned to me.

"Yeah, I do. They live large. Maddie takes Maeve to France and Italy. A month ago it was those Indian cliff-dwelling places in Arizona. If they decide it's important, it gets done. Most people just talk."

"What's your background, Angel?" I said.

She turned back to a photograph of David on top of some snow-covered mountain.

"Nothing special. Boston. North End. Regular family."

"Must be something special about them. Lots of brothers and sisters?"

"Oh, yeah. A whole bunch of them, tied down by their roots like plants."

"You're not?'

"I don't spend my whole life looking back, Jack," she said. "I'm looking forward, every minute."

She turned and leaned toward me, like she was going to tell me a secret. I could smell her shampoo, her perfume, felt my pulse quicken in spite of me.

"And another thing," Angel said, her voice husky. "That's all off the record."

"I'm not working," I said.

"Jack," she said, touching her fingers to the top of my hand. "Come off it."

And then Dalton appeared at the end of the hallway, a sweater draped over his shoulders. Angel pulled her fingers away and said, "Timmy. We were talking. Jack's interviewed Bruce Springsteen."

She started toward him, a runway swivel to her walk, and he gave her a quick look that said she was his and he was proud, and then that vanished and he said to me, "Springsteen. No kidding," but he was distracted and turned with her as she passed. It occurred to me that Angel's problem wouldn't be hooking up with men, but setting the hook so deep they couldn't be released.

7

Sandy rowed with me out to the big boat in a dinghy that was all glass-varnished wood and polished brass. The water was blue-green and the air smelled of salt and seaweed and the bottom disappeared quickly as the dinghy skipped over the chop. Sandy eased the dinghy alongside the *Escape*, while I stood gingerly and then stepped over the gunwale of the big boat and held the dinghy against the plastic fenders that kept the hulls from bumping. Sandy came aboard and tied the dinghy to a cleat on the stern. The dinghy drifted away on its painter as Sandy started for the cockpit. He started the motors and backed them into a rumbling idle and then climbed out on the narrow deck beside the cabin. At the bow he crouched, slackened the mooring line, and unwound it from its cleat.

Sandy clambered back into the cockpit, took the stick, and feathered the boat to the float. They came aboard one by one, like animals loaded on a circus train. Kathleen Kind settled onto the cushioned bench across from the helm, crossed her legs carefully, and took a copy of *The New Yorker* from her bag. Monica, unmindful of the cool breeze off the water, went to a stern seat and slipped out of her top, revealing a bikini top filled to bursting. On her right breast was a tattoo of a rose. She turned to the sun, beginning to drop from its crest in the gleaming blue Maine sky, and closed her eyes like a lizard on a rock.

Angel and Dalton began to climb the ladder to the second story of the boat, above the cabin, Angel in the lead, Dalton staring up at her buttocks.

"She's gorgeous, don't you think?" Sandy said.

I looked at him, startled.

"The very first Talaria 44 built with the flybridge."

"Really. And a flybridge is—"

"That's the upper platform."

We could hear Angel and Dalton clambering around above us. As Sandy went on about dual controls, I wondered if Dalton was married. I wondered if it made any difference.

"Know boats?" Sandy said.

"Not really."

"Well, take my word for it. This is the best yacht of its kind in the world. Unless you go totally custom, and David has the Sou'wester 51."

"This one's very nice," I said.

He launched into a recitation of the boat's attributes, going into a sort of trance, the way some people do when they talk about boats or cars or religion. I listened politely.

The hull was Kevlar and carbon fiber. The electronics were state of the art. The motors were twin Yanmar diesels and there was no propeller, just water jets. The thing was controlled with a stick, not a wheel, and could turn on its own axis. The hull drew only twenty-eight inches of water but could take eight-foot seas.

"We can go three hundred and fifty miles on a tank of fuel," Sandy said. "Cruise from here to New York at twenty-eight knots."

"Ever do that?" I said.

"Hell no. David doesn't use *Escape* to see more people. He uses it to get away."

Sandy watched gauges and threw switches, and I felt like I was on an airplane. I looked over at Ms. Kind and she'd put down the magazine and was looking out at the shoreline, where the Connellys' cottage protected the inner harbor like a castle.

She looked at me and smiled.

"I don't care about that technical mumbo jumbo," she said. "But you should see below."

Ms. Kind stood and hooked her finger at me and I stood and she opened a passageway door and eased her way inside. I followed into a dining area and galley with more appliances than my house, and on into a cabin with a massive bed at its center. Everything was gleaming cherry. Ms. Kind sat on the rose-colored comforter, leaned back, and looked around.

"This is my kind of boating," Ms. Kind said. "Sit in the harbor with a good book. Go ashore to a four-star restaurant."

"Must be nice," I said. "Can't imagine what something like this would cost."

"It's the old, 'if you have to ask,' " she said.

"So the family doesn't give away all of its money," I said.

"The Connellys aren't monastic, Mr. McMorrow. They have a right to enjoy their lives."

"True. And I guess they do."

"What makes you say that?" she said, a faint challenge in her tone, her sandal dangling on her foot like a gauntlet about to be thrown.

"The boats. The houses. The stuff you read, about him especially."

"Oh, Christ. If people knew what garbage appeared in the press, they'd never read a newspaper again."

"I probably shouldn't ask this, but it's not true? The philandering, the drugs and stuff when they were young?"

"God almighty. They never did anything that other people weren't doing then. And the philandering was ninety percent innuendo. David Connelly dating this actress. David Connelly dating this society pager. You know one paper linked him with me? We were seen leaving a Boston hotel together early one morning. We were there for a breakfast meeting with a nonprofit, for God's sake. We shared a cab back to the office."

I looked at Ms. Kind, the cool spareness of her. The thought of her having an affair with David Connelly wasn't as absurd as she made it out to be, and I wondered if it was vanity that made her repeat that story. She returned my gaze and seemed to be reading my thoughts.

"I'm old enough to be his—"

It wasn't mother, and she didn't finish the thought.

"Whatever," Ms. Kind said. "This friend of yours. Is she your wife?"

"No."

"But you're together?"

"Yes."

"A long time?"

"By some standards. Not like the couples in my town who celebrate their fiftieths at the Grange."

"But permanent?"

"Yes."

"Raises some interesting confidentiality questions, doesn't it?"

"On occasion," I said.

"Which prevails? Protecting children, or the public's right to know?"

"It's her job. I don't get involved."

"Oh, really?"

She smiled.

"I didn't intend to be here. I got—"

"Swept along by David's largesse? Join the club. We're here for mandatory bonding. We go in shifts. This is Team A."

"Some of you seem to be bonding more than others," I said.

There was a pause.

"What's that supposed to mean?" Ms. Kind said.

"I don't know. You and Monica aren't exactly chums, are you?"

"Not exactly. And I don't socialize with the guy who parks my car, either."

I didn't pursue that.

"What do you do with these numbers you crunch?"

"Somebody has to tell them how much they have to spend. It isn't a bottomless cup, much as some people would like to think so."

"And Tim Dalton, what does he do?"

"He's chief of staff. David is president and Maddie is vice president."

"What does Monica do?"

Ms. Kind hesitated and it seemed to me her eyes rolled slightly.

"She's Angel Moretti's friend. They came to the foundation as temps together last year."

"And you decided to keep them on?"

"I didn't. Someone else did."

"What does Angel do?"

"She's Mr. Dalton's—"

Ms. Kind hesitated.

"—administrative assistant."

"Huh," I said.

Ms. Kind looked at me and showed nothing but a cold smile.

"So you must feel good about what you do," I said. "Helping so many people on this large scale."

"You hope you're doing the right thing—that over time you're making a contribution. There's a certain gravity to what we do. We aren't making widgets. I mean, we promise a half-million dollars to these poor, sick infants, we'd better come through with it."

"Why wouldn't you?" I said.

"Oh, you can lose focus, overestimate revenue, start spending money on unnecessary things, extraneous—"

Ms. Kind paused. The motors rumbled and the boat began to move, the shoreline slipping past the oval-shaped portholes. There were footsteps in the passageway and Dalton and Angel came through and Angel said, "Oh, my God. This is so lovely." She hurried over, bent down, and ran a hand along the cherry bed frame. Ms. Kind rose from the bed, her icy smile still frozen in place.

"—positions," she murmured.

8

We rumbled down Blue Harbor Bay, the rock shore on both sides bristling with spruce and fir, houses perched here and there on the rocks like sightseers who had crept out of the woods to watch us pass. It was beautiful, the low chop on the water, the sun lighting the granite, the gulls above us, the ospreys launching from the woods and circling over the coves.

Monica and Ms. Kind were seated at opposite ends of the stern, separated by their social divide. Dalton and Angel had clambered along the narrow deck alongside the cabin and were sitting on the forward deck. Dalton was pointing to houses as we passed, probably identifying the owners and their net worth. I went up on the flybridge with Sandy and he named islands as we passed.

Long Island. Hardwood Island. Tinker Island. Three rocky nubs below Tinker that Sandy said were crests on an underwater ridge.

"People get in trouble in between there," he said. "Two feet of water and all ledge. Try to cut that corner and you'll hang her right up."

"Down you go?"

"More likely you sit on your side with your hull full of water and hope somebody answers your Mayday."

"Not a place to be careless?" I said.

"Hey, in the fog, at night, water fifty or sixty degrees? You can get killed out here just as easy as you could two hundred years ago."

"Is that why David likes it so much?"

"You'd have to ask him."

He paused and I didn't fill the gap.

"But I'd guess it has something to do with the water treating everybody the same," Sandy said.

"Is that why you're out here?" I said.

"Yeah," he said, "but I come at it from the other side. All that matters is that I can get a boat from Point A to Point B."

"What doesn't matter?" I said.

"The rest of it," Sandy said flatly, and then we rounded the last of the string of ledges and headed southeast into more open water. The wind picked up and the boat began to rock with the chop. Dalton and Angel stood up carefully and inched their way back around the cabin. I glanced at Sandy and he was watching them, and his jaw clenched and he shook his head almost imperceptibly. I imagined that behind his Oakleys, his eyes narrowed with disdain.

So much for bonding.

We made a wide sweep just southwest of Mount Desert Island. The island's mountains loomed above us like something that had just been discovered, rocky peaks high above the tree-lined shores. There was something grand about this coast, the scale of it, the cold, clean hardness. It was a place where for centuries people had lived at their own risk, finding a way to accommodate the landscape because the landscape wouldn't accommodate them. Cold waters as deadly as boiling oil. Hard winters. Rocky terrain. It was a place that bred humility in most people and, as we swung back up the east side of Long Island,

I wondered if that was what Roxanne was finding in the Connellys, and not the arrogance we'd expected.

I thought about that as we made our way back up the bay, the chop subsiding, the sun falling in the sky to the west. As we approached the shallower waters leading into the harbor, Sandy went down the ladder to the cockpit to bring the boat in. Ms. Kind was reading her *New Yorker* in the salon. Monica had reluctantly given up on the last rays of the sun and moved inside. Dalton and Angel were standing at the stern and Dalton was pointing to something on the shore. Sandy said he'd come alongside the float and asked me to put the fenders out on the starboard side. I stepped along the narrow deck beside the cabin and flipped the fenders overboard on their lines. When I came back to the cockpit, Sandy said, "I think I can turn you into a boat guy, Jack."

"So I guessed right on the starboard?" I said.

We moved slowly through the brightly painted lobster pot buoys and then Sandy stepped out onto the float. I moved to the bow and tossed him the line that was coiled there like a golden snake. He fixed the line to a big cleat on the float.

"Very nice," Sandy said, and gave me an easy grin. In spite of myself, I grinned back.

Dalton, Monica, and Kathleen Kind started to queue up, like the fasten-seat-belt light had just switched off. Nobody looked thrilled by the excursion except Angel, who turned back and looked the yacht over and said, to no one in particular, "I like this boat. We'll have to do this again."

And then she looked at Sandy and said, "Sandy, next time I want to go to Bar Harbor."

"You'll have to talk to the captain," he said.

"Okay," Angel said. "I will."

9

They came down the ramp to the float: David, Maddie, Roxanne, and Maeve, who was five and very pretty, all tanned with wild, curly golden hair. She hopped up the ramp as the dinghy came alongside and then hopped back down. She was wearing sneakers without laces and cutoff jeans and a T-shirt that said JACKSON HOLE.

"Hey, everybody," she said. "Did you see porpoises?"

I climbed onto the float and said, "No porpoises this time."

"Last time I went with my daddy on the small boat, that one out there, and we saw six. They were following us."

"They were," David said. "Stayed right alongside for a couple of miles."

"They're wet and black and shiny," Maeve said, and she did a hop-scotch move on the float and back to Roxanne. "Have you ever seen one?"

"I don't think so," Roxanne said, leaning close to her.

"Then we'll take you. My daddy knows where they are, and seals, too. Sometimes we see the seal babies."

"That would be fun, Maeve," Roxanne said.

"Let's go tomorrow," Maeve said. "Daddy, can Roxanne and her friend stay tonight and we'll get up really early and we'll go on the big boat, 'cause it's cold in the morning, and you can make eggs and waffles and we can have hot chocolate because Roxanne has never seen a porpoise? Can you believe that?"

She turned to Roxanne. "How old are you?"

"Thirty-two."

"And you've never seen a porpoise? You gotta go, girl."

Roxanne smiled, and Maddie said, "Sure, we'll take her out."

"Let's go," David said. "Sandy, leave it running. All set for fuel?"

He jumped aboard. I looked to Roxanne and she said, "I really don't know whether—"

"Let's go," Maeve said, and she took Roxanne's hand and began to pull her toward the boat. Roxanne smiled and surrendered and they stepped onto the gunwale and down into the boat. The others were on the float, Sandy, too, and David said, "Fix everybody up with drinks, whatever, Sandy. Food should be here soon. I told them four. We'll be back in an hour."

I climbed aboard and David stepped to the helm as Sandy shoved us off. The motors rumbled and we eased away from the float and past the Boston Whaler and the other mooring buoys and then David eased the stick forward and the yacht gathered itself up and took off with a roar, jet wakes spewing into the air. Maeve opened a locker under the stern seats and pulled out a life jacket and snapped it on. She clambered up the ladder, and Maddie followed her, and then Maeve leaned back over and called to Roxanne.

"I'll be right there, honey," Roxanne said, and she came over to where I was standing across from David. He turned to her and grinned and said, "We'll find you a porpoise, Roxanne, or my name isn't Ahab."

She smiled and he looked back at the instruments, eased back on the stick. The roar eased, too, and David settled back onto the helm seat and turned to us.

"Have a seat, guys," he said. "Get comfortable."

We did, sitting on the cushioned settees across from him. David picked up the microphone and started talking to someone, first about the weather, then about delivering lobsters to the float. I put my arm around Roxanne as the shoreline receded and I leaned close to her and said softly, "You okay?"

She turned and we looked out the port side at the islands.

"Fine. The little girl is an absolute delight."

"She back them up?"

"Completely. Said this girl Devlin was 'jerky.' I think it was the worst word she could think of. Said she squeezed her shoulder too hard and put her in the closet in the dark. Told her if she complained to her parents, she'd flush her doll down the toilet with the poop."

"Nice."

"Yeah. I still need to track her down."

"But the parents are okay?"

"Oh, they're really very pleasant, very sincere. Maeve seems close to them, don't you think?"

"Yeah. Not at all what I expected."

"The cokehead chasing the maid?"

"Yeah, although there's some chasing going on."

"Oh?"

I told her about Dalton, the aging Harvard jock, and Angel, the pretty assistant.

"Is she receptive?"

"In an arm's-length sort of way. Knows she has a ring in his nose."

"That's pathetic," Roxanne said.

"A bit," I said, and David hung up the microphone, eased off the throttle, and leaned toward us.

"If we're going to see them this time of the afternoon, this stretch in here is the best place. They chase the mackerel into the bay, drive them up this strait between the islands."

"Do we sit and wait?" Roxanne said.

"No, we'll cruise. I'll go up on the bridge. See a little better up high. Come on up."

We went up the ladder first. There were cushioned seats arranged in a semicircle with the helm, all teak and steel, on the right. Maeve was kneeling facing the bow, her hands clenching a stainless-steel bar. Maddie stepped to the helm and watched the instrument panel and then touched the stick and took over. We sat on the left side and looked out at the water, the sunlit shoreline. After a minute, David popped up the ladder, arms loaded with fleece sweatshirts. They were dark green, with *Escape* embroidered on the left breast.

"No fun being cold out here," he said. He took off his sunglasses and shrugged his fleece on. Roxanne and I did the same, and David took the helm from Maddie while she put her fleece on. Maeve said she wasn't cold but went and sat on the helm seat beside her father, one little hand on the controls.

"She's a different species, I think sometimes," Maddie said, sitting down next to Roxanne. "Little bit of a thing, not an ounce of fat on her, and she's never cold. Swims before anybody up here, first one in, last one out."

"Some kids are just like that," Roxanne said. "Must be their metabolism."

"So you don't think this will bother her in the long run?"

"I'm no expert," Roxanne said. "But she seems very well adjusted. Very happy."

"Oh, she is. Just a joy to be around. When David or I feel a little discouraged about something, we say we need some Maeve time. She's the light in our lives."

I smiled as I listened. It was refreshing to hear that a couple who had tens of millions of dollars, and no small amount of political clout, still turned to a five-year-old girl to cheer them up.

"But I don't want anything lingering. I don't want guilt or anything haunting her."

Maddie paused and then said it again, not to us as much as to herself.

"I don't want anything like that for her."

I looked at Roxanne and she caught my glance.

"So I really thank you for making this so, well, I wouldn't call it easy, but comfortable for us. I mean, the thought of the State coming to see whether we were abusive parents—I know you have to do that, but you've done it in a good way for us, and for Maeve."

She reached out and touched Roxanne's hand.

"So thank you."

"You don't need to thank me," Roxanne said.

"Now what do you think? We have a friend who's a child therapist. She practices in Cambridge and Boston Children's. She's really wonderful. We could have her talk to Maeve."

"I'd keep it very low-key," Roxanne said. "She seems so good now."

"Oh, but you don't know what they've got locked away in their little heads," Maddie said. "And the way children can work so hard to appear happy and normal. They do it for their parents, for themselves. They want their lives to be what they were before, so they sort of re-create it all."

Roxanne turned to her, interested.

"Have you studied that?"

"No," Maddie said quickly. "But when people talk, I listen. David says I have a master's degree in osmosis."

She turned and leaned across Roxanne toward me. "Now, Jack, do you write about coastal issues?"

I said I'd write about anything that affected people's lives in Maine. She said I should write about aquaculture—that a company wanted to fill this bay with a fish farm and ugly blue barrels. She'd seen them Down East and in the west of Ireland.

I listened as she filled me in. How the proposal had been defeated at the state level only after David and the Rockefellers and others brought all their political cannons to bear. How areas of the Maine coast without influence were vulnerable. Maddie talked about bacteria and fish waste and dissolved oxygen. She said the story in the *Times* was okay, but the problem hadn't gone away. She was smart, determined, and articulate. I could see why the fish farmers had retreated.

"I'll keep you posted, Jack," she said.

She leaned back as David, one hand on the stick, told us the histories of the passing islands. One had been used for raising hogs, another had been for sheep. One was home to a reclusive member of a prominent New York family. South of us were quarry islands that, at the turn of the twentieth century, had hosted small towns filled with immigrant stonecutters. Granite from these islands had been used in the construction of much of Wall Street and the Library of Congress.

We nodded and he slid back to his seat, adjusted our course to cut between two bars. We sat for a moment and then Maddie leaned over to us and said, "Do you think you'll have children?"

It was a forward thing to ask, but she seemed so earnest that it was hard to take offense.

"We just might," Roxanne said.

"Because we have friends who have chosen not to. I tell them they're missing the most wonderful, joyous thing passible. We probably won't have any more children of our own, but we're planning on adopting next year. We're working with people in the Dominican Republic. Do you place children in adoptive families, Roxanne?"

Roxanne said it was a different part of the agency, but yes, they did.

"Because I've said to David, you know, we're going so far for a child. Perhaps we should consider a child from Maine or Boston. You don't want to neglect your own backyard."

"No," Roxanne said.

"Because I think we'd be a good family for most kids. Maeve isn't possessive or jealous, at least not yet. And we'd be able to offer them opportunities that many families wouldn't."

Maddie said it so matter-of-factly, no brag at all. I looked out at the gorgeous Maine coast as we cruised in this beautiful boat with this family that seemed loving and well-adjusted and charming. I thought of the places Maeve would see, of the good she could do in her lifetime with parents like these. I wondered why these Connellys never made the papers, why they were so different from the stereotypes I'd expected.

"There they are," Maeve called out, her tiny hand pointing toward the waters in front of us. "Porpoises."

She jumped down from the seat and took Roxanne by the arm and pulled until Roxanne stood up. Maeve pointed.

"Do you see them?"

"Oh, yeah," Roxanne said. "Look at that. They're jumping."

"I told you," Maeve said, and I glanced over at her mother watching her. Maddie was only half-smiling and the other half of her expression seemed like one of worry or sadness, like all of this might suddenly come to an end. It was like she was clutching it tightly, trying to keep the scene in front of her from slipping away.

Roxanne had come to protect the daughter, but in that moment it was Maddie who seemed more vulnerable.

Suddenly she turned to Roxanne and me. "What are the chances," she said, "of this story getting out?"

10

When we got back to the house, the others were on the porch, drinks and hors d'oeuvres in hand. Sandy was drinking a Beck's and talking to Monica, who was drinking something clear from a tall glass. Ms. Kind was stretched out on a wicker chaise with her *New Yorker* and a glass of white wine. Dalton, scotch in hand, had a chart out and was showing Angel where we'd gone on our cruise. She sipped a glass of wine, looking up as we arrived.

Maeve announced the count: three porpoises, six seals, two ospreys, and a bald eagle.

"Good for you, honey," Angel said while everybody beamed. "Are you hungry? There's shrimp and these lobster things and California rolls."

She herded Maeve to the table, where the food and drinks were arranged on a white cloth. And then she turned to Roxanne and me and said, "Would you guys like a drink? How 'bout a beer? Glass of wine?"

I started to decline but David said, "How would a Guinness be, Jack? You seem like a good Celt to me. Roxanne?"

She shook her head but said a sparkling water would be great. A high-school-age girl appeared with another tray of shrimp and Angel said, "Could you get her a Poland Spring? A fizzy one."

The girl said, "Yes, ma'am," and it occurred to me that Angel Moretti from the North End was finding she liked this life very much, thank you. If the gardener had wandered by, she would have told him to go dig a hole.

David put a pint glass of Guinness in my hand, apologizing that it wasn't a draft. I said it was fine, and the caterer girl brought the spring water for Roxanne. She toasted me with a glance and a tip of her glass and sipped. Maeve bounded over and grabbed Roxanne by the hand and said, "Let's go see my room." Maddie joined them and said, "Would you like to see more of the house, Roxanne?" and Roxanne said, "Sure, that would be nice." Off the three of them went, deeper into the house.

Dalton had called David over to the chart and was asking about symbols and what they meant. Monica, looking up invitingly at Sandy, was asking him what it was like to go all the way across the ocean in a boat, and wasn't he terrified the whole time. Her lower lip nearly trembled. Ms. Kind looked up from her magazine to survey the scene, smiled smugly, and looked back down. Angel topped off her wine and sidled over to me, touching my arm and saying, "So, Jack, you writing about this outing for the *New York Times*?"

"I don't think so," I said.

"The Connelly family isn't news?"

"Only when it does something newsworthy," I said. "Going for a boat ride and eating shrimp doesn't quite make it."

"Oh, really? I've seen write-ups that had less than that happening. A benefit dinner, something at the MFA. Voila, they're in the *Globe*."

"Just a photo, though. And I don't write for the society pages."

"Why not? You get to go to parties, meet lots of beautiful people."

"I meet lots of people anyway."

"Not this kind of people. What do you write about up here in Maine? People in trailers and that sort of thing?"

"Some of them," I said. "Some of them are good people. You know, five miles from here is a different world. Where I live is a different world."

"What is it? You and all the poor people?"

"Some of them are poor. Some are just regular people. They support themselves, love their families, live good lives."

"Yuk. It's so, like, depressing. On and on forever, the same old crummy routine. Go to work for forty years, retire, get sick. What's the saying? Life's a bitch and then you die?"

"Most people in this country don't even know what a hard life is," I said.

"I know. The starving people in India and all that. My parents used to pound that into us when we were kids. I went to Catholic school and they'd have the nuns come in who worked in these countries and tell us horror stories. We had paper cups with slots in the top and we'd fill them with change and then give these nuns fifty-pound boxes of pennies. I don't know what they did with them. Who wants to count forty thousand pennies, you know? It seems so—"

"Futile?"

"Yeah."

"You sure you're in the right business?"

She looked at me blankly for a moment, like she'd forgotten what business she was in.

"The foundation, I mean."

"Oh, but that's not boxes of pennies. It's hundreds of thousands of dollars. We do a lot of good."

"I'm sure. And what do you do?"

"I'm Tim's assistant. He's the chief of staff, like at the White House. He keeps things on track and I keep him on track."

I looked at her, the big dark eyes, the delicate curve of her lips, a faint shadow of cleavage showing through her half-buttoned blouse. I bet she kept him on a track, like a greyhound chasing one of those mechanical rabbits.

As if on cue, Dalton joined us. He put a hand on Angel's back, laying claim, and then let it drop away. I checked for a wedding ring, and sure enough, there was a pale line of skin on his left ring finger.

"Beautiful coastline, isn't it?" Dalton said. "Get down here often?"

"Once in a while," I said. "It's a big state. And I cover northern New Hampshire, some of Canada."

"We love it up here," he said.

"Who's we?" I said.

He glanced at Angel and said, "Oh, all of us. David and Maddie have us up pretty regularly. Can't spend all our time at the grindstone. And they have a place in Jackson Hole. We try to get out there at least once every winter. You're going to have to join us next year, Angel."

"But I don't ski, Tim," she said.

"I'll teach you. A couple of days and you'll be doing double diamonds."

"When I think diamonds, I don't think skiing," she said, and she smiled at him, a high-voltage beam that she could switch on and off. Dalton took a swallow of scotch while he recovered.

"Pretty girl like you, I don't think you'll have a problem," Dalton began, but Angel wasn't listening. She was looking past him at Connelly as he approached.

"Jack," he said. "Have something to eat? Don't be shy. What we don't eat the crabs get in the morning. Amazing how they can sense food. Throw in a shrimp, a piece of chicken, and you can see them come running from fifty feet away, like you've rung the dinner bell."

"They must smell it in the water."

"Highly effective scavengers," Connelly said.

"It's crabs that eat bodies in the water," Dalton said. "Not fish, like people say."

"Uck, Tim," Angel said. "That's disgusting."

"Well, it's true," he said, but once again her attention was elsewhere.

"David," she said. "Tomorrow let's take *Escape* over to Bar Harbor."

"Bar Harbor," Connelly said. "In August? Now there's my idea of hell. Boats going in and out, half the people don't know port from starboard. Crowds milling up and down the sidewalks. Why would you want to go there?"

"To see people," Angel said. "Go out to lunch. Go to the shops. There must be something worth buying."

"How many T-shirts do you need?" Dalton said.

"We can't spend the whole time here looking at seals," Angel said, and I grinned. She didn't, and for a moment the beautiful young woman washed away and revealed a petulant little girl.

"Come on, David," she said, and she took him by the arm and eased closer to him, looked up into his eyes. "It'll be fun."

Dalton smiled but his eyes didn't. David chuckled, sipped his Guinness, but there was something unfunny about the tone of her voice. It was almost as though she wasn't persuading Connelly as much as ordering him.

"Sorry, Angel," David said. "Tomorrow Sandy has to get her ready. We're making a run out to Matinicus, if the weather holds."

"Does that take all day, getting the boat ready?"

"Well, not all day. It's just that we've got to fuel up, clean up, get the food all set."

"If we left early, couldn't you do that in the afternoon?"

"Jeez, Angel, I suppose but—"

"Good," Angel said, in her element, surrounded by men, getting her way. "Maybe Sandy can make reservations. There's this one restaurant I've heard good things about."

I looked away, and caught Ms. Kind watching and listening. Her gaze toward Angel was hard and cold.

11

The car doors closed. There was a silent moment and then I said, "Sorry."

"You're not supposed to—"

"I know. I didn't mean it to turn out that way. He just invited me along. And—"

"And what?"

"And I was worried about you."

"I've been to places a thousand times more scary than this," Roxanne said.

"I know. I just had a bad vibe about this."

"What? You thought they'd kill the State lady and bury her in the cellar?"

"At sea?"

"What?"

"If I were them, I'd take the person way offshore and dump them."

"Thanks, Jack. You can suggest it."

"You know what I mean. And I am sorry."

"It's okay," she said, the irritation slipping away. "I guess we're kind of in this together."

"I guess," I said. "So what's your take on them?"

"Considering the circumstances?"

"Yeah."

"They were sort of okay," Roxanne said. "Actually, they were pretty nice."

"Easier if they were complete jerks?"

"Much," she said.

As we drove, Roxanne told me about her time with Maddie. She said the house was beautiful but old-fashioned, as if changes were made reluctantly and tradition prevailed. She said the master bedroom took up both a second-floor level of a turret and the adjoining room, and there was a fireplace and a beautiful view from the bed.

"Sounds like it would be just the place for—"

"Jack."

"What?"

"This is serious."

"I am," I said, and I took her hand and held it as though we were high school kids on a date. Roxanne said Maddie was working with representatives of a consortium of foundations that was trying to figure out the best way to use its resources to combat child abuse and neglect.

"I told her it wasn't as simple as 'combating' anything," Roxanne said. "I said it's such a complex relationship between all kinds of things. Drugs and drinking and self-esteem and people who direct their self-loathing at their children."

"Did that discourage her?"

"No. She just seemed to be trying very hard to understand what I was saying. She'd just say, 'Okay. So where do we go from there?' "

"You really like her."

"Yes, I do. I think she's a serious person," she said. "I think she really wants to do as much good as she can, with what she has to work with. And you like him?"

"Yeah. I tried hard not to, but he's just a good guy. All kinds of interests, very curious about everything. He wants to come up here sometime and learn how to cut wood."

"No kidding."

"Yeah," I said. "He said they own fifty acres right on the coast south of Blue Harbor and he'd like to build a studio sort of thing in the middle of it. And he wants to use the wood off the land and he'd like to cut it himself."

"Is he serious?"

"I think it's a challenge. And maybe some sort of spiritual thing, harvesting from the land and all that."

"What's the studio for?" Roxanne said.

"He writes, he said. And she paints. He said he's working on a historical novel about Boston and Maine during the Revolution."

"I guess that never made the tabloids," Roxanne said.

"Maybe if he writes it in bed with some naked woman not his wife. I wonder how my writing would be if— "

"We'll never know, will we?" she said.

"No," I said. "We won't."

We were crossing Knox Ridge and the sun had dropped below the wooded hills to the west, leaving the sky a dappled pink. It looked like clouds moving in for tomorrow, and I wondered if Angel would get her trip to Bar Harbor.

"You know, there was a lot of tension in that group," I said.

"I sensed something but I wasn't with them as much as you."

"This Angel—for an employee, I mean, here she is, some assistant who probably wiggled her butt and batted her eyelashes to get in the door, and she was almost insolent with Connelly, I thought."

"Like a spoiled kid?" Roxanne said.

"Yeah."

"And he's too nice to put her in her place?"

"I don't know. I mean, the food and the drinks and the boat and the house. I'm sure they're wined and dined the whole time. Dalton said he flies some of them to Jackson Hole in the winter to ski."

"What's it to him? He's got the money."

"I know, but still. He doesn't have to do any of it. She shouldn't be an ingrate."

"Maybe she's done something for him," Roxanne said.

I thought about that as I came over a crest and headed down the back side of the ridge toward home. Maybe there was some truth to David's reputation; maybe that was his Achilles' heel. A few beers, the wrong woman.

"Some women just know how to push men's buttons," Roxanne said. "And she's very, very attractive."

"And he's a prime piece of—"

"Real estate," she said.

"Yeah. 'Get out of the way, Maddie, and let me stake my claim.' "

"Maybe she already has," Roxanne said.

"That would explain some of it," I said.

"But I don't want to think that."

"So we won't."

"What will we think?" she said.

"About how Maddie hit the nail on the head."

"About us having—"

"Yeah," I said. "You think she knew?"

"Some women have a sixth sense about babies," Roxanne said.

"Do you?"

"I don't know about that. I just know I want to have one with you."

And she took my hand and clasped it in hers for the rest of the ride. I steered with one hand, off the main road and onto the dirt road, and then down the narrow lane under the canopy of trees. In front of the house, I parked and leaned across and kissed Roxanne for a long time. Her mouth was warm and soft and open and we drank each other in, and when we came apart, Roxanne sighed.

We walked to the house, opened the door, and Roxanne went to the kitchen. She put the phone receiver in a drawer in the kitchen and closed it. Went back and dropped her pager in, too. Took off her sweater and hung it on the back of a chair, then went to the refrigerator and took out a bottle of Chardonnay. Poured two glasses. Handed me one and took my other hand and led me upstairs to the loft. Kissed me as we stood beside the bed and her top fell to the floor and then her slacks, and then we were swept off our feet as if we'd been caught by waves, upended and tossed, clothes torn off, rolled onto the sand and pulled back, naked, into each other's arms, clinging for dear life.

And when we surfaced, we held each other in the last light of that day and Roxanne said she loved me, and I said I loved her, too. Her eyes filled and she pulled me close and held me tightly. Her chin pressed my shoulder.

"Maybe that was the one," Roxanne whispered.

"Maybe it was," I said.

I felt her swallow, and then I felt something prick my skin. It was a teardrop. I held her closer.

12

―‒ꟺ‒―

Roxanne went to work, commuting from Prosperity to the Rockland office of the DHS. She worked on tracking down Devlin in Ireland and got as far as an aunt in County Kerry. She said Devlin may have had a bit of a mean streak, but she came by it honestly. Her father was a brute and once killed a cat by flinging it out a window onto the road. This was before he left the family and moved to Cork, the aunt said. Good riddance. And no, she hadn't spoken to Devlin in years.

I worked with my old friend and neighbor cutting on a woodlot in Appleton. The land was a tangled mess—snags and bowed trees left from the ice storm two years before. The trick was to figure out which limb was the trip wire—before you cut it. I gashed my cheek, and my nose was sore where a limb had whacked me like a cop's baton.

I told Clair I'd met the Connellys, because we had no secrets, but I couldn't tell him the circumstances. "So be that way," he said, but then he got going on rich people buying up the Maine coast, that the need to possess everything beautiful—paintings, antiques, mistresses, the sunrise over Penobscot Bay—was one of the flaws of capitalism.

"We're taught that anything of value can be bought, that our possessions are the source of happiness," he said, putting his saws back in the truck, closing up the toolbox. "So these people see a beautiful place, they buy it. It's a terrible compulsion, this need to possess things. Native Americans never had it. Buddhists don't have it. Leaves you feeling empty, ultimately. So you try to fill the vacuum. Promiscuous sex and booze and drugs. But contentment doesn't come."

"Connelly seemed pretty happy, considering the circumstances," I said.

"A facade, Jack."

"I don't know. A beautiful wife, cute kid, a ton of money."

"A recipe for misery," Clair said. "Pass me that chain oil."

"He wants to come up and cut wood with us."

"As long as he doesn't get in the way."

On that note, hot and sweaty and smelling of fumes, we got in Clair's truck and rumbled on home.

My marching orders were waiting.

I'd pitched a couple of stories to the *Times* and was waiting for Myra in the Boston bureau to tell me which one to do first. My pick was one about two guys in a little town up north who'd been best friends since kindergarten, had grown into bad drunks, and then one best friend had killed the other with an ax, reportedly chopping his buddy into pieces. Myra liked that one, the idea of a friendship that ended in horror. She wanted to know why, and she also wanted to know how many pieces.

After a shower, I tried to find out.

I called the medical examiner's office in Augusta and got Nancy, the secretary. There was nobody else in the office, but that was okay, since Nancy had been there thirty years, knew everything that went on, and was unfailingly accurate. Our conversations were off the record.

"The guy with the ax up north," I said.

"Oh, yes. Paul Bunyan."

"How many pieces?"

"Five," she said.

"Torso and all the limbs?"

"Not quite."

"Jeez. Decapitated?"

"Quite."

"And three limbs?"

"That would be the next logical choice."

"God, best friends."

"We always hurt the ones we love," Nancy said. "And now I've got a question for you."

"Shoot."

"Why aren't you out at the scene? Isn't the town of Monroe near you?"

"Twenty minutes away. Scene of what?"

"A woman. Shallow grave."

"A homicide?"

"They're still out there—but something tells me she didn't dig a hole and tuck herself in."

We crossed the ridge on back roads, slipping through the dense summer woods, past barnyards where kids stood and stared, alongside pastures where tail-flicking dairy cows stared, too. Clair drove and I rode. Cresting the ridge, we looked out toward Knox and the Waldo County farms, fields, and woods that were the backdrop of countless dramas that had been acted out here over the centuries. It was a place that was simple at first glance, complex and dense and hard to fathom when you looked closer. I wondered if the woman was local.

I wondered if she was young or old. I wondered what circumstances had led her to end up like this.

Coming down off the ridge, we rolled into the outskirts of the village and took a left. Two boys were riding bicycles, fishing rods across their handlebars. Clair slowed the truck and I leaned out the window, asked the boys whether they'd seen police. They said they had, three miles down, but a cop had chased them away. We drove on and a couple of miles out saw an unmarked state police cruiser parked against the woods. There was a uniformed trooper leaning against the car, and he straightened when we pulled in. I got out and he walked toward me, head shaved, young as a pup.

"I'm going to have to ask you to leave, sir," he began.

"I'm a reporter," I said, and I handed him my *New York Times* ID. He peered at it and then at me. The jeans and boots. The cut on my face. I took out my pad and pen and smiled.

"I need to talk to Detective Cade."

He looked at the card again, then back at me. He looked over at Clair, who had his arm out of the cab. It was tanned and muscled and the tattoo said SEMPER FI.

"Who's that in the truck, sir?"

"My assistant."

"Huh."

"Detective Cade knows me," I said.

"Is that right?" the trooper said.

He turned away and murmured into the radio, listened, and then turned back to us, disappointed that I'd pulled rank.

"Straight in and follow the tracks, Mr. McMorrow," he said.

So straight in it was, down the logging road, following the furrows between the tufts of grass and clumps of burdock. The grass got thicker as we drove, and soon you could see it had been brushed flat by the undersides of cars. The truck lurched along, branches scraping the sides and top of the cab, and then we came to a bit of a clearing where five police cars and a crime lab van were pulled into the brush. We got out and walked down the track deeper, between thickets of alder and cherry. A hundred yards in, Cade met us coming the other way.

He leaned down as we approached and picked a clump of burdock off his jeans.

"McMorrow," he said. "You the only reporter in Maine or what?"

"Seems that way sometimes," I said. "How's it going?"

"It's going."

"This is Clair Varney. We work together."

He gave Clair the once-over and they shook hands.

"What do you do?" Cade said.

"Logistics," Clair said.

"Marines?" the detective said, glancing at the tattoo.

"Right," Clair said.

"I did four in the army," Cade said. "You?"

"Twenty-two years, but time flies."

"Where?"

"Oh, here and there," Clair said.

"Force Recon," I said.

"No kidding. Huh. That's the real deal. Vietnam?"

Clair nodded. Cade looked like he wanted to talk more, but it was time for business.

"Well, maybe you'd feel right at home in the stuff we're working in. You get in deeper, it's all blackberries and vines. Dense? I guess. All tangled with these thick viny things."

"They dug a hole in these brambles?"

"No, she was in a clearing. This is a tractor path that probably once led to a pasture. Clearing where she was buried is like an island almost, with everything else grown up around it. But they had to drag her through some of the underbrush to get her where she was. Take a look."

We started down the path, Cade leading the way. He was a wiry little guy, energetic and boyish, the youngest homicide detective in the history of the Maine State Police. He lived like an Eagle Scout, was very religious, and threw himself into murder cases like they were class projects and he was teacher's pet.

"How recent?" I asked.

"Very. Could be a day."

"Young? Old?"

"Twenties, but that's a guess."

I scribbled as we walked.

"Clothed?"

"Not really."

"How can you be not really clothed?"

"She was wearing one thing. I can't say what it was."

"Where was she wearing it?"

"Around her—come on, McMorrow. Slow down."

"Injuries? I mean, is she all beat up, or shot?"

"Nothing apparent. ME will take care of that."

"Local?"

"I don't think so."

"Why not?"

"Don't know."

"Is she still out here?"

"Oh, yeah. I'm going to have to ask you to not go right up to the scene."

"How deep?"

"A foot or less. I think they got tired of digging. It's not as easy as they make it look on TV."

"Who found her?"

"Wasn't a who, it was a what. Coyotes got digging at her. Then some old guy was up here with a beagle, hunting rabbits. Dog didn't come back."

"Found something better," Clair said.

"So what's she look like?" I said.

"Dark hair, pretty. I think she was, anyway. Of course, she could be from anywhere. So recent it may be hard because there won't be missing persons reports yet. Not like somebody missing for months."

"Somebody's pride and joy," Clair said.

Cade looked at him curiously.

"That's exactly right," he said. "That's what I never forget."

"So you'll put out a picture?"

"A sketch. Picture's a little rough for public consumption."

"I'm sure," I said.

Cade reached into his back pocket and slipped an envelope out. The three of us stopped and he handed the envelope to me.

"I don't think it'll take too long to ID her," he said.

I opened the envelope, took out the Polaroid print, and turned it over.

"My God," I said.

"What is it?" Clair said.

I stared at the swollen face, purplish and misshapen like a bruised grape. Her hair was askew and there was grass in it.

"What?" Cade said.

"I know her," I said.

"Local?" Cade said.

"No," I said. "Boston."

I paused, still stunned, cradling the photograph like it was something delicate, this image of broken flesh.

"So who is it?" Clair said.

"Her name is Angel," I said. "Angel Moretti."

13

We did our talking next to the police cars, right there in the woods. There was Cade, another detective who was an older woman, and a uniformed sergeant. Clair leaned against the police pickup a short distance away, within earshot.

"You sure?" Cade said. "She's pretty beat up."

"Completely."

"How do you know her?"

"I just met her this week."

"You met her in Boston?"

"I met her here, on the coast. She was up here visiting."

"Visiting where?"

"Blue Harbor."

"Who was she visiting?"

I hesitated, my hand on the lid of Pandora's box.

"She was staying with David and Maddie Connelly. They have a summer place there."

"That's not *the* Connellys," Cade said.

"Yeah," I said. "It is."

Th cops looked at each other. The woman detective said, "No shit." Cade said, "Huh," and looked at the photograph again, as though some clue might now emerge. "So she's some Boston rich lady?"

"She was working on it," I said.

"How?" Cade said.

I pictured Angel with her hand on my arm, putting a spell on Dalton with her big dark eyes, the petulant little-girl act she used on David. "With everything she had," I said. "And she had a lot."

I recounted what I remembered about Angel, Monica, and Ms. Kind. I told them Angel seemed to be involved in some way with Tim Dalton. I told them she seemed pretty familiar with the Connellys, but it was sort of one-way, like she didn't quite understand that working for them didn't mean they were her buddies.

The cops asked a few questions but not many. I was partway through it when the ME's people brought Angel's body out of the woods, in a green bag on a shiny chrome gurney that jounced and rattled over the bumpy ground.

"I want you to see her," Cade said. "Make absolutely sure."

"Okay," I said.

He walked over to the back of the ME's van. I followed slowly, not without trepidation. I waited as one of the ME's men unzipped the bag and folded one end back. Angel stared up at me, discolored and dirty. She was still oddly beautiful, even with the life and dreams drained out of her. She looked very young, like a child who had been playing in the mud.

I stared at her, unable to look away. And then I reached down and pulled the bag lower. The technician reached out to stop me, but

I saw it. Around her neck was a white scarf. It was pulled tight and the dead flesh around it was blackened.

"Strangled," I said.

"Not for publication," Cade said.

"Is that silk?" I said.

"It's a Hermes," the woman detective said. "Expensive. I want to know more about this guy she was with."

They zipped Angel up and slid the gurney into the van. The van backed out, its warning horn beeping, and when it had lurched down the path, we talked for another half-hour. I remembered my role and asked some questions toward the end.

They told me the name of the guy who found her. They said there was no car found nearby, but they were still looking. I asked if anyone had seen any activity in the woods the previous night or day, and they said they didn't know yet, that the case was still fresh, that the investigation was just getting under way.

"You coming by, that was something dropped from heaven for us," Cade said, and then he added, in all earnestness, "Now how you going to work that into your story?"

I mulled it over in the truck as we lumbered back down the path through the woods. I'd punched in the number of the Boston *Times* bureau on the cell phone and was waiting. I wondered how Myra would want to handle it. How did the reporter know Angel? How did the reporter know the Connellys? What about Roxanne's case? Would that come out somehow?

The phone cut out and I dialed again. When we pulled out onto the side of the road, the kid trooper was still on duty. A television news crew from Bangor was setting up, the satellite dish rising from the roof of its van. A press photographer jumped out of a car and jogged toward us, a reporter with a notebook trailing after him. He pulled up short and fired off a few shots of Clair and me as Clair eased the truck up onto the pavement.

"Are they cops?" I heard the photographer say as the reporter approached.

She stopped, and I recognized her. She was from the *Bangor Daily*. She stared at me, and said, "Hey, that's McMorrow from the *New York Times*. How'd he get in?"

Clair pulled over on the crest of Knox Ridge, hoping for better reception for the phone. I dialed and waited and this time Myra answered. She sounded harried, and when I told her about them finding a body in the woods, she said, "Three inches."

I told her they'd ID'd the body as a woman from Boston, and she said, "Okay, give me six."

And then I told her the name: Angel Moretti. I said she'd worked for the Connellys at their foundation. I told Myra I'd met Angel at the Connellys' house in Blue Harbor earlier in the week. Myra said, "Oh, baby."

And then came the questions.

Myra was good—twenty-seven years old, mind like a stiletto, headed for the top of some news organization, and it was in these situations that it showed. She wanted to know whether the Connellys were suspects. How closely they'd pinpointed the time of death. What Angel actually did at Sky Blue Foundation. Where in Boston she'd lived. How she'd landed in the proximity of people like the Connellys. Had they taken her on as some sort of protégée?

"For that matter, Jack, what in the world were you doing there?"

"It's a long story," I said.

"Yeah, well, you can tell me later. I'll call New York. Keep the phone with you."

I rang off and looked at Clair. He was considering the view, the patchwork of pale green fields showing high on the wooded hillsides like blankets put down in a grassy field for a picnic.

"You know how much work went into clearing those woods, a hundred and fifty years ago?" he said.

"She likes the story," I said.

"A lifetime of work," Clair said. "And look at that puckerbrush where they found the girl. Doesn't take long for nature to take it all back."

"I've got to find out everything I can about Angel."

"Is it the fact that a beautiful young woman is dead in the woods up here?" Clair said. "Or is it the celebrity angle?"

"All of the above," I said.

So we tumbled back down toward the valley and home, slower than we'd come. When we pulled into the dooryard, Roxanne's Explorer was parked by the shed. She was home.

"I'll let you work," Clair said.

"Come in for a few minutes," I said. "You and Roxanne can help me think."

She was in the kitchen, still in her work skirt and blouse, eating baby carrots dipped in Grey Poupon mustard. She chewed and gave me a mustardy kiss on the cheek and said hi to Clair.

"I've got some news," Roxanne said. "There was a mother cardinal and four babies at the feeder a minute ago. The little ones were so cute. But that's not the news."

"I have some news, too," I said. "It's not good."

"What's the matter?"

"Angel's dead. Angel from the Connellys."

Roxanne froze in mid-bite.

"What? A car accident?"

"No. She was murdered."

Roe went pale, put her hand on the counter.

"That beautiful girl," she said.

"A blessing and a curse, being beautiful," Clair said.

"In Boston?" Roxanne said.

I told her where Angel had been found. I told her I didn't think they knew where she'd been killed.

"Monroe," Roxanne said. "Who knows about some woods in Monroe?"

"Not hard to find places like that," Clair said. "You just keep driving until you run out of road."

"My God. But who—"

I shrugged.

"How?"

I told her.

"Oh, her poor parents."

"Every parent's worst nightmare," Clair said. "When the girls first moved to the city, I used to wake up at night in a sweat. Scared me more than everything I'd done, the prospect of something happening to them."

I glanced at him, thought that this had peeled away a layer of him, revealed a part of him I'd never known.

"Who . . . ?" Roxanne said.

"Could have been somebody from here," I said. "She'd attract attention anyplace. Broken down by the side of the road. Wrong time, wrong place, wrong person."

"Was she—" Roxanne said.

"I don't think they know. They just found her. We were just there."

"I wonder if anyone has told David and Maddie," she said. "I was just talking to Maddie this afternoon."

Where was she?"

"Back in Boston."

"David, too?"

"Yeah. He was there. He said hello, in the background."

I thought for a moment, and Roxanne said, "Jack, will he be a suspect or something?"

"Anyone who knows her would be, I guess. They'll try to track her movements in the past couple of days, look for motives, alibis, start ruling people out, one by one."

"Where were you on the night of such and such?"

"Yeah. Sounds corny, but that's sort of how it works."

None of us spoke, and then Roxanne said, "Maddie asked me to come to Boston to speak to some sort of group of foundation people."

"When?" I said.

"Tomorrow afternoon."

"Can you do that?"

"I have comp time. But I'd need permission anyway."

"Because—"

"Because it's sort of a conflict of interest."

"Where would you stay?"

"She invited me to stay at their house, in Back Bay. Do you think I still should go at all?"

"I don't know," I said. "I guess so. I have to go down there, too, if that makes any difference."

"To do the story?"

"The follow. Today will be the bare bones."

"Well, that will be a little strange. Will you have to interview Maddie and David?"

"Yeah, if they'll agree."

"I can't imagine they wouldn't."

"It's a murder investigation," I said. "It changes things."

"Throws everything up in the air," Clair said. "The cards come back down and you have to put them back in order. Who's good, who's evil. Who do you really know, and who do you only think you know."

Roxanne turned to the counter, put the lid back on the jar of mustard, and folded up the bag of carrots. She put them in the refrigerator and then walked to the big glass window and stood with her arms folded, as though the room had suddenly grown cold. She looked out at the field and the woods, the birds flitting in the brush. Finches. Suddenly she turned to us.

"I like her," Roxanne said. "Maddie's a good person. We had a good talk this afternoon, and she really wants to see if she can help kids in Maine."

"She had no idea that anything was wrong?" I said.

Roxanne shook her head.

"No, she was fine. You know, they're nothing like people think. She seems completely sincere. And David—I like him, too. They're both good-hearted. But with Maddie, there's something very vulnerable about her. I don't know; this whole Connelly mystique in a lot of ways is just nonsense."

"I like them, too," I said. "But when this comes out, connected to them, the Connelly angle is going to be played for everything it's worth."

"Must be hard. Being them, I mean," Roxanne said. "You know who the police should be looking at? That Dalton creep. You know he held a door for me while we were at the house there, and when I walked by him, I swear he deliberately brushed his hand across my hip. I swear he was grabbing a little feel. I almost smacked him."

"You should have," I said.

"If this meeting is still on, I think I will ask if I can go," Roxanne said.

"I'll go with you," I said.

"So you don't think they'll be—"

"I think Angel was presumptuous with Maddie and David," I said, "and I don't think Maddie liked it."

"You don't kill people for having bad manners," Roxanne said.

"Not usually," Clair said.

"But sometimes?" Roxanne said.

Clair didn't answer.

14

The foundation meeting was at one o'clock at the Marlborough Club, on Marlborough Street in the heart of Back Bay. At eleven-forty we were inching along Congress Street amid throngs of tourists flocking like pilgrims to Faneuil Hall. It was raining softly, a warm drizzle that the kids ignored as they stood around the statue of Sam Adams. Most of them probably thought he made beer.

Roxanne leaned forward in her seat and gathered up her reports and file folders and stuffed them in her bag. I continued on into the financial district, swung left on Milk Street, and backtracked into the streets behind South Market, in a quixotic search for a parking space. I circled twice, then double-parked on Chatham Street and ran up to the bureau in South Market; Roxanne stayed with the car.

The second-floor offices were modern and new, everything a newsroom shouldn't be, but Myra had done her best to litter her office with coffee cups and takeout cartons. She would have smoked if they'd let her.

She was in, on the phone. I took a seat in front of her desk while she talked to somebody in New York about my story about Angel.

"No, he can't have it ready tonight, not the story we want to do. So let 'em swarm. This isn't the *Post*. . . . I know you know that. . . . So we're a day ahead of everybody else. We had the breaking story first, the Connelly part of it, anyway, and now we'll do the follow, the profile. . . . Yeah, McMorrow's got lots of sources. . . . Yes, he really met the victim. . : . I don't know how he manages it, either. . . . When? Tuesday . . . Yes, this past Tuesday. . . . Yeah, we talked about that, but I hesitate to overstate the relationship. I mean, he met the woman but they didn't talk into the wee hours or anything. They had one private conversation, otherwise they were part of a group. . . . No, I think we should let people speak about her who really knew her. . . . Right, a cultural thing. Not exactly rags to riches, but tradesmen's class to the world of wealth and celebrity. . . . Right. It'll be available for Monday's paper. Yes, I'll be here. Jack will be, too."

She hung up.

"So you heard where we're going with this?"

"Yeah. Who was that?"

"Simon."

"They're looking for some sort of first-person thing?"

"Well, not first-person, but firsthand impression. The scene, how Moretti spent one of the last days of her life. And a peek into the private world of David and Maddie Connelly. The oceanfront estate. The beautiful yacht."

I winced.

"You know," I said, "I'm not really comfortable with that part of it."

"I know," Myra said. "How come?"

"I wasn't there as a reporter."

"That hasn't stopped you in other situations. How exactly did you end up there? Are these the circles you've started traveling in?"

"No. Listen, this has got to be off the record."

"Jack, it's me."

People were coming and going in the foyer, so I got up and closed the door. Then I told her about Roxanne, and the complaint about Maeve, about the Irish au pair.

"So the State of Maine is investigating a child abuse complaint involving David and Maddie Connelly's kid?"

"Not anymore. Roxanne talked to the child and she talked to the parents, and once she finds this Irish girl, that'll most likely be the end of it."

"And all this is confidential."

"Very."

"I mean, we can't get it from some other source?"

"Not if you want me to ever write another word for you again."

I said it with conviction.

"Jesus. What if the au pair says she never touched the kid? The mother's a closet abuser? You know, the Connellys have a closet full of skeletons. Remember the cousin who stalked that girl? Those two kids who died in that accident in the Berkshires or someplace? And Maddie, she hasn't had it easy. Did you know her older brother killed himself when she was a little kid?"

"I didn't know that."

"Yeah. I remember hearing that someplace. She was, like, eight. He was in his teens."

"That doesn't mean she beats her child."

"No."

"Roxanne doesn't believe it, and she's done hundreds of these cases."

Myra looked away. Took off the tortoiseshell headband that held back her white-blonde hair. Put the headband back on and looked at me again.

"Okay. If nothing came of it, I guess. Jeez, this goes against my instincts, but it's a weird circumstance. Listen, just go after the Moretti woman with everything you've got. And we need the Connellys in there in every other respect. And we need that Maine place described, their life portrayed. And that's not just prurient. It puts this North End girl's life in perspective, her climb to—"

The phone rang. Myra reached for it. I got up and left before she could change her mind and started up State Street. After I told her what Myra had said, and my response, Roxanne was quiet.

"You trust her?" she said, after a minute.

"Yeah," I said. "But she's still a newspaper editor. And a good one."

"What if Devlin does deny it?"

"I don't know, honey," I said. "Let's just take this one bridge at a time."

The Marlborough Club was a four-story brownstone with a discreet brass plaque and a bay window in which someone had placed a vase full of flowers the color of bricks. Understatement was the word for the day.

I double-parked and told the doorman I'd only be a minute, then followed Roxanne up the stairs where another guy heaved the door open. We stepped inside. It was still and the carpet was thick, like moss in the Maine woods. The paneling was dark and so was the rest of the place. We waited for our eyes to adjust and then walked to the front desk.

A young woman looked up at us. She was pretty in a vapid, self-conscious sort of way, and her hair was done in a stiff Jackie Kennedy flip. Behind her was a computer and the screensaver was a photograph of the front of the club, in case she fell asleep and woke up not knowing where she was. Roxanne said she was there to meet Maddie and David Connelly, and the woman said the Connellys were in the Hotchkiss Lounge on the fourth floor.

We padded up in the funereal silence and eventually heard muffled voices. At the fourth-floor landing we looked around. David Connelly turned from the window and gave us a weary smile.

He looked older out of his shorts and T-shirt and into old-money casual. His blazer was standard prep-school issue and his shirt was denim. His tie was red with sailboats on it. His tan slacks were some sort of twill and his loafers were ancient.

"Hi, guys," he said, and he hurried over, gave Roxanne a brief hug, and gripped my hand, patting me on the shoulder. I felt like we'd shown up at a wake.

At that moment, a door opened at the end of the foyer and we heard china rattling, and then Maddie came out and saw us and said, "Oh, you made it. Roxanne, you're a dear."

She was dressed in a navy suit with a knee-length skirt and pale hose. Navy pumps, a cream-colored blouse, and pearl earrings. It was as if the couple we'd met in Blue Harbor were playing dress-up. I thought Roxanne's slacks, silk blouse, and jacket were more appropriate.

"So good of you to come all this way," Maddie said.

"I'm glad to," Roxanne said.

"We're very sorry about Angel," I said.

"Oh, God," David said. "She leaves and she's happy and bubbly, and two days later—"

"I still can't believe it," Maddie said. "I feel like I'm going to wake up any moment and say to David, 'Oh, I just had the most horrible dream.'"

"A nightmare," David said. "I saw your story, Jack. Do the police have any idea?"

"They didn't yesterday, but they were just getting started. That she was found so quickly is a big help."

"Not much of a silver lining," Roxanne said.

"No," David said. "Not much of one at all."

"Oh, it's a tragedy," Maddie said. "She was just coming into her own. A beautiful girl, and she had so much potential. She was seeing a lot of things for the first time. She wanted to travel. She'd never been to Europe, and she and Monica had talked about going to London and Paris. Some sort of package, six nights, seven days, or some such, but at least they were going. And she was so happy. And then—"

She looked away and seemed to drift off for a moment. I thought of what Myra had said about her brother's suicide. I wondered if this sort of thing could cause a post-traumatic flashback.

"Parents are kind of Old World," David said. "Italian, North End, big family. According to Tim Dalton, she was the only girl with a bunch of brothers. Led kind of a cloistered existence."

"The baby," Maddie said. "Oh, God, can you imagine what they're feeling?"

"How's Monica?" I said.

"Tim and Kathleen Kind tried to call her at home. Mother said she was in bed, in shock. Known each other since they were in grade school. Best friends."

"What happened?" I said. "I mean, after they left Blue Harbor?"

"Everybody came back Wednesday night," David said, folding his arms on his chest, protectively, I thought. "Went to Bar Harbor, like Angel wanted to; they seemed to have fun. She and Monica drove back together in Angel's car, that silver Audi. Her first car. Tim found some deal for her."

"That was good of him," I said, and Maddie and David looked at me, as though they were looking for some hidden meaning.

Maddie looked away and David said, "Well, they were close, I guess."

The door opened and a white-haired man signaled to Maddie. She smiled at him and said to Roxanne, "Well, would you like to come in and meet everyone, have coffee and biscotti or something?"

"You staying, Jack?" David said.

"No, I have work to do. I'm doing another story on Angel, actually. In fact, if you don't mind, I'd like to talk to one or both of you about her. In an official capacity."

"You do it, David," Maddie blurted, so quickly she seemed to surprise herself, and added, "David knew her better than I did."

Their eyes met, and there was an odd signal, a sign of understanding between them, and then it was gone and Maddie took Roxanne by the arm and David tapped me on the shoulder and said, "Sure, be glad to, Jack."

I said I'd be back, looked to Maddie for some sense of how long the meeting might take. She said I should go do my work and then swing by the house when I was done. Roxanne could go home with her.

I looked at Roxanne and she didn't object. She gave my hand a squeeze and, with Maddie Connelly beside her, walked to the door of the meeting room. The white-haired man held the door, heads turned from the tables, and the door swung shut.

I turned and David was watching me watch Roxanne. It was like he had some special interest in the way we interacted, and I felt for a moment that I was being spied upon. But then David gave me a touch on the shoulder, a big grin.

"Don't worry," he said, hustling me to the stairs. "Maddie'll take very good care of her."

15

D avid suggested we talk over a drink, or coffee. We took Roxanne's car and cut across to Newbury Street, where gawkers moved slowly past the chichi shops and restaurants like sailors whose ship had just anchored in the harbor. David pointed to one restaurant he said I'd like if I was into Tuscany, and then we went another block and he pointed to a parking lot and I pulled into the back side of the Harvard Club and parked.

An attendant came out and said, "Hey, Mr. Connelly," and David said, "Hey, Luis, man. How 'bout the Sox, baby. What'd I tell you? Is this the year or what?"

They low-fived on the way by and we went inside, through a labyrinth of corridors, and emerged in the big bar off the lobby. The bartender said, "Hi, Mr. Connelly. Been a while," and David said, "Been up in Maine, Gregory. Clean living out on the boat. This is my good friend, Jack. Works for the *New York Times*, Gregory, so watch what you say. Jack, what do you think?"

I was thinking that he seemed curiously lighthearted for a guy who was about to talk about a murdered employee. Or was this just his public persona?

"A single-blend?" he said, and he ordered something, the name of which I didn't catch. I said I'd just have a Sam Adams and the bartender moved away. I glanced around at the afternoon crowd, saw a couple of fiftyish women spot David and whisper and smile. The drinks came and David picked his up, handed me my beer, and said, "Let's go somewhere quiet," and I followed him through the foyer, where there was a portrait of his father that David breezed right by. He waved to the concierge and we went to the stairs and up. A left and a right and we were in a small sitting room that overlooked Comm. Ave. There was a black leather couch, a table with a cribbage board and cards. More portraits on the wall, all dour white men.

As though their mood were contagious, David turned somber.

"So," I said, putting my notebook and tape recorder on the table.

"So," he said. "I don't know what I can add to what we've already said."

"We were just talking, as—"

"Friends," he said. "And this is on the record. You know, one of our lawyers wanted to issue a statement. I said, 'Come on. I'm not a corporation. And this is a young woman who was just a guest in my home. So sorry, but I'm going to speak like a human being.' "

I hit the button on the recorder and picked up the pad.

"Okay. So how long did Angel work for the foundation?"

"I'm not sure. Tim would know. A year, maybe? Maybe more. Not two."

"How often did you see her?"

"Oh, gee. Every week? At least to wave to. She was friendly, always had something to say. She wasn't shy, which is sort of funny. Because she was sheltered, you'd expect her to be this wallflower, but it was like she had all this pent-up social energy."

"And it all came bursting out?"

"Yeah, Very bubbly. Enthusiastic. Livened up the place, really."

"Did she have friends there?"

"Well, there was Monica, of course. She knew everybody. Tim sort of took her under his wing, and Kathleen, too, when she first came to Sky Blue. What to wear in what situation, that sort of thing. There was a bit of Eliza Doolittle in her, but I wouldn't want that in the paper. She didn't know exactly what to wear to the BSO, to a luncheon thing at the Ritz."

"You took her to that sort of thing?"

"Yeah, if a group was going, representing the foundation. We try to be pretty egalitarian about the perks, if you can call them that. I'd rather stay home, but some people like getting dressed, the whole scene."

"What's Maddie think of it?"

"Not much. We're really of the same frame of mind. Rather be in Maine, given a choice. Or head out west, if it's winter. I mean—and this is off the record, if you don't mind—being in my family sometimes limits the conversations you have. Sometimes people just shake your hand and stare at you. It gets very old."

"Back on the record."

"Right."

"So Angel left Blue Harbor Wednesday night."

"Around seven."

"Did she work Thursday?"

"I don't know. I wasn't there. I popped in Thursday morning to check on some things. I didn't see her then."

"When she left, was she in good spirits?"

He hesitated, as though trying to picture her.

"Yeah. Like I said, she had a nice time in Bar Harbor. She liked boats if they were surrounded by other boats. Some people are like that. But we had lunch, she and Monica and Tim went into some shops. I think she bought some sort of jewelry. But yeah, she was good. Just like when you saw her."

"Did she make a lot of money at the foundation?"

"Well, I would guess she was paid fairly. It depends on what you call a lot. To tell you the truth, I really don't know. We leave that for other people to manage."

"I know, but the Audi. Buying jewelry. She had nice clothes."

David shrugged, almost exaggeratedly. "Hey, she was single. She lived at home."

"Where's that?"

"Michelangelo Street, North End. I always kidded her about that."

"You know her father's name?"

"Yeah. I met him. It was Rocco. Well, I guess it still is. Nice guy, very old-fashioned Italian, salt-of-the-earth type. It was like, if you wanted to date Angel, you'd have to go to him for his permission or something. But don't—"

"I won't. Between us, did he lavish stuff on her?"

"I don't know. It's not like he was a person of means or anything, although North End real estate is through the roof. Just a hardworking middle-class family, seemed to me. But I mean, the Audi wasn't new. Maddie says I'm oblivious to stuff like that. You know, whether somebody's wearing a thirty-thousand-dollar dress or a three-hundred-dollar one. Show me their boat, on the other hand . . ."

He grinned. Tossed down the rest of his scotch. I sipped my beer and he looked at his watch. I looked, if he wouldn't. It was a Rolex.

"I don't know what else I can tell you, Jack. We're very sorry about it. We liked her. We thought she had a great life in front of her. And this is tragic, and I hope to God they find who did it and put him away."

"Or her," I said.

He looked at me as he stood.

"Right," David said. "So, is that enough?"

I felt like it would have to be. "Yeah, I guess so."

"You know where to find me, if you have more questions. But I've gotta get back for Maeve. She's supposed to get home from play group at two."

I stood and picked up the recorder, took a last swallow of my beer. We made our way back down and David waved to Gregory, said "Go Sox" to Luis. He was quiet on the ride back, directing me to Marlborough. At the corner of Exeter, he waved me over in front of a massive sandstone mansion. It was four stories, surrounded by a ten-foot-high stone wall. A gated drive led to an inner courtyard and carriage house. I'd just read something in the *Globe* about a two-thousand-square-foot condo in this neighborhood going for $750,000.

David picked my notebook up off the seat and scribbled a number.

"My cell," he said, and he shut the door and waved, then patted his pockets. He produced a remote for the electronically controlled gate, hit the button, and a steel panel slid open. David turned back.

"Hey, Jack," he said as I started to pull away. "When we gonna cut wood?"

He gave me the look, endearing as a little brother.

"Soon," I said.

"Great," David said. "Looking forward to it," and for the life of me it seemed he really was. For the life of me, I was, too.

16

The map showed Michelangelo Street off Charter, around the corner from the Old North Church and Paul Revere's place. After a few wrong turns I found myself at the end of the street. There was a playground with a great view of the harbor, the Coast Guard station, the Charlestown piers. I pulled over and composed myself, knowing that knocking on the door at the home of a grieving family was nothing to breeze into. You had one shot. If you broke through, they poured their hearts out. If you didn't, the door slammed in your face.

The street was lined with brick row houses with occasional trees and cars parked bumper to bumper like elephants in a circus parade. I made one run past and scoped out number twenty-eight. It was well kept but not gentrified like some of the neighbors, with their window boxes full of geraniums and security service stickers on the doors. There was a van parked out front with Rocco Moretti's name painted on the sides. Below the name it said he did ceramic tile and marble, residential and commercial. I parked at the corner, wedging the car half in front of a hydrant, and walked back.

I went to the front door. It was open. Inside was a tiny foyer with four mailboxes and buzzers. Moretti was number one. I took a deep breath and pushed.

I waited. There was no answer. I put my finger on the button again just as the door was buzzed open.

I went inside. It was a narrow hallway and I smelled food, heard the chink of dishes. There were doors on the right and left. The door on the right clicked open and a woman's voice said, "Did you see Davie coming? He should be—"

She poked her head out. Fifties. Dark hair and skin. She saw me and jerked back like an animal slipping back into its burrow. I heard voices inside and then it was quiet. A man stepped into the hall. Forty and handsome. Tight polo shirt and jeans. Chest puffed out under a gold chain. Eyes narrowed.

"Who are you?"

"Sir, my name's Jack McMorrow. I'm a reporter for the *New York Times*. I'm here to ask you if you'll talk to me about—"

"We already told the other people. No comment."

He turned back toward the apartment.

"But if you have a second—I met Angel. In Maine at the Connellys'. I talked to her for quite a while. I'd like to include that in the story. She was very nice. I'd like to do a story that reflects that."

Someone inside the apartment said something and the guy said, "It's a reporter. *New York Times*. Says he met Angel in Maine."

Someone said something in Italian and he turned hack.

"You knew Angel?" he said.

"We chatted that one time and that was it. I was at the Connellys' on other business. Listen, I'm really very sorry for your loss. And I'm sorry to just barge in."

He turned back to the room and relayed what I'd said. Three or four people answered, men and women, in English and Italian. I heard the words *son of a bitch* and something muttered in Italian. It did not sound like a welcome.

He turned back.

"You call tomorrow, sir."

"Thank you, but I'm going to have to go back to Maine. And I'd rather do this in person. It's not something to do over the phone."

He looked at me, took a deep breath, and let it out slowly.

"Are you a relative?" I said.

"I'm Angel's older brother," he said, and then he stepped back inside and closed the door. I stood in the empty hallway and waited. Told myself that what I had said was true, even if it wasn't the whole story. Could I do the story next week? Sure. Would the *Globe* or the *Herald* have it first? No doubt, and that wouldn't do, but I couldn't tell him that. It was the only thing about my profession I disliked: the subtle manipulation, the carefully tailored half-truths. But all for a good cause, I believed.

Most of the time.

The door opened. The brother poked his head out, said "Come in," and then he went back inside and left me to follow.

I stepped into a room full of relatives, red-eyed and grim. The brother motioned to a place on the couch beside a woman in her forties, a tissue held up in front of her face like a burka. The brother said his name was Joey. His mother's name was Maria Moretti. The father, Rocco, was a short wide man with massive hands folded on his lap. He sat to my right. Next to him was Georgie, another brother, who looked at me like I was a child molester. Filling out the room were aunts and uncles, several cousins, and a grandmother. The girl cousins looked like they'd been crying. The boy cousins looked like they wanted to fight. The grandmother was seated in an armchair with crocheted things on the arms. Her eyes were blank, her gnarled fingers worrying rosary beads. She looked at me and hissed in Italian.

Joey stood in front of me.

"What did she say?" I asked him.

"*Non c'è rispetto per i morti.* No respect for the dead."

"Actually, I have a lot of respect," I said, and I nodded toward the old woman. She glared back, dark eyes glowering.

"What you want to know?" Joey said.

"What Angel was like."

"She was a great kid," he said.

"The only girl?" I asked, beginning to write in my notebook.

"Angel was the baby," her mother said suddenly, her voice faraway as if she were all alone, talking to herself. "A beautiful little girl. Never gave us a moment's trouble, not like a lot of these kids today. Out taking drugs and standing on the corner and no respect for anything. Angel was a perfect lady."

I glanced up at the brothers, a sister-in-law who was very pregnant. I thought I detected a flicker of something, an eyebrow raised.

"She won the Blessed Virgin Prize four times at Saint Anthony's," Mrs. Moretti said.

"Nobody's ever won it four times," her husband said, staring at his hands as though they belonged on someone else.

"A beautiful child," Mrs. Moretti said.

She had a framed photograph on her lap, facedown. She tipped it up, bit her lip, and choked back tears. Turned the photograph toward me.

It was Angel Moretti at eighteen or so, a high school portrait? Dark, welcoming eyes. A full mouth turned upward in a gentle smile. Olive skin with a touch of pink on her cheeks. She was beautiful, but in her expression there was a hint of resignation. Had she known then that there was a bigger world out there?

"Do anything for anybody," Rocco Moretti said. "You put that in your story. Give away her lunch if somebody was hungry. Remember when she did that? That new kid, didn't have money or something? Angel gives the kid her goddamn lunch. That's the kind of girl she was."

"She was the one to take in the new girl, put her under her wing," Maria Moretti said.

"What about her adult life?" I said.

The parents hesitated. Georgie stepped in. He said Angel went to Bunker Hill Community College for business, worked with computers and as a secretary.

"Administrative assistant," the pregnant sister-in-law said. "They're not called secretaries."

"Different places," her mother said. "She moved around a lot."

"Around the country?"

She looked at me, horrified. "No, she didn't leave Boston. Different jobs for an agency. They sent her to different places. And then she went to the Sky Blue place, the Connellys. She stayed there. They like her there."

"I met her, you know."

"That's what Joey said," Maria Moretti said. "Then you know what she was like. A beautiful girl. So sweet."

"Yes, she was very nice."

"You're a friend of the Connellys?" the father said, a new wariness in his voice.

"No," I said. "I'd just met them, too. They seem like good people."

"Oh, yeah. Mr. Connelly. He treated Angel very well. She was going to the parties, the Boston Pops. She got me tickets to the Red Sox, right on the third-base line, right on the railing. She said Mr. Connelly said he wasn't gonna use 'em, asked Angel if her dad was a Sox fan. He didn't have to do that. He treated her good."

"And Mr. Dalton, her boss?"

A dark flicker passed through the room, like the shadow of a bird. The parents looked at each other, and Rocco Moretti said, "Mr. Dalton, he—"

"He gave my sister lots of opportunities," the brother, Joey, said quickly. "They liked Angel there at the foundation. Everybody liked Angel. She was good at math, and all around she was a great kid."

He said it like he'd summed up her entire character. Now I could go.

I looked to Angel's parents and smiled—soothingly, I hoped.

"She seemed to be doing very well. A nice car, nice clothes. Was she very happy?"

"Oh, yeah," the mother said. "Things were going great for her. But it was hard work, a lot of functions, weekends at work. Meetings and conferences in Providence and Connecticut. She worked a lot. One time she had to go to New York."

"Did she stay in touch with friends in the neighborhood, even though she was in this, I don't know, this sort of glamorous world?"

"Angel didn't forget where she was from," Joey said. "She got a job for Monica at the same place, 'cause Monica wasn't working."

"I met Monica, too," I said. "That was very nice of Angel."

"Wonderful child," Maria Moretti said. "Angel didn't forget her friends. Or us. Tell him about the cruise, Rock."

"Yeah, this is the kind of girl she was. She started making good money. What does she do with it? She sends her parents on a cruise. We went to Nassau, outta Miami. Angel pays the whole freight. I never saw so much food in my life."

"That was very nice. She still lived at home?"

"Oh, yeah. We were very close," Maria Moretti said.

"Monica live in the neighborhood still?"

"Oh, yeah. With her parents on Snowhill, across from the playground. Angel stayed there sometimes if Monica's parents had to go away. Monica's aunt in Rhode Island has inoperable cancer and they wanted to spend time with her before—"

She stopped talking, started to sob. The brothers leapt from their seats and each took a shoulder. The angry one, Georgie, said, "Maybe you'd better go."

Nobody disagreed. They just looked at me with their grim, hard faces as I tried to formulate a question that would break through all this surface stuff, something that would provide even a hint of who Angel Moretti really was.

"I will. And I'm really sorry to bother you. Just a couple more questions. She was very pretty. Did she have a steady boyfriend? Anybody she dated?"

"All the guys liked Angel," the pregnant woman said. "She was so nice to everybody and everything, and—"

She glanced at the brothers and stopped. I looked at them and they still were glaring at her. Clearly Angel's love life was off limits.

"But nobody I should talk to? No longtime boyfriend or anything?"

The father suddenly held his hands out like he was quieting applause. He turned to me with deep sad eyes.

"Do you have children, sir?" he said.

"No. But I hope to."

"Well, sir. You're a smart man, to do what you do. Work for the *New York Times* and write about important people. We're simple people. I have my business. I have my family. That's it. And unless you have children of your own, you can't know how I feel in here."

He put a hand on his chest. I watched him, wrote in my notebook.

"It's like my heart has been torn out. It's still beating, you know what I'm saying? But the pain is almost too much for me. And it doesn't go away. It's the last thing I feel before I sleep. It's the first thing I feel when I wake up. It is the last thing I will feel before I die."

He paused. The room was deathly quiet, and then someone sniffed and one of the women let out a muffled whimper.

"But the man who did this to my Angel, he'll pay. He'll burn in Hell, and he'll pay before that, too. We'll make sure—"

"—that the police find him and he gets the death penalty," Georgie said. "They have it in Massachusetts now."

"But not in Maine," I said.

"Nobody in Maine killed my little girl. Angel didn't know nobody in goddamn Maine."

"She knew the Connellys," I said.

"Yeah, but nobody else. Went up there and sailed on their sailboat. I told her, 'What you want to do that for?' I says. 'Your great-grandfather came over on a boat, almost killed him. What if the goddamn thing sinks?' "

"She said, 'Oh, but Daddy, it's so quiet and pretty.' Some goddamn hundred-year-old ship?"

"You mean, their powerboat?"

"No, a big sailboat thing," Maria Moretti said. "She said it has a mast eighty feet tall or something. They'd go around to the harbors up there and they'd row into the dock and go out to dinner. She said the boat was peaceful and quiet, just the sound of the wind ruffling the sails or whatever. She talked like that."

"She had a way with words," Rocco Moretti said.

"She was happy after that trip," the mother said. "Remember that? How happy she was, going to work, dressed like a million dollars. And now—"

"This is the bottom line. Some shitbum killed my beautiful little girl," Rocco Moretti said, his voice rising, looking me in the eye like he was issuing a challenge.

"Dad," Joey said.

"Let him talk, Joe," Georgie said.

"Put this in your story," the father said, his voice trembling with rage and grief. "Somebody killed Rocco Moretti's little girl. And we're gonna find this animal and—"

"That's right, Dad," Georgie said, calming his father. "We'll find this son of a bitch and we'll handle it."

"Who?" I said. "Your family?"

Georgie looked at me and didn't answer. The old man stopped talking and stared straight ahead, deep into his own grief, his fists clenching as if they were squeezing an imaginary throat.

17

Snowhill ran alongside a playground a couple of blocks from the Morettis', toward the harbor. I parked, illegally again, and asked the first three people I saw where Monica Vitale lived. An old woman hurried away without speaking, a young woman said she'd just moved there and didn't know her. Some kid in a Celtics hat and big shorts pointed to a house up the street and said, "That'll be twenty bucks."

I smiled and kept walking in the sultry city heat.

It was a gray clapboard tenement with tubs of geraniums on the sidewalk by the door. The flowers had just been watered and the run-off had, spilled onto the pavement like blood. In a second-floor window, an air conditioner droned.

I went to the door and rang the bell. I waited and then there was a fumbling, knocking sound and the door rattled and opened the width of a security chain. A slice of a woman peered out. I could see purplish permed hair, red lipstick, one narrowed suspicious eye.

I told her my name, said I was from the *Times*, that I was working on a story about Angel Moretti. I said Monica knew me from Maine. We'd been at the Connellys'. I didn't say Monica hadn't said boo.

"I don't know," the woman began. "I'm her mother."

I went through the same entreaties. They didn't seem to be working until I said I thought a story about Angel and what a good person she was might exert pressure on the police to work harder to find her killer.

"Oh, they were good friends," Mrs. Vitale said. "Since they were little kids. Is that the kind of thing you want to know?"

"Yes, it is," I said. "Now, this must be very hard on your daughter."

"Like losing your sister," she said.

"Can I talk to her?"

She hesitated.

"Right now?"

"If you don't mind. I don't think it would be right to do it over the phone, given the circumstances. It would seem disrespectful."

Mrs. Vitale weighed that and then she closed the door. I waited. In a moment it opened up, chains jangling like Marley's ghost.

"What's your name?"

I told her again.

"I'll ask," she said. "But you gotta remember. This is very upsetting to Monica. It's almost like she's blaming herself."

I waited for Monica on the couch in the living room. The room was dark and cool, with lacy cloths draped on dark mahogany furniture and family photographs on the wall. Mrs. Vitale, her husband, and Monica between them. Monica alone, Monica as a little girl, and Monica graduating from high school. An only child, it appeared.

The husband was a fleshy, weak-chinned guy with tinted glasses, like Elvis wore in the last years in Vegas. Monica was soft, too, and they had the same cautious smile. Their pictures hung alongside a crucifix and a painting of the Sacred Heart, blood red with a crown of thorns, which made Monica and Dad look a little like martyrs.

A clatter on the stairs and then a murmur and Mrs. Vitale stepped in.

"Here she is," she said, as if she were introducing a princess at a ball. Monica came in behind her, and she didn't look like a princess. She looked like a scared kid, wide-eyed and wary, drawn into a big gray sweatshirt like a turtle.

"Hi, Monica," I said. "Good to see you again, but I'm sorry it's under these circumstances."

Monica nodded, barely.

"Could we sit and talk?"

Monica moved to a chair, sat, and pressed her legs together, her toenails now painted silver, digging into the ends of the same plastic Adidas sandals. From a shorts pocket she dug out an elastic thing and pulled her hair back into a ponytail. Mom took a chair next to her, ready to translate.

"So this is hard, I know," I said.

She didn't respond.

"But I have to ask you these things. Try to put together a good picture of Angel in the story. So anyway, I understand you were together a lot?" I left the notebook on my lap, like a camera in a bird blind.

"Yeah, a lot."

"Even after you got out of school?"

"Yeah," Monica said.

"Like sisters," Mrs. Vitale said. "I know a lot of girls, they have sisters and they aren't nowheres as close as these two are. I mean, were."

Monica put her hand over her mouth and bit her lip.

"I know it's difficult," I said.

"It's a nightmare," Mrs. Vitale said. "I tell you, I wouldn't let any child of mine go off to Maine, those animals out in the goddamn woods."

I began to take notes, one eye on Monica.

"So Monica," I said. "You and Angel didn't come home together?"

She nodded, pulled her hair out of the scrunchy, tied it back.

"No, I wanted to go earlier. I went with Ms. Kind."

"How was Angel when you left?"

"Fine."

"Happy?"

"Yeah."

"She liked working at the foundation?"

"Yeah, she did. They were nice to her there."

"Were they nice to you?"

"I guess."

"She got you the job? Is that true? Somebody told me that."

"Who?"

"Her parents."

"She had to apply like anybody else," Mrs. Vitale said, suddenly defensive. "Angel told her there was this job to apply for."

"Who'd you interview with?"

I could see a new wariness fall over her like a tossed sheet.

"I don't know."

"How long ago was this? I'm just trying to get a sense of when Angel was there, when she helped you."

"About six months ago."

"She kept the job on her own," her mother said. "She got good evaluations, didn't you, babe?"

"Yeah, I got along good with everybody."

"Ms. Kind?"

"Yeah, she was okay."

"Mr. Dalton?"

"He was all right."

"It was a lot of responsibility," her mother said. "I mean, they have millions of dollars, those people."

"I know," I said. "I saw their house in Maine. Now, did you and Angel spend a lot of time with the Connellys themselves? David and Maddie?"

"Not much," Monica said. "More Angel than me."

"Why's that?"

"I don't know. It just worked out that way. Mr. Dalton, she worked for him directly, and he went to a lot of stuff, parties and benefits, and he gave Angel extra tickets."

"Did you go with her?"

"Twice."

"Did the Connellys go, too?"

"Sometimes."

"That must have been fun."

"It was okay. Not great. Rich people all knew each other. One time it was a lot of speeches and whatnot. Boring."

"But Angel went a lot?"

"More than me."

"Would she get all dressed up?"

"Oh, yeah. Gowns and heels."

She stretched out her feet and eyed her toes.

"Where'd she get fancy gowns? Go and buy them?"

"Yeah, I guess. I didn't ask her."

Two twenty-one-year-old girls and one goes to a black-tie thing in a gown and they didn't talk about the dress? I didn't think so.

"But Angel did get to hang out with the Connellys?"

"I guess," she said. It was beginning to feel like a cross-examination. I smiled, tried to make her comfortable.

"Monica," I said. "Here's what I'm trying to figure out. I have a picture in my mind of this young woman who grew up in Boston in the North End and then she gets introduced to another part of Boston life and she takes to it. Is that right?"

Monica looked away, fiddled with her hair.

"Well, I'd say so, wouldn't you?" her mother said to her. "I mean, the clothes and the car, and one time she got her picture in the paper. She was in the background at some party for AIDS or something and David Connelly was beside her and there she was. She looked like a million dollars, hair up and all done just so. You never woulda known it was our Angel."

I wrote that down, every word.

Mrs. Vitale paused and then she reached out and stopped my pen.

"This isn't for your write-up, but her father is a real miser," she whispered. "Owns that building and two more he rents. I mean, what's that worth around here now? A shoe box goes for a thousand a month. It's crazy. And this is a kid, senior year in high school, her father gave her five dollars a week for allowance. That's it. Didn't let her work or anything. She never had money at all. I bet she never held fifty dollars in her hand. And all of a sudden, money everywhere around her."

"So that would have impressed her?"

"It did, kinda," Monica said. "She was into it. Me, I don't know. I got kinda sick of those people."

"Was it hard work?" I said.

"It was okay," Monica said.

"You worked very hard," her mother said.

"What about the overnight stuff and the conferences?"

Monica looked at me blankly for a moment, then seemed to catch on.

"Well, that wasn't me as much as other people."

"She never had to go out of town," her mother said. "I wouldn't have liked that. I really wouldn't like it now, after all that's happened."

"But Angel had to do that?" I said.

"Yeah," Monica said, then hesitated. "Sometimes."

"She did?" her mother said. "Why didn't they ask you to go?"

"I don't know, Ma," Monica said. "They just didn't. We had different jobs."

"I thought you did the same job?" her mother persisted.

"Sort of, but they were sorta different. Jesus, how would I know? We didn't sit at the same desk, for God's sake."

Mrs. Vitale looked taken aback.

"It's okay, honey," she said. "You've been under a lot of strain and stress. Mr. Morrow, I think we've had enough for today."

She wrapped a protective arm around her daughter's slumping shoulders. I pressed on, not knowing whether there would be another time.

"But Angel was generally happy," I said. "She liked the boat trips last week. I heard she went sailing with the Connellys, too."

Monica looked at me blankly.

"They didn't invite you to go on this sailing thing?" Mrs. Vitale said. "Why didn't they invite both of you?"

"I didn't know about any sailing thing," Monica said. "I just went on the big cabin cruiser."

"This week."

"Right."

"You didn't hear about a sailing trip?"

"Nope. But I tuned those people out a lot of the time."

"Monica, you pay attention at work," her mother said.

"Ma, just chill out."

Her mother started to say something, then caught herself.

"What was she like, then? If you had to sum her up."

Monica suddenly started to cry. It seemed contrived, but her mother pulled her closer.

"It's okay, baby."

"She was a great kid," Monica said, through the tears. "We were still best friends, no matter what happened."

I looked at her.

"Like what?" I said.

"I don't know," Monica said.

"It's okay, honey," her mother said. Monica's head was on her shoulder now, tipped to the side at an awkward angle as if her neck was broken.

I shook that image off and said, "You mean, if she had a lot of money and dressed in fancy clothes and hung out with rich people?"

"She didn't hang out with him," she said, tears trickling down her cheekbone onto her mother's arm.

"Hang out with who?"

"It didn't make any difference. I know it didn't. We were still best friends."

"Sure you were," her mother said. "Mr. Morrow, I think it's time for you to go. I don't see the point of all these questions. I don't think Monica's father would like this."

"Why?" I said.

"Because you're upsetting her, sir."

"Well, murder is upsetting, Mrs. Vitale," I said. "There's no way around it."

18

I drove back to the Connellys' at rush hour, inching along Tremont Street like something terrible had happened and they'd given the order to evacuate the city. On the Common there were people jogging in the heat, coasting on bicycles. A couple in business clothes walked hurriedly alongside me, briefcases swinging, the guy my age, gray showing above his ears, the woman, fifteen years younger. They were unsmiling, faces tense, and at one point the guy tried to take the woman's free hand, but she shook him off like he was dirty.

Angel and Dalton.

I thought about them all the way to the Connellys', wondered what Monica had meant: "She didn't hang out with him." What? She just took gifts, let him buy lunch, blew him off at quitting time? My hunch was she'd given him enough encouragement to keep his flame fanned. Slept with him, maybe on a weekend trip. But where would they have gone, if they didn't really have to work? A nice hotel? It would have to be someplace private, where you could just roll in and roll out, unnoticed.

Someplace like this.

I double-parked in front of the Connellys' house, went to the gate, and pushed the button. A woman came on the speaker and I identified myself and she asked if I had a car. I said yes, and she said okay, and I still was standing there when the big gate across the drive rolled open. Then started to close. Then opened again, then closed and opened.

I jogged to the car and waited until there was a space wide enough to drive through. I did, as passersby on the sidewalk peered in. The gate closed on them and I was left in the Connelly sanctuary.

It was a cobblestoned courtyard shaded by tall horse chestnut trees. Two of the cars from Maine were parked there: the black BMW and the Suburban. Inside the garage of the carriage house I could see a BMW motorcycle and some sort of sports car under a canvas cover. Beyond the carriage house on the lawn was a soccer goal, a cedar swing set, and a small bike with training wheels.

I got out of the car; David emerged from a side door of the house, grinning like I was an old buddy from Harvard.

"Sorry about the gate. Mrs. Donovan is a peach, been with me since I was a kid. But she doesn't take to technology."

"It's fine. I waited and made my move."

He shook my hand and gave me the shoulder pat again.

"Good to see you. Roxanne's inside, but I think they're still talking business."

"That's fine," I said. "Whenever she's ready."

"Ready for what?"

"Ready to go."

"Go? It's already been decided. You're staying, and not in some hotel. Stay here. We'll have a drink, go get some dinner. Sox are away or we could go over to Fenway."

I tried to decline, but he wouldn't hear of it, and insisted on bringing in our bags. I followed him up a cobblestone walk to the side door.

"This is a nice oasis in the city," I said.

"I call it Fort Apache," David said. "Told Maddie I want catwalks on the walls so Maeve and I can keep lookout."

I smiled. He opened a heavy door, like the door to a vault, and we went in.

Inside it was cool and very still. We were in an entryway and David said to leave the bags, Mrs. Donovan would take them up to our room. He said the girls were in the kitchen and led the way.

It was like a museum, high ceilings and tile floors, photographs and paintings and prints in between. Our footsteps echoed as I followed David, and heard Roxanne's voice. When we came into the kitchen, Roxanne and Maddie were sitting at a long dark-wood table. There was a bottle of white wine between them and one of Pellegrino. A stout white-haired woman was unwrapping a block of cheese at a counter across the room.

"Jack, this is Mrs. Donovan, the car crusher," David said, and she turned and smiled and said, "Now, David, that's quite enough out of you."

"Okay, car denter," he said.

Maddie said, "Hi, Jack," and Roxanne did, too. David went to the refrigerator and took out two bottles of Sam Adams, opened them, and presented me with one. He raised his bottle in a toast and said, "Here's to—"

I thought he was going to say Angel, but he didn't.

"Roxanne was a tremendous help," Maddie said. "We're thinking of stealing her from Maine and keeping her for ourselves."

"Ask in February," I said, "and you might have a deal."

"They had some great ideas," Roxanne said.

"I think it might lead to something," Maddie said. "I think we're going to start finding ways to make real progress on this."

"Good," I said.

"How did your afternoon go?" Roxanne said.

"Interesting," I said. "But sad."

"Where'd you go?" David said, very attentive.

"Talked to Angel's family. A whole room full of them. And Monica and her mother."

"How are the Morettis?" David said.

"Grieving," I said. "Father is very angry."

"That's understandable," Maddie said. "And it's not like just a tragic death. A murder, and whoever did it is still out there loose."

"That might never change," Roxanne said.

"I've written about unsolved murders," I said. "Saddest thing is when the parents die without any sort of justice."

"That must be terrible," David said. "How do they reconcile themselves to that? I mean, jeez. What a thing to go to your grave with."

Maddie looked at him and he met her glance and looked uncomfortable for a moment, then brightened as he looked back to us.

"Maddie," he said, "now you can give the tour. She was waiting for you, Jack."

"Do you like old things?" Maddie said.

"Sure," I said.

"Oh, a live one for you, Mad," David said. "If I don't hear from you in a day or two, I'll send for help."

So the three of us went; David said he'd go upstairs and see if Maeve was awake. We walked through a couple of rooms to a center hallway, and from there to the formal living room to the left of the front door. A massive marble fireplace, floor-to-ceiling windows, and a concert grand piano.

"I love old things," Maddie said, like she was talking about her grandmother's china. "I'll bore you to death if you let me. That's a George the Third sofa. And that's a Chippendale lowboy. Made around 1770 in Philadelphia. I mean, the craftsmanship was just astounding. Someone was sitting in that the day they signed the Declaration of Independence. I just find that fascinating. Across the room is a settee. In 1820, it meant you could live graciously. This is a wonderful example, Duncan Phyfe. See the paw, how it's almost horizontal? Most of them are more erect. In this one the lion is crouching. It's one of a kind."

She was animated, intent, enlivened by the history. It was oddly endearing, her passion for this, nothing blasé about it. It was like this was the real Maddie, the woman behind the looks and money. She touched the settee, stroking it like it was a pet.

David came into the room, Maeve in his arms. She blinked sleepily, her legs hanging limp. He made a snoring sound and Maddie pretended to glare at him, like she was the teacher on an eighth-grade museum tour.

She was talking about corner cupboards made of walnut and fruitwood, late eighteenth century. Paused at a pine valuables cupboard, William and Mary, around 1700. The kneehole desk was George II.

"Got all the dead kings covered," David said.

"Who did the collecting?" I said.

"My grandmother," David said. "She was an antique, too."

"David doesn't care about any of this," Maddie said.

"It's furniture," David said.

"It's history," Maddie said. "How can you love boats so much and not care about this?"

"You can't sail a sofa," he said.

She gave his arm a squeeze and smiled. "My darling Philistine"

David grinned and she pulled him a little closer so their hips touched. It seemed a funny time to be playing the cute couple, but I supposed people dealt with death in different ways.

So on we went, Maddie pointing out priceless antiques, David schlepping along at the rear. Maddie led the way through a study with duck paintings on the walls, photographs of Connellys fishing in Scotland, hunting in Montana, David on the deck of a racing sailboat. MARBLEHEAD TO HALIFAX—FIRST IN CLASS the inscription read. Along one wall were glass-fronted cabinets (Edwardian) filled with antique guns. Rifles and shotguns, revolvers and derringers. The Winchester was Civil War, forty-caliber and rare. The pair of dueling pistols was early nineteenth century. Ditto for the blunderbuss.

"Your grandmother again?"

"Grandfather. I'd like to donate all of it to a museum."

"David, they're part of the family's history," Maddie said.

"So? Doesn't mean we have to live with it."

While David lagged, we moved into a salon sort of room at the rear of the house. The windows overlooked a walled garden brimming with flowers. Hanging here and there were two Andrew Wyeths, a Frederick Remington, and a Picasso drawing. On one wall were framed photographs of Connellys with famous people. David as a toddler cowering beside Lyndon Johnson. Young David and Maddie with young Bill and Hillary. David at twelve or thirteen, looking over at a long-haired John Kennedy Jr., other Kennedy cousins beside them.

"You knew John Kennedy?" I said.

"Not then, not well," David said. "Better years later. His projects and our projects overlapped sometimes. Very nice guy."

"Sad," I said.

"Very," he said. "For all the family baggage, he carried it well. I mean, he could have been a basket case, a total screw-up."

"All the tragedy in that family," I said. "And who knows what else, because I'm sure there are things that have never been made public."

As the words left my mouth, I could see an odd look from Maddie. She swallowed and seemed to retreat inside herself. It was as though her mind had suddenly wandered far from these photographs, from this room, from us, to a sad, disturbing place.

David said, "Maddie, how 'bout Mistral for dinner?"

His voice was cheery, almost jarring, and Maddie came back, but slowly. I glanced at Roxanne, saw she was watching Maddie, too.

"Sure," Maddie said. "That would be nice, David. Why don't you call?"

And then to us she said, "Had enough? There's a great seventeenth-century piece in the first-floor study."

"Looks like they made it with an ax," David said.

"Where did you grow up, Maddie?" I said.

"Western part of the state," she said. "Dad and Mom both taught at Amherst."

"That must have been a nice life," Roxanne said, "growing up around a college."

Maddie didn't answer. Instead she turned away, and the distant expression crept back.

"Yeah," David said quickly. "It was. It was a good life for a kid, knocking around the campus, right, Mad?"

His wife snapped back, her bright eyes suddenly focusing. "Yeah," she said, her voice off-key. "It *was* a good life."

We turned to leave the room, Maddie leading the way. I touched my hand to Roxanne's and she pressed back.

19

Mistral was on Columbus Avenue, just over from Berkeley. On the ride over, Maddie driving the BMW, David said he liked it because the food was straightforward. Maddie said she could go and just have dessert. "And the people, are very nice," she said.

And they were.

Pulling up in a line of livery cars, our doors were opened, all four of them. The head valet looked like Antonio Banderas.

"Hey, Mr. and Mrs. Connelly," he said. "How goes the battle?"

David said it was going fine. Maddie didn't answer.

There was a line of people waiting to be seated but we breezed right through, everybody on the staff greeting the Connellys like old friends. The black-clad blonde woman who seated us gave David a little extra snap in her eyes and her walk, but he seemed oblivious, waving to a couple as we crossed the stark, gray-walled room.

"John Kerry's here," he said as we sat, and then to Maddie, "Did you ever call him back?"

The waiter, who was French, asked the Connellys when they were going to take him to Maine to catch lobsters. They said soon, Jacques, soon. He explained the specials and we ordered: sea bass and smoked salmon, Dover sole and beef and potato pizza. Maddie recommended the chilled yellow corn soup, with lobster and avocado. David said we should try the scallop ceviche. He said if the Sox had been in town, we might have run into Nomar Garciaparra.

Maddie ordered wine without looking at the list: it was a South African pinot noir. Maddie said she liked it and felt that we should support the post-apartheid economy there. Roxanne had more Italian sparkling water.

So we talked about South Africa and an organization there that raised infants born with HIV. The foundation had just given it a lot of money. We talked about Italy and the Amalfi coast and how Venice was sinking. Maddie asked if I missed New York. I said, not often.

When the wine came, David offered a toast: "To our new Maine friends," he said. "And to Prosperity. The town."

Appetizers arrived: the soup, mussels, and endive salad.

We ate and drank and talked and the Connellys asked lots of questions. They both wanted to know about the inner workings of the *Times*. David asked Roxanne about how she handled parents when she was all alone, whether she was ever afraid. Roxanne said she had developed a sixth sense when it came to things like that, and had managed to sidestep risky situations.

All of us knocked on wood. The soup was delicious.

Long before the entrees, David ordered more wine. The room grew more boisterous around us. The candelabra flickered and it occurred to me that Roxanne looked very beautiful. I noticed David studying her, too.

I asked them about the foundation, whether they were deluged with requests. They said they were but that was why they had a staff.

You needed a professional buffer, David said, or you'd never be able to say no.

"Is Tim Dalton good at what he does?" I said.

"Very," Maddie said. "Very organized, very efficient. Has good sense of the players in the city, who's for real."

"There are a lot of bullshitters in the not-for-profit world," David said, "if you'll excuse the expression."

"How 'bout Kathleen Kind?"

"A total professional," David said. "You never need to tell her what priorities should be. Place runs like clockwork, but it's because she's on top of things."

"Are they married?"

"To each other?" Maddie said, shooting David a quick glance. "Oh, no. Tim's wife, Diana, is a lawyer in town. She's a very well-regarded litigator. A big deal, actually."

"And Ms. Kind?"

"Divorced. Her ex-husband is with a bond house. No kids. I guess he was spending more time with one of the aspiring young analysts than with her, and one thing led to another. That was just before she came on board with us, three years ago."

"Seeing anybody else?"

This time David looked uneasy. The entrees had come. He picked at his salmon and caviar.

"Actually, she and Tim dated for a bit. He was separated for six months or so. Another case of careers taking precedence over a marriage. But the Daltons pulled it back together."

"And Angel?"

"You can tell you're a reporter, Jack," David said.

"Just trying to get everybody straight in my mind," I said.

"Angel was a beautiful girl," Roxanne said.

"And she was built," Maddie said, "to put it bluntly. Talk about physical gifts."

"Her parents seemed to treat her like she was fourteen," I said. "Very protective. They didn't like it that she worked out of town."

"For us?" David said.

"I think maybe that's why there was something immature about her," Maddie said. "It wasn't that she was shy. But she seemed hesitant to enter into a real relationship."

"So she flirted and fooled around instead?" I said.

Maddie looked to David. He shrugged.

"It's hard," he said. "At what point do you become the morality police, you know? And we were all young once. You do dumb things, you learn from them. You go on."

"But Tim Dalton isn't all that young," I said.

Roxanne kicked me under the table.

"And he's married, right?"

She kicked me harder.

"Yeah," David said. "I thought you must've noticed that, up at the house. Maddie and I talked about it the night they all left. I mean, I guess something had been going on, but you try to tell yourself it's in your head. Or it's just foolishness, harmless foolishness. Midlife crisis run amok. But it was getting out of hand. We decided I was going to have to tell Tim to cool it."

"And I was going to tell Angel," Maddie said.

Suddenly, even in the din of the restaurant, our table grew quieter.

"And did you?" I said.

"Oh, yeah," David said.

"Me, too," Maddie said. "It was . . . uck. I just hate that kind of thing."

"And what was their reaction?" I said. "If you don't mind me asking."

"Well, I wouldn't want this in the story, Jack. For her family's sake."

"Jeez, for Tim's sake," Maddie said. "His wife would clean him out in a heartbeat."

"If I get it, it won't be from you," I said. "But the police might bring it up, and then I have to report it."

"I don't want Tim to think I was gossiping about him," David said. "That wouldn't be very good form, now would it?"

"No," I said. "But what did they say?"

"Tim told me it was just fooling around; he'd never even kissed her."

"Angel looked at me like I was crazy," Maddie said. "Said they were just friends, just being silly; didn't I ever flirt when I was young?"

"Ouch," I said.

"I know," Maddie said. "The little hussy."

"Maybe she was right, that's all it was," Roxanne said.

"We'll never know now," David said.

"I wouldn't count on that," I said. "The cops aren't going to let go."

"And you know what, Jack?" David said, the big grin flashing, starting to turn to summon the waiter. "I don't think they're the only ones. I can see you're part bulldog. Just be careful, will you? I mean, we're talking about a murderer here. And what is it they say in the cop shows?"

"I don't know," I said.

"The second murder's always easier?" he said. "But you'd know more about crime stuff than I would."

"I don't know about easier," I said. "But sometimes it's inevitable."

"It sets off a chain reaction," Maddie said, almost as though she knew and could speak with authority.

I looked at her.

"What cop show was that?" I said.

"Oh, I don't remember," Maddie said. "They're all the same, aren't they? Good guy gets the bad guy and they all live happily ever after."

Now there was a curious tinge of bitterness in her voice. Roxanne looked at her; David took the wine bottle and topped off our glasses.

"That's not the way it works in real life?" I said.

"Only in the movies," Maddie said.

"Should we get another bottle?" David said quickly. "Maddie, what do you think? Did you want to stay with the South African? Where's the steward? Have you two ever been to South Africa?"

I watched Maddie as she retreated into herself, looking past us, past this place. David brightened as she faded.

I shook my head.

"No," Roxanne said.

"Gorgeous, parts of it," he said. "But such a horrible past. Isn't it funny how terrible things happen in beautiful places?"

"Like Maine," I said. "The beautiful Maine coast."

Maddie and David both looked at me.

"You mean Angel?" David said.

"Yeah. I don't think she went exploring in the boonies."

"No," Maddie said, back with us now. "The country didn't interest her at all. She was a city person. The question is, who brought her to that godforsaken place?"

"Yes," I said. "That's it in a nutshell."

20

We stayed late: dessert, coffee, cognac. David talked a little about Angel, and a lot about boats, sailing, what it was like to be in the mid-Atlantic in a storm. He said it was the closest he'd been to death and the most alive, at the very same time. I asked him if they'd ever taken Angel sailing and he thought about it and said no, that she'd been with them a year and *Serendipity*, the family's Hinckley sloop, had been out of the water for longer than that for a complete refitting.

"She told her parents about some sailing trip," I said. "Said the mast was eighty feet tall, how peaceful it was without the noise of a motor."

"Not with us," Maddie said. "But I'm sure we're not the only people she knew who had access to a sailboat."

"Anybody can charter," David said. "That's how a lot of people get in trouble. The ocean isn't anything to fool with."

Neither is the land, I thought, picturing Angel in the ground, the grass in her hair.

There was no check. David said they knew the owners and would take care of it later. Roxanne drove home and we said good night to them in the kitchen. There was back-patting all around; David gave Roxanne a kiss on the cheek. The wine? Maddie went up to check on

Maeve and David showed us to our room, which he called the honeymoon suite.

It was on the fourth floor, with a view of the Charles and the lights of Cambridge beyond the river. The bed was a four-poster with a dark red canopy and the down comforter was turned down. Our bags were set on top of a blanket chest along the wall.

"If you want to know what king the thing was made under, you'll have to ask Maddie," David said. "I lose track."

He left and we were alone. Roxanne inspected the room, said, "My God, Jack. Look at this vase. It's probably Ming Dynasty or something."

"Maybe it's Filene's Dynasty," I said.

She kicked off her shoes and sighed. Unbuttoned her blouse and tossed it onto the dresser. Slipped out of her slacks and threw them aside, too, and then took her makeup case to the bathroom. The water ran, and then she was back. She took a nightshirt from her bag and pulled it over her head and said, "Oh boy, am I tired."

I opened the drapes so we could see the lights from the bed. And then I turned off the lamp and stripped down to my boxers and slid in beside her.

"Good day?" I said.

"Yeah. I think it went well."

"You glad you did it?"

"Yeah."

"You like them?"

"Yeah; you?"

"Uh-huh," I said. "They're very nice. Very real. Maddie has a melancholy to her."

"Yeah," Roxanne said. "Like maybe this charmed life isn't all it's cracked up to be."

"Or something sad that the charmed part can't undo."

"You know she's not what I expected," she said. "He is, sort of. But not as full of himself. It's like he doesn't take himself too seriously."

"Maybe that's his defense against all this Connelly stuff."

"Maybe, but she doesn't have the same confidence."

"She's not a Connelly."

Roxanne turned on her back and looked up at the canopy over us.

"It's not just that," she said. "There's something very fragile about her. I've seen it in children who have had some sort of trauma. You see it years later, when they're with good families and everything is fine. There's something different about them, no matter how well they're doing. I see that in Maddie, too."

"Maybe the brother dying."

"I don't know."

"I'd say it was Angel, but I saw it before she died. Maddy's sad side, I mean."

We were quiet for a minute. Roxanne intertwined her legs with mine. Leaned over and kissed my shoulder, then fell back.

"Do you think they'd come see us?"

"Why not?"

"Well, where would they sleep? We only have one bedroom."

"In the addition."

"What addition?"

"The one for the baby," I said.

I could feel Roxanne smile.

"You know, today I thought I felt a tingle."

"Really. Is that what happens?"

"I don't know. Maybe it was my imagination, but I just felt different all of a sudden."

I kissed her cheek. A minute passed and I thought she was drowsy, falling asleep, but when I looked over, her eyes were open wide. Outside there was a siren, tires screeching.

"Jack, do you think we're right to trust them?"

"You mean, after someone in their company has been killed?"

"Yeah."

"I don't think they're serial killers."

"I don't think they're bowled over with grief, either," Roxanne said.

"No. But maybe they didn't know her that well."

"If Angel had come on to you, I mean, *really* had come on to you, would you have resisted it?"

"Yeah. Sure. And I'd have tried not to laugh."

Roxanne smiled, pulling the covers up under her chin. "I don't think you would have laughed. You wouldn't have wanted to hurt her feelings."

"No."

"So you won't laugh when I ask you one more thing?"

"I don't think so."

"Would you lock the door? It's got a bolt thing you turn."

I got up and crossed the room. The house was silent. I turned the knob that moved the bolt, and I didn't laugh at all.

21

I was dreaming that I was in an office and there was a fire alarm and I couldn't get out from behind the desk. Then I woke up and it was morning, gray light pouring into the room, Roxanne asleep beside me. The alarm was my cell phone ringing, and I groped for it on the nightstand and answered it.

"Mr. McMorrow?"

A young woman's voice, very young. She said she was sorry to bother me. I rasped that it was okay, I'd been up for hours. She said her name was Annie, that she was an intern at the *Times* bureau.

"There are two men here to see you," she said.

"What do they want?"

"They say they need to talk to you about Angel Moretti. The woman who was killed?"

"I know," I said. "Are they cops?"

She hesitated.

"They didn't say that. If they are, they're not like any I've ever seen."

"Why?"

"One's really big and he's got a tattoo on his neck and the other is smaller and, I don't know, I just don't think they're police."

"Where are they?"

"They're sitting out by reception reading the paper."

"Did they ask for me by name, or just to see a reporter?"

"You. I said you weren't here, that you didn't really work in the office. They asked if I could call you, and I said I guessed I could, and then they just said they'd wait, and that's what they're doing."

"Were they polite?"

"Yeah. The big one is sort of cheerful."

"You're all alone there?"

"Yeah. I came in early to work on some stuff."

"I'll be right over."

Roxanne murmured in the bed as I grabbed jeans and a T-shirt from my bag and headed for the shower. When I emerged, she was asleep again, dark hair against the white sheets, and I wrote a note on a pad and tore off the page. I left it on my side of the bed. It said I loved her and I'd gone to the bureau. I'd be right back.

I opened the door and closed it behind me, but there was no way to lock it. The house was quiet but I could smell coffee from somewhere below me. I made my way down the stairs, eventually found the kitchen. Mrs. Donovan was sitting at the table drinking coffee and reading the *Herald*.

"Good morning," she said. "Are you ready for breakfast?"

I thanked her but said no. I said I had to run over to my office for a bit. She said she'd make me something when I got back.

"Do you know how to open the gate?" she said.

I figured it out, punching the button in the post and driving through quickly before the gate closed behind me. Marlborough Street was quiet, Boylston, too, the streets still and the air cool and slightly damp with dew. Joggers in silky shorts ran in the road and bicyclists signaled with their hands as they turned, as though that alone would keep them safe. It was like everything menacing in the city had been a dream and now we were all awake. Pretty to think so.

It was almost eight when I was buzzed into the bureau offices. They looked up.

Two white guys in their thirties: one very big and barrel-chested, wearing a black T-shirt and black jeans and a Red Sox hat. Red hair stuck out from under the hat like a cat hiding under a rug. He had a tattoo of a shamrock on his neck and a diamond in his left earlobe. The other guy was smaller. Dark hair and a sharp, narrow face. He was chewing gum and somebody was wearing cologne. It was the big guy who spoke.

"You McMorrow?"

The other guy was watching me.

"Yeah."

"Great," the big guy said. "Just the man we're here to see. We come over to talk to you."

They both stood and the big guy was quick, coming out of his chair like a football lineman. He held out his hand, a massive rosy paw that made my hand seem soft and delicate.

"I'm Mick. This is my business associate, Vincent."

Vincent looked at me but didn't speak.

"Hey, I like your work. I read your story in the paper there, the one about the girl they dug up in Maine. Good stuff. No bullshit, you know what I'm saying? Gets right to the point."

"Thanks," I said.

He smiled. One of his front teeth was capped in gold.

"So, it just so happens, I got a friend who'd like to talk to you about that girl."

"Is that right? What about her?"

"I really can't speak for him, you know what I'm saying?"

"I know what you're saying. I don't know why you came here."

"I can take you to him."

"Why doesn't he come here?"

"He'd rather be confidential. His position is what you might call sensitive. But he has some information that you'd be very interested in."

"What kind of information?"

"You need to talk to him."

"I need an idea of what he's going to say. See whether it's worth my time."

The big hand came out and tapped my shoulder. It was like being whacked by a piece of oak.

"Sure. You're an important guy, working for the *New York Times*. You can't be running around chasing every nutcase who wants to bend your ear."

"That's right," I said.

The little guy watched me, so still he didn't appear to be breathing.

"He knew the girl."

"So did a lot of people."

"He knew her real, real good."

"Her boyfriend?"

"No."

"Brother? Father? Second cousin?"

"I'm not at liberty to say."

"I don't think so. Have him call me, he wants to talk."

"He wants to talk right now. He's waiting."

"Waiting where?"

"A place where we can have coffee and whatever. He'll buy you breakfast. He woulda come here but he was nervous 'bout somebody seeing him coming in and out. Then there's a story. They put two and two together, you know what I'm saying?"

"Listen, I'm pretty busy," I said. "I can call him later."

"I know, Jack. Mr. McMorrow. But this guy, he said it's important he talk to you right now, before you write another story about this girl."

"I don't know."

But then I thought for a moment. What did he know about Angel? Did he know who'd killed her? Had he heard something on the street? I nodded to the intern, Annie, who was peeking out from Myra's office. We went out the door, the three of us, waited for the elevator and stepped in. The door closed and there was a moment of silence.

22

The elevator opened. We went out the door, Mick in front, me in the middle, Vincent bringing up the rear, which made me feel like I was being escorted.

Mick led the way to a dark blue Cadillac parked in a handicapped space on Chatham Street, behind the building. There was a cardboard handicapped permit on the dash. He reached in and tossed it onto the seat.

"Came with the car," he said.

We rode out Congress Street. I sat in front with Mick and Vincent sat in back. The car smelled like cigarettes and Mick drove like a New York cabbie, stomping the gas and the brakes, one finger spinning the wheel. He was telling me about how he was starting to write stuff, how he'd never really done it before but he found himself with some time, that it beat watching the TV.

"That's what most guys do. Sit in front of the tube."

"Where's this?" I said.

"It's called Cedar Junction, aka Walpole. The state prison. Me and Vincent, we was in the same cube."

I didn't flinch.

"How long have you been out?"

"Coupla weeks."

"How long were you in?"

"Me? Eight months, two weeks, and four days. Vincent a little longer."

I smiled.

"But who's counting?"

"That's right," Mick said. "You count the days, lemme tell ya. Ain't that right, Vincent?"

Vincent didn't answer.

Mick drove south, cutting through alleys, stopping to let women in short-skirted business suits cross the street. They hurried, knowing they were being ogled, but we took our time until we popped out on Summer Street. Mick drove across the bridge and the water in the channel was gunmetal gray, and then we were off the bridge and into the treeless landscape of Southie.

There were storefronts and tenements, a few white kids out on the corners, hunched against the wind that blew cold off the harbor. We pulled over in front of a bar called the Double Diamond Lounge. The sign in the window advertised Rolling Rock and luxury rooms. The window was covered with a wrought-iron grille, like a fence around a cemetery.

We sat in the car, the three of us. Mick rested his arm on the seatback beside me, like a guy on a date about to make his move.

"You know Southie?" he said.

"Not really."

"I grew up here. Know every square inch. Like Vincent and the North End. My old man came from the Old Country, Donegal. Fit right in with the rest of the fucking brogues around here. You still got 'em. That bar across the street? All green cards. You'd think you were in goddamn Limerick."

"Is that right?"

"You oughta do a story on Southie. Nobody's done a good story on Southie. Place is changing. I mean, look at this gook here."

A man was walking down the sidewalk toward us. He looked Cambodian.

"Ten years ago, this guy wouldna shown his face in this neighborhood. Now look at 'im. Walking down the street like he belongs here. Of course, he isn't here at night, is he? He isn't stupid. Hey, but I'm not disrespecting these people. No way. In the joint these fuckin' gooks are mean motherfuckers. These nineteen-year-old kids from Lowell, Lawrence, you don't mess with 'em. But they don't mess with the Irish guys, either. Lemme tell ya, there's some crazy motherfuckers from Southie and Dorchester doing time in Walpole. Isn't that right, Vincent?"

Vincent's agreement was assumed. He got out first and we followed and stood and waited to let the Cambodian man pass us. He stared straight ahead but Mick gave him a big smile, said, "Whaddya say, Jackie Chan?"

Mick turned to me as we crossed the sidewalk.

"They'll cut your throat before you even know they're in the room," Mick said. "They're very good."

Mick held the door. I stopped in front of him and he smiled and I said, "Was your friend in Walpole, too?"

"Hell no," he said. "He's a very careful man."

23

We sat in a booth in the back beyond the pool tables. An older woman—red hair piled high, the rest of her packed into skintight sweater and jeans—headed over. She left her cigarette burning on the edge of the bar like something left to light a fuse.

"Mick, good to see you're back," she said, like he was home from college. "You made out?"

"Fine. You treat people like you want to be treated, Terry."

"The Golden Rule, Mick," she said.

Mick said we wanted a big breakfast and the woman left.

"So where is he?" I said.

"I don't know. He musta been held up."

"I thought you said he was waiting?"

"He was. His pager musta gone off."

"What's he do, he needs a pager?"

"A littla this," Mick said. "A littla that."

The waitress came back with coffee. I had mine black. Mick poured in four containers of half-and-half and four sugars. Vincent watched me like a begging dog, his black eyes fixed on mine. Mick smiled again and sipped his coffee. In his fist the cup looked like it was from a kid's tea set.

"Vincent don't do caffeine," Mick said.

Vincent shook his head. I felt like telling him to quiet down.

"You Irish?" Mick asked me.

"And half Scottish."

"Same thing. Fighting the fucking English."

A guy with a big belly walked by and said, "Hey, Mick," and Mick waved his hand but didn't look at him.

"So what line of work are you guys in?" I said.

Mick looked at me. The smile was still there but the eyes were vaguely threatening.

"I'm in business," he said. "Wholesale, retail. I buy truckloads. Washing machines, TVs, refrigerators. Sometimes it's hard to determine where your stock, how should I say, originated."

"So that's how you ended up in Walpole?"

The smile slipped another notch, the gold tooth disappeared.

"A business risk."

"And you do your time and go on?"

"I can take a pinch. I don't rat anybody out."

"You don't mind that?"

"Hey, inside's like anywhere else. You got money, you live okay. You got commissary. You put money on your card, you can buy clothes. You hire a house mouse, do your laundry, make your bed. You can buy decent sneakers. Racks of tuna. Racks of tuna are very big. Everybody works out and prison food's got shit for protein."

"Is that right?"

"Yeah. You oughta write about prison. Nobody's written a good story about Walpole."

"No?"

"It's its own world, you know what I'm saying? And then you come home. I walk in here, it's like I never left. It's weird."

"You just go back to work."

"That's what I'm doing right now."

"Oh, yeah?" I said. "I don't need a refrigerator."

"I got sidelines," Mick said.

At that moment the redheaded woman arrived carrying three plates of sausage, potatoes, and eggs. She left and came back with a plate of toast and a plastic bottle of ketchup.

"You boys enjoy," she said.

"You're an angel, Terry," Mick said.

Vincent took his fork in one hand and a napkin in the other and started to eat. I picked at my plate, took a few bites of toast. Mick hunched over his eggs and didn't look up until the plate was clean.

He pushed it away, wiped his face with a napkin, looked at my plate.

"You don't like your Irish breakfast?"

"Lost my appetite."

"Yeah?"

"I'm wondering what business this is that you're doing. I'm wondering where this guy is. I'm asking myself whether you're jerking me around."

"No way, Jack. I'm delivering something."

"Delivering what?"

"A message."

"For your friend?"

"Yeah. I guess he ain't coming, so I'll do it for him, long as you came all the way over here."

"So spit it out," I said. "I've got things to do."

His eyes narrowed. His grin turned mean, a predator's curl on his upper lip.

"Some people prefer you leave the dead alone, don't go picking at their grave."

The three of us were silent, and then I said, "What grave is that?"

"Angel Moretti's grave," Mick said.

"And who's saying this?"

"Friends of hers. They'd like you to respect the dead."

"I do. But if somebody's murdered, they deserve more than that."

"But these friends, they appreciate what you've done. They just think you've done enough."

"So?"

"So just leave it alone. For this girl's sake."

"That's the message?"

"Yeah. I mean, I don't think it's unreasonable, do you? Poor girl gets killed and buried in the woods and whatever else happened to her. Twisted bastards. I'd love to get hold of 'em."

"Yeah?"

"So there's that terrible tragedy and now you go rooting around in her life, gonna hang it out there for the whole world to see. The feeling is, this kind of thing should stay . . ."

Mick paused, searching for the right word.

"Stay what?" I said.

"Private."

"Meaning?"

"The rest of Angel's life. Just leave it alone."

"So who sent you? Her family?"

"It's immaterial."

"So the Morettis send an Irish guy."

"I run an equal opportunity business."

"That's why you have Vincent with you?"

"Vincent knows people in the North End. He's got connections in that part of the city. I do business there. I do business in Roxbury, Dorchester. All over."

I paused. Looked at the eggs congealing on my plate. The red-haired woman came back and leaned over me and said, "You didn't like your breakfast?"

"He hasn't been feeling good," Mick said.

"That's okay, honey," the woman said, and she took our plates away. Mick put his big hands on the table.

"So consider this a courtesy call, Mr. McMorrow. You got some people for whom these stories are hurtful. And these people been hurt already. You got kids?"

I didn't answer.

"Well, you can picture how these parents feel. Their flesh and blood, murdered in this way. Hey, I didn't know Maine was that kind of place, rapists and murderers out there waiting in the woods. So this is this poor girl's last hours on earth, being tormented by these guys. This is a hard thing for her friends and loved ones to take, as you can—"

"It's not up to them."

"What?"

"Whether I write a story."

"Well, I can see how you feel. You got space co fill. Hey, why don't you write about Walpole prison, what it's like on the inside? I could tell you some stories that'd sell papers. I'm serious. The shit that goes down, you wouldn't believe. And then they toss these guys back into the community. No wonder we got crime."

I didn't answer.

"So I'd help you with that story. I'll help you with the Southie story. But I'm here to tell you that this story about this dead girl is not a good thing."

"For them or me?"

"For anybody."

"I don't agree."

"Then I guess we got to persuade you to take us seriously, right, Vincent?"

I looked at Vincent. He was breaking into a hint of a smile.

"You're supposed to say, 'Yes, master,' " I told him.

"Vincent got jumped by some of those Jackie Chans in Walpole and took two of 'em right out," Mick said. "Self-defense, so he didn't get hammered too bad."

"I could kill you," Vincent said, his voice an odd high-pitched whisper.

"With your breath?" I said.

"You're dead," he said.

"I'm outta here," I said. "Thanks for the meal and the nice conversation."

I stood up. They did, too. The red-haired woman was wiping glasses, acting like she'd just gone blind and deaf. I started for the door, heard chairs slide behind me. Two old men glanced up from their morning Budweisers, then looked away. Outside, the air was heavy and still and it had begun to drizzle. I started up the block, and Mick and Vincent fell in beside me, one on each side.

"Hey, listen, McMorrow," Mick said. "Let's chill. Maybe I came on a little rough. I was thinking of a different clientele. But I mean, think of this poor kid's parents."

"So how does this work?" I said, still walking. "You get so much to deliver the message? The rest if I agree?"

"When you agree," Mick said.

"Yeah, right," I said, but then the big paw was in my armpit, the little guy on my other arm.

"Hey," I said, but I was off the ground, feet dragging, into an alley and up against the wall, cold brick against the back of my head.

24

"I'm asking politely" Mick said, pinning me to the wall by the shoulders.

I stared into his eyes. Black pupils. Blood vessels like pink veins in white marble. Vincent stood and waited, a little dog waiting for the big dog to take me down.

Prison rules. They were still playing by them.

"You're wasting your time," I said through clenched teeth.

"I got time," Mick said.

"I don't," I said.

"I could just break your fucking wrists."

"Then we put two reporters on the story."

"I could send somebody around, burn down your house."

"Three reporters," I said. "And I'd find you."

"Is that right?"

"Yeah."

I held his gaze.

And suddenly he smiled. Relaxed. Released me from his grip and I felt myself slide down the wall.

"That's what it's like inside," Mick said, grinning. "Right, Vincent? Happens just like that."

Mick snapped his fat sausage fingers. Vincent nodded.

"You gotta understand that to write about prison. You gotta know how it feels to always be on your toes, every second, even when you're fucking sleeping. When I'm inside, it's like I never sleep, not really. It's like I'm totally wired, all the time. You wouldn't know it to talk to me. Hey, it's like I'm joking around, I'm bullshittin' with some guys in the gym, but part of me is always ready."

"So what was that? A demonstration, or a warning?" I said.

He gave me another quick thump on the upper right arm. I rocked to the left and shifted to regain my balance.

"Just givin' ya some real-life stuff for your story, stuff only a con is gonna know. Readers'll think you're giving 'em the real inside juice. You can start your story, 'Mick didn't sleep for a fucking year.' Except you gotta take out the 'fucking,' 'cause you got kids might read it. So it goes like this."

He held out his hand, brushed it across an invisible movie screen.

" 'Mick hasn't slept in a year. Not like you sleep, in your soft bed in your nice, safe house. Mick dozes like a fucking watchdog. A sound that ain't right and bam, he's wide awake before you can stick a shiv in his back. And remember. In prison, that ain't no figure of speech.' And so on and so forth. Whaddya think?"

"I think your friend should deliver his own messages," I said.

"I like this writing stuff. You write books?"

I didn't answer.

"Somebody oughta write a book about me, the shit I've seen."

"I'm sure."

"So how much?"

"How much what?"

"To drop this story. Leave it alone."

I shook my head.

"I got a guy wants to save the family from this trauma."

"What trauma? She's dead. They've already been through that."

"That's why they can't take any more."

"What is it?" I said. "They don't want the world to know she was screwing around?"

He looked at me.

"Who's saying that?"

"That she was with a guy who was married?"

"Jesus, who's telling you this crazy shit?"

He leaned closer. The shamrock on his neck wrinkled.

"You're getting into deep shit here, McMorrow. I'm trying to tell you. This is the real deal."

"I know that."

"I don't think so, 'cause if you did, you'd be washing your hands of it. Ain't fucking worth it, man. Real bad things can happen. You got loved ones? You want 'em to lose you? I'm not threatening you, McMorrow. I'm trying to give you some advance warning."

"Of what?"

"Of what can happen if you cross the wrong people."

"If I—"

"If you drag this family's name through the mud."

"Why don't they want the guy caught?"

He looked at me and smiled and the tooth glinted.

"Get a clue, McMorrow. Just 'cause the cops, can't find him, that don't mean justice hasn't been done."

Mick's smile widened and the image appeared, looming behind his carnivorous grin. Some guy beaten, tortured, shot. Buried at sea, in a foundation, in pieces in a landfill. For the first time in the conversation, I was afraid.

"When did this happen?" I said.

Mick didn't answer.

"Because the Morettis were still after him when I talked to them. That was yesterday."

No answer.

"So did you find who did it?" I said.

Mick was looking into my eyes like he finally had me, finally had found the leverage point.

"So what's it gonna be, McMorrow?" he said, his gravel voice softer now. I looked at him, the tooth, the glittering wolf's eyes. Vincent watched and waited.

"I'll write whatever I want to write," I said.

Mick's smile melted away.

"That's not what they're gonna want to hear. I can't guarantee your safety, they hear the kind of story you're talking about."

"And you come near me or anybody close to me, I can't guarantee yours," I said. "And I'm serious."

I turned and walked out of the alley and up the block. As I walked, I listened. I waited for the sandpaper sound of footsteps.

Nothing.

I crossed the street. Passed the Irish bar and took a right. Cut across to Congress Street and looked around. Kids. A couple of cars. No Cadillac.

At the T stop on Congress Street I looked back. Still nothing. I turned to the steps, grabbed the rail, and as I did, a car horn honked and I looked up. The Cadillac was coming toward me. The passenger window came down and Vincent leaned out. Rested his right wrist on his left forearm. Shot me twice with an imaginary gun, then pulled his gun hand back into the car and blew past the tip of his finger.

Mick drove on.

25

Back in the car, I got on the phone, I called Cade in Maine on his cell phone and got a crackly hello. He took my number, said he'd call back. When he did, I was on Beacon Street, by the Common. My head hurt where it had hit the wall.

I told Cade I'd been rousted by a couple of guys and told not to write about Angel Moretti. I said they were hired messengers and he said that was interesting, but who would have sent them? I said I didn't know, that's why I was calling him. He said to call a Boston detective named Sullivan. I said that didn't narrow it down, and he said the detective's first name was Sinead and she was a woman, very tough. I said I figured that, at least the woman part, and he said he hadn't, because what kind of name was that? He gave me the number. I asked whether she'd be working on a Saturday morning and he said she was always working. Her husband left her for their best friend, and she'd been working 24/7 ever since.

"And besides, today's the funeral. You going?"

I said I didn't think I'd be welcome.

"When did that ever stop you before, McMorrow?" Cade said, and he laughed like that was a very clever joke.

I called the number for Sullivan and it was a pager. I punched in my cell number and almost rear-ended a car at the corner of Charles Street. Two blocks later Sinead Sullivan called me back.

"You were on my list, sir," she said, traffic noise in the background. "Where are you?"

I told her and she asked if I could find the State House. I said I could, and she said to go to the Hancock Street side and wait. I took a right and made my way back toward Beacon Hill, then wound through a maze of tree-shaded one-way streets. For a while it seemed the gold dome of the State House was a mirage, always beyond reach. And then there it was, looming over me. I pulled over and parked by a hydrant. Five minutes later a blue Sable pulled up behind me. A woman got out and I did, too.

She had short red hair, fair skin, and a round face. Her walk was all straight-ahead determination, her expression, too, like she'd grown up in a house full of rambunctious brothers and had to wrestle her way through every day.

We traded names and shook hands, and her arms were strong and her shoulders had bulk, like she lifted. We went back to her car and climbed in and she turned down the police radio that was on the console, the talk radio, too.

"Imus," she said. "So somebody doesn't want you asking questions about our deceased?"

"No. Or at least they don't want me publishing stories about her."

"Tell me about it, right from when they first contacted you."

I did. As she listened, she stared straight ahead. She didn't take notes.

"Mick Egan and Vincent Tucci," she said, when I'd finished. "Leg breakers."

"That's what they are?"

"Yeah. Muscle. Enforcers. You owe a bookie a lot of money, late with your payment, he sends people like Mick and Vincent."

"He said he was in business. Appliances or something."

"Does some tailgating if it lands in his lap, but muscle is his mainstay. You got a guy won't give you a contract to haul your trash, they come knocking. They won't kill you, but if a talk doesn't do it, they'll come back and beat the crap out of you, burn your house down."

"Why doesn't somebody just shoot them?"

"Probably will eventually. They'll pick the wrong guy to roust. Vincent's just a sociopath. Keep him on a leash. But Mick, he's been around for a while, knows people, does all the talking. He knows how people are probably gonna react. Guy like him knows human nature. Fear, especially. It's his stock-in-trade."

"I see."

"So what did you tell him?"

"To kiss off."

She looked at me, gave a little snort.

"Detective Cade said you were a tough nut."

"I don't know about that."

"So did Mick get physical?"

"Put me up against a wall, but then he made it sound like he was joking around."

"That was a test," Sullivan said. "If you'd crumbled, fine. When you didn't, he had to consider how far to go. A reporter—he's playing with fire."

"I told him that."

"He knows. So he goes back to whoever hired him and says, 'The guy didn't crack. What do you want me to do?' "

"Who would want me to back off this story?" I said.

"Who have you talked to who was hostile?" Sullivan said.

"Her family. They weren't thrilled to have me knocking on their door."

"But they talked."

"Yeah. They said they'd find the guy and deal with him themselves. You think they could?"

"Ah, who knows. It's not like they're directly connected, but I'm sure they could go down the block and Moretti could talk to somebody who could take care of it, if they had a name."

"What? Like 'The Godfather'?"

"Yeah. They might have to pay something, though."

"Brothers made it sound like they'd do it themselves."

"Talk," Sullivan sniffed. "Makes 'em feel better."

"Mick said something about that, too."

"Smokescreen," she said. "You don't know who would want to keep you from asking about Angel?"

"I don't know. Depends on what they think I'll find out."

"Who was she screwing from the office?"

I looked at her.

"You're asking me?"

"I have a pretty good idea, but I haven't been hanging with the Connelly posse the way you have."

"How do you know that?"

"I'm a cop, Jack. I find things out."

"I was only there one afternoon. Their place in Maine."

"And now you're staying with David and Maddie Connelly."

"I knew them before all of this happened."

"You know them before your friend went to visit them in Maine?"

I hesitated.

"No."

"So they're newfound friends."

"You could say that."

"Fast crowd you hang with."

"I haven't found it to be."

"Ten years ago we busted a couple of David's buddies. Us and the DEA. They brought a big sailboat up from Jamaica, filled to the brim with marijuana."

"What about David?"

"He loaned them some of the money. Something like six hundred thousand. He said they told him it was to buy a bar. May have been true—we couldn't prove otherwise—but back then he definitely tended to collect some questionable hangers-on."

"Liked to live dangerously?"

"Lots of rich people are risk takers. They get bored, not having to work for a living."

"Now he just hangs out with his wife and kid," I said. "Talks a lot about boats."

Sullivan shrugged, looked out the window.

"Maybe," she said. "People grow up. And sometimes they don't. So who do you think Angel was humping?"

"Humping?" I said. "Where'd you go to finishing school?"

"Okay. Involved with."

"I don't know. I only met her once."

"And who in that group of people seemed interested in more than her remarkable data-entry skills?"

I hesitated again.

"Who do you think?" I said.

"Well, of the guys? I'd say Dalton. What do you say?"

"Am I a confidential informant or something?"

"If you want to be."

"I can help you, I guess."

"So Dalton?"

"He was all over her. It was uncomfortable. He's married and forty years old."

"Irrelevant to ninety-nine percent of the male population," Sullivan said. "Nobody else was interested?"

"The guys were just me, Sandy, and Connelly. So I'd say no."

"The women?"

"Interested in Angel that way? Not that I noticed. Kathleen Kind, from the office, she thought Angel was trash. It was the Tim and Angel show, pretty much."

"They didn't argue or anything like that?"

"No, he kept one hand on her at all times. She played up to it, like she knew she had him on the line and could reel him in or cut him loose."

"You think she could have told him to take a hike that night or the next day?"

"I think Angel knew the effect she had on men. I think it may have been new to her, this realization that she could make these rich guys swoon, but she was aware of it. I think she was—"

"A player?"

"Maybe."

"You think she boffed Connelly?"

"I don't know. He didn't seem particularly interested in her that way. But she—"

A capitol security cop rolled up and slowed down beside us. He saw Sullivan and nodded, looked at me curiously, and drove on.

"Nosy son of a bitch," Sullivan said. "I hate it when he does that. So Connelly didn't seem interested but she did?"

"No, it wasn't quite like that. It was like he was trying to be polite but she was sort of forward. David this, David that. It seemed presumptuous. This guy's the big boss and she's at the other end of the food chain, but she's acting like they're—"

"Sleeping together?"

"Like she's got a hold on him."

"And sleeping with him would give her that leverage," Sullivan said.

"But he wasn't acting like that at all. It was like she was just somebody from the office."

"But his wife was there. He wouldn't be dragging her onto the poop deck or whatever with his wife around."

"No, but you can tell if there's something between people, don't you think?" I said.

"I suppose," Sullivan said. She adjusted her gun, a snub-nose on her right hip. "So to summarize, we don't know who killed her. Yet. We don't know who's hiding something and doesn't want you poking your nose in. Yet. Of the possibles, the Moretti family is most likely to know bad guys. But Connelly has the clout and he used to hang with drug dealers. Dalton, now that Angel's gone, might not want the world to know he was screwing around with a twenty-year-old."

"Was she twenty?"

"Actually twenty-one. Same difference. So who do you put your money on, Jack?"

"For which? Mick or the murder?"

"Both."

"I don't know," I said. "I don't like Dalton because I don't like liars. But then Kathleen Kind, from the office, gave Angel a look on the boat that could have killed."

"The woman scorned, maybe," Sullivan said. "Maybe had the hots for Connelly herself, been eyeing him for years, and then this little piece of work sashays in with her mediocre typing skills and scoops him up."

"Or it could be just some random pervert who grabbed Angel on the side of the road in Maine."

"Maybe. Detective Cade's still thinking that way, but odds are against it. I'm looking for somebody who Angel had her pretty little claws into. Somebody she was squeezing in some way, and she squeezed too hard."

She took a pad and pen off the console. Asked for my numbers and I gave them to her, but as I recited the digits, I was thinking about Angel, something she'd said and the way she said it. It replayed in my head, not just the words but the inference in the presumptuous, petulant lilt in her voice.

David. Tomorrow let's take Escape *over to Bar Harbor . . .*

26

I called ahead. When I pulled up in front of the house, the gate slid open. I pulled in and the BMW was there; the Suburban was gone. The drizzle had stopped and Maeve was on the edge of the back lawn, standing behind a table. Taped to the front of the table was a cardboard sign that said, "Drinks, ten cents." The letters had run. She began to jump up and down.

"Mommy, a customer."

Maddie, in shorts, bare feet, was sitting in an Adirondack chair in the shade, a book on her lap. I walked across the cobblestones and up to the booth and dug in my pocket for change. I dropped it all in a mug that served as the cash register. Maeve picked the mug up and peered in. She was wearing a jumper with straps and I looked for bruises. There was one on her tiny collarbone, but it was fading, a barely discernible smudge.

"It only costs a dime," she said.

"I'm very thirsty," I said.

"I don't have that much punch."

"I'll start with one cup and see how I do."

"Okay, Jack," she said. "Jack in the Beanstalk." She giggled. "That's the only other Jack I know."

"He's one of my favorites," I said.

"He beat the giant," she said.

"That's why I like him. I like it when the good guy beats the bad guy."

"You do, don't you," Maddie said.

Maeve poured my punch into a paper cup. The punch was pink. I sipped it and it tasted like weak grapefruit juice. She spilled some and ran off to get a towel, and I walked over to Maddie and sat in the chair beside her. She took off her sunglasses and propped them on top of her head.

"It's a theme," she said.

"What is?" I said.

"In your stories. I did a search in the *Times* archive. You write about injustice and sometimes you write about people who right wrongs."

"It doesn't happen much in real life," I said.

"No, it doesn't," Maddie said. "Life is one continuous roll of the dice. Some people win and some people lose."

I looked around at the house, the grounds, the walls and wealth that sheltered this family from so much of the unpleasantness in the world.

"Do you consider yourself one of the winners, Maddie?" I said.

She looked at me, surprised by the question. Hesitated, then said, "Sometimes I've won, I guess. The question is, do you win when it counts the most? Are you lucky in business, unlucky in love? Are you wildly successful but your children are a mess? Do people rave about your books or your films or whatever, but your husband dies of cancer?"

"Or you're young and beautiful and somebody kills you."

Maddie turned and gave me a long look.

"Exactly," she said.

Maeve came out of the house with Mrs. Donovan trailing her, paper towels in hand.

"David and Roxanne went sailing," she said. "He heard she hadn't been in a sailboat in ten years and he wouldn't take no for an answer. They went over to the Basin. They'll be back by noon. The funeral is at two."

"Nice day for it," I said.

"Which?" Maddie said. "Sailing or a funeral?"

"Sailing."

She looked up at the trees.

"A decent breeze, but for David it isn't good sailing unless it's blowing a gale."

"Roxanne will like that," I said. "She's been working too much and too hard."

"On the unending crusade, eh? You're very alike, you two. I can see why you're together."

"That's one of the reasons," I said, and Maddie looked at me and smiled.

"Did you meet in New York?"

"Maine, right after I moved up there."

"A match made in heaven?"

"Something like that."

"That's nice," Maddie said, and paused. "You know, I did see that pattern in your stories. And this story about Angel is perfect for you, Jack. Young damsel is murdered and the knight won't rest until the villain is brought to justice. When you look at your stories as a body of work, you're not like other reporters."

"That's what my editors said. I was a thorn in their side."

"Uncompromising," Maddie said. "And unrelenting."

"I don't think people should get away with things like this."

"I don't either. I think of that girl, her last moments on earth spent in agony. I think they should catch the person and lock him up forever."

Maeve and Mrs. Donovan had finished cleaning up the spill. Mrs. Donovan went back inside and Maeve took up her position behind the table.

"So you're on the story and nothing will stand in your way," Maddie said.

"Two guys tried to stop me this morning," I said.

"Really?" Maddie said. She turned toward me, hand on her chin, a cluster of diamonds and emeralds glinting in the sun. It struck me again that she was intriguingly attractive.

"What did they do?"

I told her.

"My God," she said. "Who would do that? I mean, it must just make you want to do the story even more."

"You're right."

"Well, it would have to be the murderer. Who else would object to you writing about it? Whoever killed her is afraid you'll find something out that will expose them. Which means, you know, that it wasn't some crazed person in Maine. If it was some random thing, then you writing about Angel wouldn't have anything to do with the murderer. Unless you were writing about what bars she went into or where she stopped for lunch."

"Very true."

"So it's not random," Maddie said. Her voice dropped and she turned away from me and said, "Huh."

"Yeah," I said. "Huh."

"I was hoping, you know," she said. "I mean, if it was something to do with her work at the foundation, or with people she met through us. God, at the benefit parties she was like the Pied Piper with these guys following her. You saw her. Picture her with her hair up, cocktail dress. I mean, it was like moths to the flame."

"And Dalton won out?"

"I don't think anybody won out. I think she just enjoyed being chased."

"But Dalton was the lead hound."

"I don't know. It appeared that way. I mean, you were there last weekend."

"That's what the police think," I said.

"They're seriously looking at Tim? Oh, Jesus. What that would do to Sky Blue, my God."

"I think it's out of your control."

"Oh, I know, but still."

We were quiet. Maeve was restless behind the lemonade table. She had taken the coins from the mug and lined them up, stacked them by denomination, piled them in a single stack like a leaning tower. They fell in a jingling heap.

"Of course, the foundation wouldn't fall apart," Maddie said, half to herself. "Our work would go on. We're not responsible for people's personal lives."

"Unless the family decided to sue you, say you hadn't protected her from sexual harassment or something. Just the name 'Connelly'—"

Maeve skipped over and jumped on her mother's lap. Maddie wrapped her arms around the little girl as though she were protecting her. And then she hugged her tightly and Maeve hugged back.

When she turned to kiss Maeve on the cheek, I could see that Maddie's eyes had filled. She pulled her sunglasses back down and gave Maeve another squeeze.

"Oh, no," Maeve said, looking toward her table, where a yellow jacket was circling the pitcher of punch. She squirmed loose and ran to shoo it away.

"So, Maddie," I said. "You act like something amuses you about me chasing stories like this."

"Oh, it's not that. I think you do a good job."

"Then what is it?"

She tucked her legs up underneath her and for a moment she looked very much like her daughter, vulnerable and small.

"'Nothing," she said.

"What?" I said, and I grinned.

"Oh, it's nothing. It's just that, all this stuff about justice and not letting somebody get away with something. It assumes that it's possible to do that, to get away with something terrible you've done and just go on with your life. For some people, maybe. A total sociopath. But most people, they still carry that with them. They carry it for the rest of their life."

"On their conscience, you mean?" I said.

"With every fiber of their being," Maddie said. "It hovers over them like some sort of black cloud that nobody else can see. But they can see it, and it makes everything they do, normal things, seem like a charade. Like you spend your whole life playing the role of somebody else."

"I suppose," I said softly. I looked at her curiously, this person who was not what I'd imagined, whose layers peeled back like pages in a book.

"I'll bet for a lot of these people, being caught is the best thing they can hope for," Maddie said.

"You've thought about this," I said.

She turned to me and brightened, gave me a version of the smile that had probably won David Connelly's heart: pretty, charming, and slightly flirtatious.

"Oh, yeah," Maddie said. "I think about a lot of things. David says that to me. He says, 'Maddie, I can't believe the stuff that goes on in your head.' "

The gate opened and the nose of the Suburban poked through.

"Mommy," Maeve cried from her table. "Customers."

Maddie smiled and got up from her chair, the stuff inside her head safely tucked away for another day.

27

There had been no visiting hours, so the funeral was Angel's only public appearance. We drove over to the North End separately, David and Maddie in the BMW. David kept pulling over to keep from losing us. As we drove, I filled Roxanne in. She told me about her time with the Connellys.

"It was fun," Roxanne said, as we followed down Washington Street. "You know, he's really a very nice guy. There's a gentle side to him. Patient and kind."

"Sullivan still has him as a suspect," I said.

"He's a good man," Roxanne said. "I'd almost stake my job on it."

"Roxanne," I said. "I think we both already have."

The Mass was at Sacred Heart, a brick steepleless church on North Square, a few blocks from the Morettis'. Paul Revere's little wooden house was across the square, and when we pulled up, tourists turned and watched, in case Angel's funeral was the next stop on the Freedom Trail.

The Connelly link apparently was out, because there were three TV crews and at least two newspaper teams waiting outside the church as we walked around the corner with the other family and friends. You could pick out the family because they were the ones who told the press to go to hell. Georgie, Angel's brother, came out of the church and shoved a TV cameraman back.

As the cameraman stumbled, still shooting, the reporter with him spotted Maddie and David and the knot of reporters and cameras converged. I moved off to the side and out of range. Roxanne was with Maddie and David as the TV cameras rolled and the newspaper guys barked questions. One TV reporter, a made-up young woman with lacquered black hair, squirmed her way up to David and said, "Mr. Connelly, why are you here today?"

"We have no comment," Maddie said.

"Mr. Connelly," the woman continued, holding David by the sleeve of his blazer. "Angel Moretti was visiting your summer house in Maine before her body was found. Do you feel in any way responsible for her death?"

"Excuse us, please," David said, smiling patiently. "We need to get inside."

The reporter tried one more time, shoving the microphone up to Maddie's face.

"Mrs. Connelly, how well did you know Angel Moretti? Were you in Maine when your husband had Miss Moretti up to visit?"

"You heard her," Roxanne said. "No comment."

She pushed the microphone aside, and then there was a flurry of motion from the church door. Two big men in dark suits moved through the crowd and stood in front of the cameras, saying there'd be no press inside.

"Who was that woman?" the TV woman said to her cameraman. "Is she a Connelly? Did you get her?"

I waited outside with the press and a few tourists who'd had enough of Paul Revere. When the last of the funeral goers had gone into the church, one of the men in suits took up a sentry position outside the front door, arms folded over his big chest. An organ started to play and I sauntered away, looking for someone who could tell me something more about the young woman who lay dead in a coffin in the front of the church.

In a half-hour, this is what I came up with:

A retired priest who knew the Moretti family and claimed to remember baptizing Angel twenty years back. "Such a pretty baby," he said, standing by the back door of the rectory next to the church. "You know the Devil is very much alive and working in the world today."

A cleaning lady at the rectory who knew Angel's grandmother and said she was a wreck. "The whole family is in my prayers," the cleaning lady said, on the corner waiting for the bus. "That's all you can do these days is pray."

It wasn't much, but every little bit added to the depth of the story. Standing on the sidewalk behind the church, I made a mental list: Roxanne could tell me something of the scene inside the church. I had the cops and David Connelly and Angel's father. And there was Monica—in a short black dress, stepping out of the side door of the church, fishing a pack of cigarettes from her bag.

I walked over and she saw me as she exhaled the first drag.

"Hi, Monica," I said.

"Hey," she said.

Her eyes were red and she sniffed and wiped her nose with the back of her hand. Standing there on the concrete step, she leaned down and took off one of her shoes, a black high-heeled thing with straps. She flexed her bare foot.

"God, these shoes hurt. It's hot in there, you know. Your feet swell."

"How's everybody doing?"

She shrugged.

"Terrible. Her mom is like a basket case. Her dad was crying, too, but you couldn't hear him. Georgie tried to do the reading and he got all choked up, and some lady from the church had to finish it."

"It's hard," I said.

"It sucks," Monica said.

She snaked her shoe back on and then caught sight of her black bra strap, which was showing. She tugged at it but it slipped back out and she gave up.

"God, I could use a drink," she said. "I need a break from this."

"Is there a place nearby?"

She looked at me.

"Just a quick glass of wine?" she said.

"Sure," I said.

We walked back to the square and out to Hanover Street. There was a restaurant around the corner with a bar at the front, and we walked in and Monica put her bag on the bar and we sat. She dug out another cigarette and started to light it but then saw a no-smoking sign. She dropped the cigarette on the bar. The bartender, a handsome kid with two hoop earrings, said, "Hey, Monica, how's it going over there?"

"Shitty," she said.

"I woulda gone but I couldn't get off work," he said.

"No problem," Monica said. "She got plenty of people showed up."

She ordered a white wine. I ordered a Budweiser. There was a guy at the other end of the bar and he looked Monica over as she perched on the stool. He saw me watching him and he turned away. When the drinks came, she drained half of her glass in one long swallow and closed her eyes and sighed.

"It's hard, I'm sure," I said.

"I never had anything like this, you know what I mean?" she said. "My grandmother died, but this—I'm talking to her one day and then she's in a goddamn hole in the ground in goddamn Maine."

"You cared a lot for her, didn't you?"

"She had brothers. I had nobody. My mom had a hard time having me so she got her tubes tied."

"Huh," I said.

"So we were like sisters, you know? When we were eight and twelve and fifteen, she was like my sister, my friend. Except we didn't really fight like sisters do. We just talked, and even when guys started hanging all over her, she always came back to me to go over things, you know?"

She started to cry and took the napkin out from under her glass and dabbed at her eyes.

"Even now?"

"Now what?"

"I mean lately. Did you two still talk things over?"

"Yeah, I mean, some of this stuff she was into, I don't know, I just didn't care. There wasn't one of these rich guys gonna marry me, you know what I'm saying? I'm North End. I'm not gorgeous. I marry some guy, we'll move to Saugus, if I'm lucky. That's who I am."

"And Angel?"

"Oh, with her looks she had possibilities. Maybe some guy with bucks would decide he just had to have her and they'd move to friggin' France or someplace. End up like Maddie Connelly there, married to a pile of money, hanging around your big houses, riding around in your yacht. You know she wasn't rich at all before she latched onto David?"

"I know that."

"Parents were teachers or something. But she's good-looking and smart. Very nice body, even now. She could make the big jump. Angel was smart, too. She coulda done it."

"How was she smart?"

"Lots of ways. She was quick. Me, I gotta think about stuff. She just gets it. Money stuff. I mean, 'cause of where we work, she's reading up about investments and taxes and shit. She's saying things to me like, 'You know there are places you can put your money in the bank and the government can't find it?' The Cayman Islands and all this. I said, 'If I go to some island, I'm going for the beaches, not the banks, and what do you care about that crap?' She said, 'You never know.' I said, 'You been hanging with these rich bastards too much.' She said even the ones that aren't supposed to be rich have money. I think she meant that she had a chance, too. You didn't have to be a goddamn Connelly or whatever."

"Like who?" I said. "Who had money who wasn't supposed to?"

"I don't know. Mr. Dalton. He just worked there and his kid had, like, all these horses and shit. Ms. Kind, she was just like, some kind of accountant, and you know Angel found her passport in her desk or something? She worked in her office on some project thing. Angel could be pretty snoopy. Anyway, she said Ms. Kind went all over the place. She'd go to places like the British Virgins for two days, fly home. 'British Virgins,' Angel said, like she knew what that was. I said to her, 'It figures the American Virgins wouldn't be good enough for that snobby bitch.' "

"That's a quick trip," I said.

"Must be nice, huh?" Monica said. "I said to Angel, 'Why don't we get to live large?' She said, 'Well, let's go.' We were supposed to go in three weeks to Grand Cayman, me and her. She got me a ticket and everything. I got a new bathing suit."

Monica seemed like she might cry again but she fought it off. I sipped my beer.

"So she was doing pretty well at the foundation?"

"I don't know. I guess. She had a better job than me. Everybody's friggin' rich around that place. She always had enough cash. Kept it in her piggy bank."

She smiled, drank more wine.

"She still had a piggy bank?"

"No, that's what she called her box at the bank."

"A safe-deposit box?"

"Yeah. I'm like, 'Angel, what if the bank burns down? What if a jet crashed into it like on nine-eleven?' She's like, 'Yeah, Monica. And what if an asteroid hits Boston.' She was funny."

"So what did she do? Cash her check every week and put the money in a safe-deposit box?"

"I don't know. She didn't tell me all of it. She knew it wasn't my idea of fun, sitting around talking about money. I'd talk about hot guys. Or clothes. God, she had some really nice clothes. We went to New York, like, a month ago and she just went wild."

"Paid with what, plastic?"

"Cash money. She had a wad of it. And she told me she had some jewelry, kept that in the box, too. Her mother yesterday, you know what she said? She asked me if I wanted some of Angel's stuff. I'm like, 'Jesus, thanks, but no.' Wouldn't that be creepy, wearing your dead friend's clothes?"

She shuddered. Downed the last of her wine, leaving lipstick on the empty glass. Picked up her cigarette and slid off her stool. She jiggled her hips unselfconsciously as she pulled her dress back into place.

"Monica," I said. "Did Angel have a real lot of money?"

"I gotta go back," she said, as though I hadn't spoken. "My parents are there."

And she slipped out the door. I stayed and paid the check. Walked out of the cool bar and into the damp blanket of summer air. I turned and headed up Hanover, Monica long gone. A car horn honked and I looked over.

The Cadillac.

It rolled up and slowed and the passenger window rolled open. I stopped as Mick leaned down and called across Vincent, "Hey, McMorrow. Nice-lookin' lady you got. I wouldn't leave her alone, if I was you. Not around here. Not in Maine, neither. You know what I'm saying? You write about one dead girl, you could end up with two."

And the window buzzed up and the car moved slowly away. I started for the church, breaking into a trot.

The hearse was out front and the funeral home guys were loading Angel's coffin into the back, like they were returning her to the shop for repairs. TV cameras rolled as they closed the doors and the family streamed out of the church, women dabbing their eyes, guys holding the women up. Guys from the church shoved their way through and the family piled into three limos and the procession pulled away.

I searched the crowd for Roxanne and finally she came out of the church with David and Maddie. Cameras swung toward them and reporters began calling as they turned down the sidewalk, David's arm around Maddie's shoulders, Roxanne close to his side. He said, "No comment. Sorry," and kept walking. I strode past the press and caught up at the corner beyond the church. I touched Roxanne on the arm and she jumped.

I took her arm and asked her how it had been inside. She said it was very sad, that the parents were wrecks, the whole family had been crying and sobbing.

"It was very hard," Maddie said, brushing a finger over her cheekbones, checking her makeup. David shook his head and said nothing.

We rounded the corner of the square and headed for the parking lot. I kept hold of Roxanne's arm and she clutched mine to her side. It didn't seem like there would be an easy way to say it, so I just blurted it out. "Those guys were here. They drove by when I was up the block talking to Monica. Mick said I should watch out writing about a dead girl because I might end up with two."

The three of them stopped.

"He said I had a nice-looking girlfriend."

"Call the police," David said. "He can't say that."

"No, Jack," Maddie said. "Isn't that against the law, to threaten someone?"

"His word against mine," I said.

Roxanne was quiet. I saw her put her free hand on her belly.

"I'd still call the police," David said. "You want me to make some calls? My uncle, he's in Florida, but he can get on the phone and shake things up. He knows the commissioner very well."

"No. I'll just tell Sullivan, the detective. She knows this Mick guy. She can go talk to him."

"Talk to him?" Maddie said. "I wouldn't talk to him. I'd lock him up. You can't get away with that."

We were moving now, other funeralgoers walking beside us. Roxanne didn't say anything for a moment, and then she said, "I took some notes."

I looked at her, smiled, and held her close.

28

I called Sullivan from the Connellys' kitchen, left a message, then stepped outside onto the stone terrace with the phone to wait for her to call back. I sat in a chair in the shade and looked up at the city sky. A turkey vulture circled high above and I wondered what dead things it would find in the city. I thought of Angel in the ground and wondered how long it would have taken for vultures and ravens to find her, after the coyotes had exposed her.

Not long.

Sullivan called back and I told her about Mick and what he'd said and she said she figured he still was all talk, but it was time to bring him in and seriously rattle his cage. She said she'd looked for him at the funeral but hadn't seen him.

"You were there?" I said.

"Yeah," she said. "I saw you leaving. What'd you get out of Monica Vitale?"

I told her about what Monica had said about Angel having money. The clothes, the trip, the safe-deposit box.

"Did you have all that?" I said.

"This for the record?"

"Yeah. I've got to get a story out of this, you know."

"Egan didn't scare you?"

"We'll go back to Maine," I said. "If he comes up there, he'll be on my turf, and I won't be alone."

"Your lady friend okay with that? Just curious."

"Yeah," I said. "She wants this person caught."

"I thought that was my job, Jack," Sullivan said.

"I keep it in the public eye," I said. "I keep asking questions because somebody wants me to stop. I keep sweeping things out from under the rug. And you swoop in and get all the glory."

"You are the real deal, aren't you?"

"Whatever," I said. "So are you following the money or what?"

"I can't say anything that would compromise the investigation."

"Come on. I know about a lot of it."

"Write what you know," she said. "Leave me out of it."

"The question is, where would someone like Angel get money to blow."

"Look around you, McMorrow," Sullivan said. "For these people, it grows on trees."

"What, are you following me?"

"Not you," she said, and, she rang off.

I hung up and David came out of the house carrying a tea tray. There were three mugs on it, two big and one small, and a plate of cookies. He set the tray down and Maeve skipped out of the house and took the smaller mug and a cookie and trotted across the lawn to the swing. I thanked David, took my tea and sipped.

He looked up at the sky and said, "Hey, a vulture."

"I saw it," I said.

"You know, I saw three of them by the side of the road in Weston the other day? They were eating a deer that had been hit. Looked like the Wild West."

"Feels like it sometimes," I said.

"How long are you staying in Boston?"

"Just long enough to write the story. I'll go into the bureau shortly."

"We're leaving, but you and Roxanne can stay," he said.

"No, that's okay."

"No, please stay. Mrs. Donovan will be here. She'll take good care of you. She'll be like your mother, waiting up for you."

"Thanks," I said. I sipped the tea again. "David. Can I ask you a question? For the story?"

"Sure."

He put his mug down and looked at me and waited.

"Did Angel make a lot of money at the foundation?"

"Angel? No. I mean, I'm sure we paid her the going rate and then some. We believe strongly in a living wage, and in Boston, that's not peanuts. Housing is nuts."

"Enough to buy tickets to Grand Cayman? A cruise for her parents? Go on a shopping spree in New York? Keep cash in a safe-deposit box? That car?"

David was quiet. He held the mug up to his mouth and touched his lips to the tea. Lowered the mug.

"I know what you're getting at."

"Dalton," I said.

"I don't know. I mean, he doesn't have limitless money. He's got a job for a reason. And his wife, she's going to notice if he's draining the accounts."

"She didn't notice Angel," I said.

"I've met her," David said, picking up a cookie. "Let's just say she probably keeps closer tabs on the money than on Tim. And don't put that in the paper. I really think they both had what you might call 'extracurricular activities.' Some marriages evolve to that."

"Couldn't he give Angel a few thousand dollars?"

"I suppose. But I'd hate to think that. Why would he?"

"If Angel was his mistress."

"I don't know, Jack. Maybe they were just having a fling. How much money do you think she had?"

"I don't know. I think more than she let on. She was talking to Monica about offshore banks where you could hide money from the government. She said she learned about that at the office."

David smiled and shook his head.

"Probably fantasy, Jack. I used to see her in the office reading magazines like *Forbes* and *Fortune*. The money stuff at the office was pretty new to her. It can be sort of seductive at first."

I was doubtful but I didn't say it.

"But did we pay her well? I guess so. And maybe living at home, parents probably pampered her the best they could. Say she takes home, I don't know, five hundred a week. She feels like she's in the money, takes out a few cards. Charges the trips, the clothes. I think maybe she could give the appearance of having more money than she really had."

"A safe-deposit box full of cash?"

"Angel's version of putting it under her mattress. She was really pretty naive in a lot of ways. Maybe she liked going down there and running her hands through the one-dollar bills."

"You don't want to believe the worst about her, do you?" I said.

"No," David said. "I always try to think people are good, unless shown otherwise."

"You must get burned, on occasion."

"Hey," he said, reaching for another cookie. "I'd rather get burned once in a while than go through life being suspicious and cynical."

"You think she was killed by someone she knew?"

David paused and swallowed. "I don't want to think that, either," he said.

He clapped me once on the shoulder to end the discussion, then called to Maeve, said they had to get ready to go.

"That's why we need to get back out on the water, Jack," David said. "We'll get away from all this sad stuff. The four of us. We'll take a week. Take the boat and go to Canada. You ever been to Campobello?"

"*Escape*," I said. "It's aptly named."

'Yes, it is,' David said.

"Except sometimes there are things you can't get away from," I said. "You can look away, but when you look back, they're still right there in front of you."

His eyes clouded and he gave a short, quick sigh, then recovered, like he was fighting off some sickness, mind over matter.

"But you can't dwell on the sad stuff all the time. Especially things that are out of your control. Things happen, you know? It's in the past."

"Not yet," I said.

He looked at me and then clasped my shoulder once and went inside. It was David's way, I was learning. Confronted with something unpleasant, he just grinned and walked.

I stayed at the table on the terrace, writing down as much as I could remember of my conversation with Monica. I'd been scribbling for fifteen minutes when Roxanne came out and I told her I was going to go to the bureau and do the story, if that was okay with her. She said of course it was, but then she said she had two things to tell me. She crouched beside me, her hand on my leg.

"Maddie's all upset," Roxanne whispered. "I went by their bedroom on the way down and I could hear her crying."

"Really crying?"

"Yeah. Sobbing. And David was saying it was okay."

"Maybe she knew Angel better than we think."

"But he was saying, 'It's going to be okay. It'll be all right.' Like there was something that could be fixed. How do you fix Angel being killed?"

"You catch somebody, I guess," I said. "Maybe she's afraid. You know, that someone else will be next. And she's in this small circle of people that Angel knew."

"Maybe," Roxanne said.

"And maybe it's all just caught up with her," I said. "Angel, the funeral, this situation with Maeve. That's got to be stressful, even though it turned out okay."

"That was my other thing."

"What?"

"I just checked my messages. Devlin, the au pair, called."

"From Ireland?"

"No, Jack. From Maine. She said she never left. She never left Maine at all."

29

Roxanne said she checked the exchange of the number Devlin left and it was for Castleton, a little crossroads about ten miles inland from Blue Harbor. When Roxanne called, she got a machine with a message that said Gary wasn't home. Roxanne wondered what Devlin had done with the plane ticket to Ireland, and I said she probably sold it for a hundred bucks. Why hadn't she gone home? Probably for the same reason she'd left.

We were talking about it when David and Maddie came back outside with Maeve and a couple of duffel bags and a suitcase. Maddie looked like she'd put makeup on to try to disguise her red and swollen eyes. David said they were headed for Maine, that Mrs. Donovan would be glad to make us dinner, and not to hesitate to ask her for anything. She didn't mind. He said to use the BMW if I needed a car and didn't want to leave Roxanne stranded. The keys were in the top left kitchen drawer.

I thanked him. Roxanne looked like she was wondering whether to say anything about Devlin, but then there was a flurry of handshakes and hugs and, "Call us right away when you get back to Maine," and David was carrying the bags to the Suburban.

Maeve climbed in the back, buckled herself in a booster seat. Maddie waved and got in the front. The gate slid open and they rolled out onto Marlborough Street like soldiers leaving the fort on patrol.

"You think we should stay?" I said.

"We've been here this long," Roxanne said.

"But with Devlin here, does that mean your case is, I don't know, more open?"

"I don't know," she said. "I'd prefer to think it's closer to ending."

"Yeah," I said. "The alternative would be—"

"Disturbing. It would be like I was no judge of character at all."

"That's not true."

"No, but what is going on with all of this, Jack?" Roxanne said.

"More than we know, I think."

"But I'm not sure David and Maddie know, either."

"They do seem like sheep."

"Surrounded by wolves?"

"No. More like dogs that steal food off the counter."

"That's your story, isn't it?" Roxanne said.

"It's the story I want to write."

"In a way it's the story I hope is true. That David and Maddie and Maeve are all victims, in a way."

"Then we'll have to find it," I said. "If it's there."

Mrs. Donovan did make dinner: broiled salmon and green beans and baked potatoes, served at the big kitchen table with the Red Sox on the radio. Mrs. Donovan sat with us and chatted, but guardedly, her loyalty to the Connelly family unflinching. She did say she'd worked for the family for almost forty years, that of the three brothers (Patrick Jr. in Aspen, Michael in London), David was the cheerful one, who always had a good word to say. Maddie was a dear, and Maeve was like both of them, happy like her dad but with a quieter side like her mom. I asked her if it was hard for Maddie to come into the Connelly family and she said no, she didn't think so, but didn't elaborate. Roxanne asked where David and Maddie met, and Mrs. Donovan said she wasn't sure, and were we ready for tea or coffee?

End of conversation.

After dinner we attempted to help in the kitchen, but Mrs. Donovan herded us out. We went upstairs, Roxanne pausing to peer in at rooms along the way. From the guest room Roxanne tried Devlin's number again, got the same machine, and left another message. I called directory assistance for Dalton's number. T. A. Dalton III was listed as a resident of Pride's Crossing, an old-money North Shore town. I called and a teenage girl answered and sounded disappointed that it was only me. She said her dad was at the office and I thanked her and got the number of the Sky Blue Foundation from the operator. I called and a machine answered, giving me office hours, so I called David in the car. I asked him for Dalton's direct number, and he said he didn't know it. I asked if Maddie would know and he covered the phone for a very long minute, then came back on.

He gave me the number but he sounded distracted.

"You okay?" I said.

"Bloody traffic," he said. "Saturday night, too. You'd think half the world was driving to Maine."

He paused.

"You know, Tim might not be real eager to talk," David said.

"That's okay," I said. "He can always say no."

I said I'd try Kathleen Kind, too. David said he thought her number in Cambridge was in the book. I hung up, started to dial. Stopped.

Put the phone down and looked over to Roxanne, stretched out on the bed, flipping through a magazine.

"I'm going over there," I said.

"You don't want him wriggling off the hook, do you?" she said.

"No."

"Was David trying to shield him or something?"

"I don't know. I think he was just warning me I might not get a warm reception. Don't forget that nobody wants their organization in a murder story. David or Dalton."

"Would it help if I were there?" Roxanne said.

"Maybe if I talk to him in his office, you could just look around a little."

"For anything in particular?"

"Anything Angelic," I said.

So we told Mrs. Donovan we'd be two or three hours. She said she was going to a grandson's birthday party and might be out. She gave us a remote for the gate and a key to the side door. She said she wouldn't wait up, but there were cookies in the jar on the counter, beer in the refrigerator in the pantry.

We took the Explorer, drove across the city to the financial district, where the office towers were empty but lighted, like ghost ships adrift without their crews. We were looking for Batterymarch, off Milk Street, in the shadowed narrow streets where brokerage firms managed billions of dollars out of sight of the city's milling masses. Two seventy-eight was on the right, an art-deco building with a small glass-walled lobby. I parked out front and tried the door and it was locked, so I went back to the car and called. On the fourth ring, Dalton answered.

"Yeah?"

"Tim?"

"Who's this?"

"Jack McMorrow. David gave me your number. I need to talk to you about Angel. Your general impressions as her supervisor—"

"Not direct supervisor," he said.

"Then indirect supervisor," I said. "And friend."

"Listen, Jack, I'm getting ready to head home."

"I'm right outside. Roxanne and I were out and about. Thought I'd just try you."

"How long will this take?" Dalton said.

"Not long," I said.

There was a long pause. I could hear him breathing. Finally he said, "I'll buzz you in."

He did. With the car double-parked, flashers on, we stepped in and it was cool in the marble foyer. According to the directory behind the locked glass case, Blue Sky was on the eleventh floor. We took the elevator up and stepped off into a small carpeted foyer, and faced another set of doors, steel with small reinforced windows. There was another buzz and we pushed through into a dimly lighted waiting room.

There were paintings hung on the off-white walls. American Impressionists. Antique wing chairs and couches, or maybe replicas, and Oriental carpets on the floor.

We waited. Heard footsteps, and then Dalton rounded a corner and came toward us. He was wearing a big smile, a dark-green polo shirt and khaki shorts, sunglasses around his neck on a cord.

"Jack. Roxanne. Welcome," he said, whispering in the hushed, empty room. "Good to see you."

"Sad circumstances."

"Oh, awful. Still doesn't seem real. Were you at the funeral?"

"Roxanne was," I said. "They didn't want press in the church."

"Oh, yeah. Funny, I forget you have a working capacity. Come on in."

I followed him as he led the way past small empty offices arranged like burial chambers in a tomb. Then we swung through a door and into an office with dark paneling, two couches, and a couple of big chairs, all black leather. The desk was dark red wood like mahogany, and there were bookshelves behind it, to the left. I saw a photo of Dalton and a blonde woman who looked a little like Martha Stewart. In another photo a small girl sat on a big horse, her mouth set resolutely like she was headed into battle. A third had all three of them, dressed up at a party. Only Dalton was smiling.

We sat.

"So," Dalton said. "Just came in to catch up. Being in Maine and all, things piled up. Can you believe we were all there, having a nice time. Angel—it seems like years ago now."

"Who could have imagined?" I said.

"It's unbelievable. I mean, what animal could hurt that girl? My daughter's a counselor at a camp in Maine, on one of the islands. Makes us think twice, I'll tell you."

"So you think it happened up there?" Roxanne said.

"Don't you?"

"I don't know," I said.

"Well, I don't know why somebody would do it down here and go all the way up there in the woods."

"Maybe they thought nobody would find her," Roxanne said.

"Seems like a lot of trouble. Oh, Jesus. Listen to us. Like it's some murder on a TV show."

I smiled, sympathetically I hoped.

"You're right," I said. "You have to remember things like this aren't games. They involve real people with dreams and hopes and people who cared for them."

"Exactly," Dalton said, then seemed to draw back. "Her poor parents. The mother at the funeral . . ."

"Which brings me to this story."

Roxanne stood and said she'd wait out by the main doors and Dalton didn't protest. After she'd left, I explained to him what I was doing. He listened attentively, tanned arms folded in front of him on the gleaming desk. I talked about making Angel more than a name and a face from a crime story. I said I was talking to her coworkers, her family, to David, Maddie, and Monica.

"What did Monica say?" Dalton said. His tone was neutral.

I took out a notebook and opened it.

"Let's see. That Angel liked working here, that she seemed really to take to this world, which was different from what both of them grew up with."

"That's true. It was new to her, but Angel was a quick study. Very adaptable. She would have ended up someplace interesting. I mean, you'd put her in a new situation and there was this brief sort of adjustment period and you could see her figuring it out, practically hear the wheels turning. And then it was like she'd always been there. A few of us were at this BSO thing once and I looked around and she's talking to Derek Bok. I said to her after, 'Did you know he used to be president of Harvard?' She said, 'Yeah. I was asking him, What the hell does the president of a college actually do? Is it the courses or is it all money?' Angel could do that. It was like it didn't occur to her that she didn't belong there."

"Maybe she did."

"I think so. Like I said, a very quick study."

"But she had help."

"Oh?"

"Monica said she had beautiful new clothes, jewelry, got invitations to parties that Monica didn't."

"They're different. I mean, Monica . . . well, you met her."

"Yeah."

"She doesn't have Angel's—and this is totally off the record—her social mobility."

"Class," I said.

"Don't get me wrong. Monica's a good kid. She's just more thoroughly rooted in her background. Angel was looking to explore, and this job was her entree."

"And you assisted her?"

He looked at me warily.

"What do you mean by that?"

"Well, Monica said you got her into the parties. Bought her things. Dresses, jewelry."

"There may be a bit of jealousy there," Dalton said, "between us. But yeah. I bought her some stuff. I mean, it was either that or send her to a black-tie at the MFA in her prom dress. I didn't want to see the poor kid humiliated."

"Nobody else stepped up to help her out?"

"No. And don't put this in, but some of the women here, well, you know how women can be. A little catty. Backstabbers. And David, he'd invite her to come along to some benefit and I'd say, 'Jeez, David. You think she's up to it?' He'd say, 'What do you mean?' He's like that. Just because he's socially gifted, the family thing and all, he's oblivious to the fact that for some people, these sorts of events can be intimidating."

"So you helped Angel out?"

"Yeah. A couple of dresses, shoes. I'd say to them at the store, 'This is the kind of event we're going to. Make sure she has everything she needs.' "

"That was nice of you," I said.

He seemed to puff up a bit.

"Yeah, well, it was no big deal. I'd say to her, 'Just be yourself. Smile and chat and don't chew gum. Go easy on the mascara."

"So you were Henry Higgins and she was Eliza Doolittle."

"Oh, God, don't put it in those terms. If you mention that at all, please put it diplomatically. I don't want to insult her family. They're good people. It was just that she was in a new game and she needed the uniform."

"How'd she look in it?"

"Like a million dollars," Dalton blurted, and then checked himself. "She looked very nice. She was a very pretty girl, as you know."

"So she stood out, even at a party full of beautiful people."

"Oh, yeah. Let's just say her dance card was full. I mean, guys lined up. She had a great time, too. She just ate it up. The whole scene. She was very open to new experiences. It's really a shame. What happened, I mean."

I paused, caught up with him in my notes. And then I said, "Speaking of a million dollars, I'm told Angel seemed to have a lot of money, relatively speaking."

"Really. Who said that?"

"A friend. She said Angel went on a shopping spree in New York, bought jewelry. Her parents said she sent them on a cruise. She was going to the Caribbean in a few weeks and she was taking Monica."

"I don't know. I mean, when I was helping her out, with the clothes and stuff, I assumed she was just living on what we paid her."

"Which was?"

"I'm not sure. You'd have to ask Kathleen or somebody. Kathleen is our spending overseer. I mean, I'm sure it was a fair wage, but it wasn't buying her too many cruises. Of course, she could have just started saying yes to all those credit card offers that come in the mail. You could run up a couple of hundred thousand in a hurry that way."

"Other people have said that. But one source said she kept cash in a safe-deposit box."

"Huh. I don't know about that."

I watched him but it was hard to tell whether he was surprised that Angel had money or surprised that I knew.

"Now, one more thing, Tim," I said. "And I'll just come right out and say it. Another source has told me that you and Angel were involved romantically."

His face reddened and he leaned forward.

"Bullshit," he said. "Who told you that?"

"I'd rather not say."

"You aren't putting that in the paper."

"I'm trying to put a true story in the paper."

"Listen," Dalton said. "You publish that and I'll have you in court before the ink is dry. And I'll make sure you never write for the *New York Times* or anybody else ever again. You understand that?"

"So you're saying that you weren't involved with Angel in that way?"

"No," he spat. "No way. Which of those bitches told you that? That's slander."

I kept writing and he pounded the desk once with his fist.

"You can't print that. It's libelous."

"I just have to ask the question."

"It's preposterous," Dalton said.

"I understand."

He wheeled around in his chair and took the photo of his family off the shelf and whirled back and slammed it down on the desk. He and Mrs. Dalton stared coldly from the frame.

"This is my wife. Nineteen years of marriage and I'm very happily married. She knew Angel. In fact, she's the one who told me to get Angel a suitable dress the first time. She said, 'You can't let that poor girl walk in there looking like she just stepped out of the mall. They'll tear her apart.' That's how involved I was with Angel."

"Maybe I should talk to Mrs. Dalton," I said.

"Yes," he said. "I mean no. The *New York Times* comes to her and asks if her husband was having an affair with some young thing at the office? A woman who was murdered?"

"I wouldn't phrase it quite like that."

"It doesn't matter. She'd have a coronary right there. Half the goddamn country reading this story, all of her friends? And my daughter? My God, man. You can't do this to me."

"I don't know that I will use it. I'm going over to talk to my editor tonight," I said. "But Tim, I had to ask the question. What if you said yes, you were involved with Angel. You loved her and you were leaving your wife and you and Angel planned to get married. I don't know what your situation is until I ask."

"I've told you my situation."

"I understand," I said. "And what you told me helps re-create a portrait of Angel. This young woman who was eating up all these new opportunities. And people like you and the Connellys helped her navigate this new world."

"We did. I did. David and Maddie did. They liked her. We all liked her."

I hesitated, then said, "Why?"

"Why did we like her?"

"Yeah."

"Well, she was a hard worker and cheerful and very pretty and—"

"Maybe I shouldn't say this," I began, "but on the boat I thought she seemed sort of pushy. Presumptuous. She was pleasant, but there was an edge to her, like she was, I don't know, in charge or something. Like when she wanted David to take the boat to Bar Harbor."

"Oh, that was just Angel. That was her way."

"She was like that all the time?"

"No. I remember that particular thing, I thought she was maybe a bit out of line with David. But in general she was very nice. Maybe it was the wine."

I scribbled, then looked up at him.

"And maybe I shouldn't say this, either," I said. "But I saw you on the boat with her. I can see how someone might get the impression that there was something between you other than just a platonic work relationship. You seemed—"

I hesitated.

"Familiar."

"Oh, come on, Jack. We were kidding around, for God's sake. She was just being silly."

I didn't answer.

He leaned forward, put his hands on the desk like he was laying out his cards.

"Listen, can I tell you something, off the record? Between us?"

I didn't answer and he took it for agreement.

"Yeah, she was a bit of a flirt. And yeah, I'm a middle-aged man, almost. I'm in shape but the hair is getting thin, a little gut I can't seem to get rid of. I can't keep up with the young guys on the lacrosse field anymore, and doesn't that piss me off."

He paused

"You saw her, Jack. She was very attractive."

"Yes, she was."

"So maybe I played along a little. Maybe I was a little flattered by it. The male ego, you know? But that's all, man. I helped her out a little. Maybe I got a little kick out of being around her. I'm terribly sorry about what happened to her."

"And you don't know where she would have gotten a windfall of money?"

"No."

"You didn't give her large amounts of cash?"

"You kidding? My wife's not stupid. Even with the dresses, she was the one who said, 'Just send her to someplace like Saks, Tim. No need to have her going hog wild.' "

"Sensible of her."

"Exactly. It all makes perfect sense."

"Except the killing part."

"Right. That makes no sense at all."

"Yet," I said.

30

When we finished, I'd filled a few pages of the notebook. Dalton asked me when the story would run and I said I had to stop at the bureau that night to check, but it looked like it would be published Tuesday. He got up from his desk and stared out the window, but it was dark outside and he seemed to be looking at his own reflection. Checking the waistline, perhaps. Wondering what his vanity had gotten him into.

I let myself out, and when I got back to the reception room with the couches, Roxanne was gone.

I opened the steel door and she wasn't in the outside foyer. I went to a window and looked down and could just see her car in the street, flashers still blinking. I walked down the hallway toward Dalton's office again and his door was closed and he was talking, apparently on the phone. I heard him say, "In an hour. Tell your mother."

But no Roxanne.

There was another corridor on the opposite side of the waiting room. It was dark, but I walked down it. I stopped halfway and listened. Heard voices, then music. I kept going and turned a corner and saw a door half-open on the right, blue television light spilling out.

I walked to the door, heard a woman saying, "I know this isn't politically correct, and God knows I feel terribly sorry about what happened. But the girl was, if not sleeping her way to the top, then certainly something close to it."

"There's no death penalty for being attractive," Roxanne said.

"Oh, but there is, don't you think? If Miss Moretti had been some dumpy, plain girl, do you think she would have been invited to this office retreat in Maine? And if she hadn't been in Maine, if she hadn't been able to bat her big eyes and convince people to take her to Bar Harbor, to dinner, to wherever else her whims pointed her, then she would have been home. She would have been safe with her working-class parents, would have eventually met some hardworking schmo from Dorchester or some such place and settled down and had babies and lived to be eighty. Instead she ended up here and one thing led to another."

"But Kathleen," Roxanne said. "Being pretty and flirtatious didn't kill her. Somebody killed her."

"But it did, Roxanne. Let's say she was waylaid in the boondocks of Maine. What would have attracted somebody? Her looks, the way she was dressed."

"How was she dressed when she left?" Roxanne said.

"Jeans down over her hips, the way they wear them now. Her belly hanging out, not that it wasn't flat as a board. A little sweater that left very little to the imagination. Picture her with a flat tire with that outfit on, some pickup truck full of rednecks comes rolling up. But look at this for a minute. These people make this point in a very accessible way for young girls."

A tape started, music and a voice-over saying, "what if none of us were pretty girls. . . ."

I stepped into the room. They turned and smiled.

"Jack," Roxanne said.

"Hey," I said.

"I borrowed her," Kathleen Kind said. "There's this organization that we've funded. They produce educational materials for adolescent girls. I was showing Roxanne."

"Go right ahead."

"But you have to get on with your work," Kathleen said. "More interviews?"

"I have to go talk to my editor," I said.

"Well, here," she said. "I'll let you take this with you, Roxanne. If you're interested, give me a call."

Roxanne said she would. Kathleen Kind ejected a tape from a VCR and handed it over, then took a folder from a shelf and gave that to Roxanne, too. I asked Kathleen if she had a few minutes and she said sure, but only a few because a car was coming to pick her up. I said I'd be quick, and she invited me to sit. There were two chairs in front of the desk and I took one and she took the other. Roxanne sat away from us, by the door, and opened the folder and read. I glanced at Kind: khaki skirt, black short-sleeved sweater, low-heeled black shoes.

And a cool smile that was as impenetrable as a mask.

I took my notebook out of my back pocket and flipped it open. She didn't flinch. I said I was sorry about Angel and she said it was horrible, that she used to feel safe in the country but she never would again. She started to go on about how the notion that rural areas were safer than cities was a fallacy. I interrupted and asked how much Angel had been paid.

Kind looked mildly irritated but swallowed it and her smile returned, as if it were lipstick she could take off and put back on.

"She started at twelve dollars an hour. After two months, she went to fifteen. After six months she went to seventeen-fifty."

"Seven hundred a week?" I said.

"Very good," Kind said. "A reporter who can do arithmetic."

"Sometimes you get lucky," I said. "That's not a lot of money in Boston, do you think?"

"It is if you have an associate's degree, average clerical skills, and no prior experience in foundation work."

"Did you hire her?"

"Tim hired her," she said, as though nothing more needed to be said.

"And Monica came with her?"

"A few weeks later. Once Angel had established herself."

"How was Angel as an employee?"

"Fine," Kind said. "She could be very personable."

"I understand she went to some of the social events with other people here."

"Yes."

"She liked that?"

"Who wouldn't? Free champagne and all the jumbo shrimp you can eat."

"I'm told she was socially, I'm not sure what the word would be . . ."

"Facile?"

"Yes."

She didn't say anything.

"Did you think so?"

"Miss Moretti was a very confident young woman, after she'd been here for a while."

"And when she first arrived?"

"Much less so. I think her confidence grew exponentially the longer she was with us."

"Why?"

"You'd have to ask people who worked more closely with her."

"You didn't?"

"Not really. She worked for Tim, who is more on the grant assessment end, does this project meet the foundation's goals, what will it achieve. I work with the financials."

"Did you explain some of that to her?" I said.

"Not really. There was no need. She wouldn't have understood anyway. Most of the people here don't understand what I do, and they've been here for years."

"Well, here's a question for you. Monica said Angel talked about offshore accounts and ways to hide income. How would she know about that sort of thing?"

"I have no idea. And I can assure you, Jack, she wouldn't have learned about that sort of thing here. The money goes the other way here. My job is to make sure too much of it doesn't go at once."

"But where would she get these ideas?"

Kind's smile almost turned to a smirk.

"Television, perhaps," she said. "Nefarious characters are always hiding money in numbered Swiss accounts or some such thing."

"I was also told she seemed to have a lot of money, all of a sudden. Kept at least some of it in a safe-deposit box. Called it her piggy bank."

"Cute."

"How would she get her hands on a lot of money?"

"That depends on what you call a lot."

"Let's say thousands."

"Thousands isn't a lot, Jack."

"It is for someone like Angel."

"In the circles she was at least on the fringes of, it's pocket change. The people she was seeing at benefits and functions—I mean, there are people in this city who make the Connellys look positively middle-class."

Out of the corner of my eye, I saw Roxanne look up.

"But how would Angel end up with any money?" I said.

Kind didn't answer at first, and the long pause was full of innuendo.

"I'm sure I don't know," she said. "And I wouldn't care to speculate. But some people at this level of income can be rather free with their money. If they take a shine to someone. . . ."

The cool smile again.

"But short of someone just handing her a bag of cash—she didn't work anywhere else," I said. "As far as I can tell, she'd really immersed herself in this place. So where else could extra money come from?"

"Not from here. That's one thing I take very seriously. I have to because some of these people think there's this unlimited amount of money. I mean, and this isn't for print, they've grown up in a world where there were no limits. And the money was earned by somebody two generations back. They don't think of the sweat that went into that. They think it grows on trees, if you'll excuse the cliché."

"Somebody else said that. And you reminded them it didn't grow on trees."

"I come from modest circumstances. My parents came here from Poland with five dollars between them. They worked every waking minute so I could go to Smith, I could get an MBA at Wharton. My dad worked in this company that made hoses. I mean, actually made them. He came home all dirty, smelling like rubber. My mother did tax returns for the immigrant community in Quincy. Nothing was handed to them, not like some people in this world. We do a lot of good, don't get me wrong. But I don't forget that money comes from sweat. On my watch every penny is accounted for and it goes where the foundation is committed to putting it. And there are strict regulations governing that."

She lifted herself in her chair.

"Are we through?"

"I guess so," I said. "If I have questions, I'll call."

She stood and smoothed her skirt. I stood, too, stuck the notebook in my back pocket. Roxanne started for the door.

"So what do you think happened?" I said, more confidentially.

"To Miss Moretti?"

"Yeah."

"Off the record? I think she crossed paths with the wrong person in Maine in that wasteland you have to cross to get home from Blue Harbor and she was killed. Happens all the time in this world, unfortunately. Women are prey. Of course, that doesn't minimize the tragedy."

I paused. She didn't look choked up, but that wasn't her style.

"Did she get any bonuses or anything like that?"

"No, not that came through our operating accounts."

I must have looked perplexed.

"Jack," Kind said, gathering up a briefcase and bag from her desk. "You should go to one of these functions, the big ones. And this is totally off the record. The museums, the BSO—it's wall to wall with silver-haired men and a lot of younger women. The men make seven figures and have alpha-male egos to match. The women, a lot of them, are wife number two or three, former administrative assistants who saw their chance and went for it. And then some of them, like Angel, are new to the game, just there for show."

"To watch the show, you mean?"

"No, Jack," she said, pausing by the door. "They *are* the show, all decked out in slinky dresses. There's a term for it. It's a little crass. Oh, what is it?"

"Arm candy?" Roxanne said.

"That's it," Kind said. "Walk into the Oak Bar at five o'clock and see the guys in their sixties and their pretty young things."

"You're saying Angel was one of those pretty young things?"

"Off the record, Jack. And I know it's a terrible thing to say, given the circumstances. But it's the truth."

She opened the door and we stepped into the hallway, and she closed the door and locked it with a key from her bag.

"But what does that have to do with money?" I said.

"Oh, come on now, Jack," Kind said as we started down the hall. "These young women may be trophies, but the smart ones, they make sure they get something in return."

"And Angel?" I said.

"Miss Moretti," she said, "wasn't stupid."

31

A livery cab, a black Town Car, picked Kathleen Kind up out front for the ride home to Cambridge. We got in the car as the cab pulled away and I said to Roxanne, "What do you think?"

"Not exactly warm and fuzzy," she said.

"I guess they need somebody to keep the bleeding hearts in check."

"And remember, it's not her money they're giving away."

"No, and it's a good gig," I said.

"If you're good with numbers and tax law and a little snooty."

The Town Car swung around the corner and out of sight.

"And Angel?" I said.

"I think for a nice girl, Angel sure stirred the pot."

"Maybe that's my lead," I said.

"That is the story, isn't it?"

"I'll tell Myra it's changing."

"Yeah," Roxanne said. "It's not Cinderella getting killed on the way home from the ball."

I called the bureau from the car and Myra's line was busy, which meant she was in. I swung over to State Street and up and into traffic, not a parking space within two blocks. It was Jazz at the Marketplace, according to the posters, and in the distance we could hear music. I started looking for a space, looping in widening circles, and ended down past McKinley Square and the Custom House hotel. It was dark beyond the hotel and deserted and Roxanne held my arm as we walked back up to South Market. The music was loud, bouncing off the buildings like flies off glass.

I called up on the intercom and Myra buzzed us in.

She was standing at her desk, barking into the phone.

"Right, you'll see it tomorrow afternoon, early. . . . Right. McMorrow. He's been working on this since they dug her up. Yes, the Connelly connection is strong. She worked with David directly. I mean, it's his family's foundation and he's the main one there. The others just sit on the board. Right, in Maine, but not really close to where the Connellys' house is. . . . Well, listen, he just came in; hang on."

She put her hand over the phone.

"It's Alice. They want a tagline for the national budget."

I thought for a moment, but not more.

"With a Connelly entree, murder victim was poised on edge of Boston social whirl."

"That's good," Myra said, and she repeated it into the phone and rang off, turned to me and said, "Okay, where do we stand?"

Roxanne went to the restroom and I told Myra whom I'd talked to and what they'd said. Leaning on the front of her desk, she listened. When I was done, she said, "Cops have the box?"

I said I didn't know but I'd find out.

"So the question is, who was her sugar daddy?"

"Dalton denies it."

"Nah, he's a small-time nine-to-fiver. I picture somebody with serious bucks. Somebody who could promise Angel the condo in Antigua, a ride down on the Citation Two. Somebody who could pick her up like she was a mint on the way out of the restaurant. 'Here, honey. Here's ten grand. Go get yourself something nice.' "

"What if nobody gave her anything?" I said.

"You mean, what if she stole it?"

"Or something like that. What if she landed one of these guys and then threatened to go to the wife."

"Then they'd pay her off, or—"

"But if she tried it with the wrong guy," I said.

"Then somebody kills her," Myra said. "It fits, maybe."

"Right. She gets some money but wants more. Pushes somebody too hard and they decide she's a liability. Have her killed. I start to ask questions and they bring in somebody to make me stop."

"And when you don't stop?"

"Like the detective said, they're leg breakers. They're not hit men."

"Why do I not find that particularly reassuring?" Myra said.

Roxanne came back and we talked about the story. Myra said she'd love to use Dalton's wife talking about the prom dress. That would take the focus off Dalton as the apparent boyfriend. She thought we needed Maddie Connelly, too, and something more from the Moretti family to address the premise, which was that Angel was stepping across class lines.

And we needed whatever we could get about the cause and place of death, the amount of money and whatever else was in the safe-deposit box. I said I'd try to get Maddie and Mrs. Dalton that night, and the others in the morning.

And then there was small talk, Myra talking to Roxanne about her work, Roxanne telling Myra about the group Maddie had for the talk about child abuse, Myra asking me what David Connelly was really like. I said he was a good guy, very interesting, and not bad-looking, either.

"I think he's a hottie," Myra said.

"So does his wife," I said.

"If I had been Angel, that's the one I would have gone after," Myra said. "You don't think—"

"No," I said.

"He's got the money."

"No, he's a good guy."

"With a wife and a kid, and something to lose," Myra said.

"No," I said. "David and Maddie are very tight."

And then I thought of Maddie crying after the funeral, David telling her it was going to be okay.

"No," I said.

"Maybe she jumped his bones on the way home from the office Christmas party. She threatens to go to Maddie and tell all if he doesn't come through with the cash and a job for her North End buddy."

And a ride to Bar Harbor on the boat?

The phone rang and Myra answered it, started talking about the New England news briefs. I grabbed a couple of notebooks and some pens and Roxanne and I went down and out. The lobby was deserted, but the music was blaring and people were all over the marketplace. We walked out to State Street and started down and the crowd thinned, just a few college kids shuffling along, baseball hats on backward, a homeless man picking like a raccoon through a trash can. We were near the Custom House when I heard someone behind us, turned, and saw three young guys and a woman—shorts, muscle shirts, baseball hats.

They were bounding along, a couple of the guys pushing each other, one of the guys and the woman holding hands. They whooped and laughed and two of the guys broke into a sprint, like they were racing to their car. I turned and moved out of the way and the pounding footsteps approached and I started to turn back.

The shoulders. Something hit me. I stumbled, lost my grip on Roxanne's hand, and fell.

32

There was a swish of fabric behind me, a rush of steps, Roxanne saying "No."

I was just back on my feet when someone landed on me, rolling me into the street, wrapping his arms around my shoulders, climbing on my back.

I staggered, tried to spin him off, reached behind me for his face, but then the other one was on me, balaclava masks on them now, pushing me around the corner and into a service sort of alley. It was dark and I hit the wall with my shoulder, lashed out with my left arm, and caught one of them in the face. He jerked his head back, tried to grab my arm, but I wrenched it free. Turned and used the guy on my back as a shield, but then both of them ran me into the wall, my face scraping the hard brick. I bellowed but someone wrenched my head back and looped a gag over my mouth. It caught on my teeth and they pulled harder and it went into my mouth and I felt like I was choking. Someone grabbed my wallet from my back pocket and said, "Check it," and I heard another one say, "Yup."

Roxanne came around the corner, the guy and the woman holding her, the guy's hand over her mouth as she writhed and kicked and stomped at their feet. Then she was behind me and someone said, "Use this," and she cried out and then her voice became muffled. I screamed "Leave her alone" into the gag, and they yanked my hands out from the wall and I kicked blindly, hit a shin, stomped on a foot. They started kicking and hit behind my right knee and my leg buckled but they yanked me up by my shirt and I felt the cold air on my back. I tried to turn and kick but I fell onto my side at the base of the wall, saw Roxanne on her knees, the woman on Roxanne's back, an arm locked around her neck. They were kicking me in the arm, the shoulder, the chest, the side of the head, a flurry of blows and then someone was standing on my chest. I rolled and he stumbled off of me. I wrapped my arms around his legs and twisted and he fell heavily to the pavement, his head making a hollow sound like a coconut.

Two of them fell on me, grabbing for my wrists, but I twisted free, saw the woman in front of Roxanne now, the guy holding her hands behind her. She slapped Roxanne and then grabbed for the top of her shirt and yanked and the shirt tore and I could see Roxanne's bra and the woman reaching again.

I bellowed and bulled my way to my feet, taking the guy on my back up with me. Turned and charged backward into the wall, feeling his head slam the bricks, his teeth against my shoulder. And then I ran through them, hit the woman from behind, and she flew past Roxanne, sprawled on the ground, and Roxanne ducked and I hit the guy behind her in the face, felt teeth and wetness and he spun and fell and one of the guys said, "His hands, get his hands."

But I was loose now, Roxanne, too, and she pulled the gag off and ran onto State Street, screaming, "Help, help me," and I heard other voices in the distance, someone saying "What's that?"

And they were on me, but I was swinging and one stumbled and I kicked him in the belly and elbowed another as he reached for my wrists. I stomped on their feet, lashed out at their shins, and they were bending my hands back, trying to break the fingers, the wrists. One finger was bending way back but I whipped the other hand loose and grabbed for faces and eyes. I gouged and scratched and tore and one of them let out a shriek, blood streaming from his eye and then there were voices approaching. Like a flock of sparrows, the four of them fell away in unison and started running back up the street, away from the square.

One turned back and screamed, "We'll come to fucking Maine and kill you," and then two men rounded the corner, one with a Custom House insignia on his shirt, both with fists up, the older man breathing hard. They looked at me, the blood running down my face, and then at the backs of the others, fading into the darkness. One said, "You okay? What happened?" and Roxanne came around the corner then, one hand holding the torn shirt up, a gray-haired woman scurrying along behind her.

Roxanne was crying and she came to me and said, "Are you all right?" and she pulled the rag off my mouth and I said I was, and she said, "Did they break your hands?"

I shook my head.

"They tried," I said.

"They don't want you to write this story," she said, still panting. "You're going to write the best story you've ever written, those dirty bastards."

She started to sob loudly.

"You're going to write that story, you're going to write it, Jack McMorrow. You're going to write it, write it, write it."

33

Outside the emergency room at Mass General, the ambulances came and went, like wasps around a nest. We stood in a little circle in the parking lot on Fruit Street, Roxanne and I, Myra and Sullivan. My left little finger was splinted to the finger beside it and my whole hand throbbed.

"So let's say Mick didn't want to show his face," Sullivan said. "He could sub the job out, get any number of kids to come to your office there and wait. And you say the people at Connelly's place knew you were going there. Who else?"

"I don't know. Mick himself could have followed us from the Connellys' and made a quick phone call."

"Could have brought the kids himself," Sullivan said. "Let them loose like dogs."

"Will you find him tonight?"

"I'll look around. My bet is he'll be at one of the bars and everybody in the place will say he's been there all night."

"So what do you do?" Myra said.

"This isn't for print?"

"No," I said.

"I've got to be careful, standing around with reporters. Don't want something I say to come back and bite me in the—"

"It's okay," Myra said.

"Well, you look for some leverage. You find a firearm, somebody who Mick assaulted who we have something pending on, maybe they'll consider bringing charges in exchange for a break. You get something on Mick that could put him back inside and then you bargain with that. Or we go after Vincent. He has a brother out on bail for assault. Maybe we trade something there."

"An assault for a murder?" Myra said.

"You always want to trade up," Sullivan said.

"So you think that whoever hired Mick knows who killed Angel?"

"They know something we don't know."

I spoke and my voice was hard and jarring, edged with impatience.

"What is it you know, exactly, Detective? For the record, for this story."

They all looked at me but no one said anything. I took out my notebook and flipped through the pages with my taped hand. Sullivan hesitated, then pulled a cell phone out from the back pocket of her jeans and turned around and walked a few feet away. Roxanne turned to the Charles and the lights on the Cambridge side and said, "The city really is pretty, isn't it? You'd never know all this stuff was going on."

"The other day I was talking to this woman who teaches at Harvard," Myra said. "She studies all those little bugs in the sand in the ocean. She said if people knew what was under there, they'd never walk on the beach again."

I almost smiled. Sullivan was talking and I overheard her say, "We need him, too," and then she turned back to us, said, "Okay, Jack. This is what I can tell you."

We sat in the front of her car, just the two of us. She gave me a clipboard to set my notebook on. I scribbled; she talked.

She said the Audi was found on a side street in Chelsea, one window broken, the CD player gone. Forensics people matched grass and other flora from the underside of the car to the path that led to the gravesite in Monroe, Maine, and there was a gull's feather hanging from the rearview mirror, like she'd just been to the coast. But Angel's parents said she came home the night she left Maine, which meant whoever had killed her had driven all the way back north. They were checking tapes at the tollbooths on the Maine Turnpike but hadn't come up with anything yet. That just meant the car might have been driven up Route 1—with a body in the trunk.

Angel died from strangulation. The scarf was the murder weapon. Her clothes were on the backseat of the car, strewn about.

Killed during sex? Prior to? They didn't know. There was no evidence that Angel had been sexually assaulted, or that she had had intercourse in the days before her death.

No random murder?

They didn't know that, either. She could have been waylaid upon her return to Maine. They didn't know why she would have gone back there. She'd called in sick on Wednesday, the day before the body was found, but had left for work as usual. Her family said Angel gave no indication that she was going anywhere other than Sky Blue.

To meet someone? Was Dalton in the office that day?

"The investigation is ongoing," Sullivan said.

"Come on," I said.

"Jesus, McMorrow," she said. "Most of what I just gave you is new. The *Globe* doesn't have some of this stuff."

That made it a sidebar, Myra and I decided, still standing in the parking lot after Sullivan had driven away. I said I'd come in early in the morning and write both stories. She asked me how early, and I said, "Very," and she said to call and she'd meet me at the bureau. She asked me if the story had changed, and I said, "Not really," but that wasn't entirely true.

"What is it?" Roxanne said as she drove out Storrow Drive, the banks of lights on one side, the banks of the river on the other. I looked out at the darkened park, the shimmering expanse of black water, the lights on the far shore that glimmered but really illuminated nothing.

"I thought I knew a lot about Angel," I said. "I thought I had a good sense of all of them."

"And now you're not so sure," she said.

"I feel like I know less and less."

"No, Jack," Roxanne said, her pretty hands, now scratched and scraped, gripping the wheel. "I think the problem is that the more you learn about this, the more you realize that it's going to take the biggest piece of the puzzle to put it all together."

"And we're getting closer," I said. "But I don't know exactly what we're getting closer to."

"It's not a what, Jack," Roxanne said. "It's a who."

34

Someone moved in the window at the side of the house when we pulled in. Motion-sensitive lights had flicked on and the gate had rolled closed behind us. I got out of the car and looked back at the house but the person wasn't there.

Mrs. Donovan, I presumed, and when we unlocked the side door and stepped in, she was there, in her bathrobe and slippers.

"Had to turn off the alarm," she said, like it was letting the cat out. "And now if you're in for the night, I'll just turn it back on."

She punched a button in the panel on the wall and a green light showed. I thanked her for waiting up so late and she said she'd just gotten back. She'd gone to her grandson's birthday party in Arlington, and he was three and what a sweetheart, but she stayed late to talk. She saw my hand and asked what had happened. I said we'd gotten into a bit of an altercation on the streets and she looked shocked and ashamed. She asked if we were okay, and I said we were fine, and she said she didn't know what the world was coming to; when she was young you could walk all over Boston any time of day or night and not worry about a thing. I started to say it was just one of those fluke things, and then I stopped.

"Mrs. Donovan," I said. "Somebody doesn't want me to ask questions about Angel Moretti. For the newspaper, I mean."

"Why on earth?" she said.

"I'm not sure."

"Such a pretty girl. What a shame."

"You knew her?" Roxanne said, smiling.

"Oh, she'd been to the house. One time Mr. Dalton sent her over to pick up something. Another time she came with David so they could get ready for some meeting or other. She had the loveliest skin. Like a baby's. Why would they not want you to ask about her, unless— oh, my goodness."

"Yes," I said. "It's a bit scary, so you be careful. If anyone calls or tries to get in."

"I will, by God."

"Had you seen her recently?"

"Oh, a few weeks ago. She liked it here. She seemed to really make herself at home. Just a child, though. What a terrible thing."

I looked at Roxanne and our eyes met. I wondered what sort of meeting David and Angel would have had to prepare for, and I heard Angel's voice again: *David, let's take* Escape *over to Bar Harbor.*

Mrs. Donovan said there was fettucine in the refrigerator. Cookies and milk. Cold beer and soft drinks in the pantry, and red wine in the closet at the back of the kitchen. There was a corkscrew in the drawer to the left of the big slate sink. Our room was all set, but she'd opened the windows to air the fourth floor because it heated up during the day, and now we might be cold.

We thanked her and said good night, and I went to the refrigerator and took out a Beck's. Roxanne seemed to deflate before my eyes, her color draining. I went to her and put my arm around her shoulders. I thanked her for staying beside me. I said I was sorry she'd been drawn into the mess. I said I'd write the story and we'd be out of here by noon, headed home to Maine. I asked her if she'd felt any more of those twinges, and she smiled wanly at me and said no, but she'd been busy.

So up to bed we went. Roxanne went into the bathroom, then came out and slipped off her clothes and got into a T-shirt and under the covers. She closed her eyes and sighed and I said, "I know," and awkwardly started to take my shirt off.

The phone rang. I ignored it and it stopped and I had my shirt off when there was a knock on the door, Mrs. Donovan saying, "Jack, that call is for you, dear."

I looked at Roxanne, who opened her eyes.

"Myra or Sullivan," I said. "Or Clair. They're the only ones I gave this number to."

I thanked Mrs. Donovan, then looked to the cordless phone on the bureau but the receiver was gone. I opened the door as Mrs. Donovan started down the stairs and asked her if there was another phone on this floor and she said no, but there was one in David's third-floor study, and she'd show me. I put my shirt back on and followed her. She led the way downstairs and down a hall, opened a door, and turned on a light. The study was dark-paneled and book-lined and there was a phone on the desk. I could see a light flashing. Mrs. Donovan headed back to bed.

It was a phone and answering machine and intercom and who knew what else. I picked up the receiver and said hello but got a dial tone. I looked at the buttons and saw that there were three phone lines. I pushed another button and got nothing at all, then hit another button and the machine started to play messages. It said the Connellys had six. I didn't know how to turn it off.

Six messages. I grabbed a piece of paper from a brass tray, a pen from the matching cup. Started to take the messages, the numbers, part of me feeling like I shouldn't listen, but it was too late.

Kip wanted David to call him about a trip following whales south from Baja, three weeks in October. Cassandra wanted to talk to Maddie about Dylan getting together with Maeve, but if they'd left for Maine, it was too late. John from the boatyard called with a question about *Serendipity*, he'd try David in Maine. Patrick called, said he'd gotten wind of a very interesting deal on land outside Jackson Hole, call him back. Somebody from John Kerry's office for David or Maddie, saying they were playing phone tag.

The next message began with a hiss and a rattle, and then the voice, not human but a machine.

"Hello, Maddie and David," it said, monotone with an odd inflection, like a robot. "Relaxing? Well, don't. Because you're not off the hook. I know your secret. I have the book."

A chill went through me. I stopped writing, then started again.

"I won't tell. Not yet. I want to be fair and give you a chance to make an arrangement. We will talk. And don't call the police because I'll know and the secret will be out."

There was a moment of hiss, then a car accelerating. Traffic noise. A robot at a phone booth? A tape played into a pay phone.

I stood there, the pen in my hand. The machine made a musical flourish sort of sound that meant all of the messages had been played. I wondered if it saved them and I looked at the machine to see if there was a way to do that. I'd want Maddie and David to hear it.

Or would I want them to know I'd heard it, too?

You're not off the hook. I know your secret.

Questions rushed at me. What secret? What hook? What sort of arrangement? Blackmail—it had to be. Why would they be off the hook? Because of Angel?

I stood in the stillness of the room and felt sick, that nauseating flutter of betrayal. I looked at the machine but it was silent now, its lights off, like some sort of venomous snake recoiled after striking. I backed away from the desk and turned off the light. Paper in hand, I made my way upstairs through the dim hallways, back to the room, where I closed the door behind me and turned the key in the lock.

"Who was it?" Roxanne said from the bed.

"I don't know," I said.

35

We talked well into the morning, lying there in the darkness, hands intertwined, our world shrunk to this string of words uttered by a machine. I told Roxanne it was the voice of a computer reading text. Most word-processing programs had it. My best guess was that someone had typed the message, taped it by holding a recorder up to the computer speaker, then replayed it into the receiver of a pay phone.

"Should we call the police now?" I said.

"I don't know," she said. "David and Maddie are our friends. Maybe we should go to them first."

"Maybe they need help," I said.

"If they aren't off the hook, that means they've been on one."

"And someone knows their secret."

"What could that be?"

"I don't know," I said. "It could be your abuse report. Maybe something leaked out."

"But that's nearly over. And remember, Maddie was crying. David saying it was going to be okay."

"Maybe it isn't going to be okay now," I said.

"We have to tell them, don't we?" Roxanne said.

"Because I don't know if the message is still there. We can't just pretend we didn't hear it."

We talked a while longer, but found no easier solution. Then we slept, holding each other close. When I awoke, light was streaming in and I could hear traffic moving. I looked at my watch. It was almost seven-thirty. I eased out of bed and stood and I hurt everywhere, my back, my legs, my shoulders, even my feet.

As the pain jabbed, the events of the previous night cornered me again. How to tell David and Maddie, and when. I moved to the bathroom and closed the door and turned on the shower. I stood under it for a long time, my taped fingers held outside the spray, and some of the pain eased. The situation remained unchanged.

I got out of the shower and dried myself. I was shaving when Roxanne opened the door, peeled her T-shirt off, and turned the shower on.

"I'm going with you," she said, as she held her arm out to test the temperature. "I'm not staying here alone."

So we ate Mrs. Donovan's scones and tea, listened to her stories about the birthday party. We tried to hold up our end of the conversation but we were distracted, and after half a cup of tea, I went upstairs and got our bags and brought them down. I thanked Mrs. Donovan for all of her help and she said it was nothing, she hoped we'd be back. I handed her the piece of paper with the messages from the night before.

All but one.

The morning was a blur. I spent it at a desk in the bureau, notes spread around me, still working the phones. I got Dalton's wife, Sylvie, who was very patronizing to me and Angel both. But she did say she suggested "Timothy" outfit the girl so she wouldn't embarrass everyone at a dinner. If she thought her husband had had an affair with Angel, she didn't reveal that to me.

I got Mrs. Moretti, but she didn't seem to understand what I was driving at with my questions about Angel stepping out and up. Finally I asked her what she thought of her daughter hanging out with all these wealthy people, and she said people were people, money didn't matter.

And I talked to Sullivan again. She asked how I was feeling, said they were still looking for both Mick and the kids who attacked us. I asked about the safe-deposit box and Sullivan said that was still under investigation. Off the record, she said they'd just located a box in Angel's name, but it was empty. They were checking to see if there were more.

And then Sullivan said, "You got anything to tell me?"

I opened my mouth, felt the words nearly spill out. But then I said no, I didn't have anything at the moment, but I might have something soon. She pushed but I held fast. And then I settled in and wrote for two solid hours, the words pouring out of me, or as fast as they could pour with my finger broken and the background of the story a tangle of secrets.

BOSTON—*In the months before she was murdered and buried in a shallow grave in the Maine woods, Angel Moretti had begun to explore a world both close to and light-years away from her life growing up in the North End.*

"You'd look around and she'd be talking to the president of Harvard or some major philanthropist," said Timothy Dalton, Moretti's supervisor at Sky Blue Foundation, the charitable organization run by David and Maddie Connelly. "Just like she belonged there. She was a very quick study."

And Moretti, who was strikingly attractive, was equally at home in the foundation's staid offices in the financial district, at a black-tie benefit, or with the Connellys themselves. Just last week David and Maddie Connelly invited Moretti and a few other foundation staff to visit the family's oceanfront summer home in Blue Harbor, Maine, a stay that included trips on the Connelly yacht, Escape.

But if her entrée into the World of Boston's wealthy upper crust was an escape of sorts, Moretti didn't forget her roots. She still lived at home with her parents on Michelangelo Street and got her closest friend from childhood a job at Sky Blue, too.

"She was a great kid," said Monica Vitale. "We were still best friends, no matter what happened."

At this point, police don't know.

I gave Myra the story at twelve-thirty. She gave it an initial read and liked it, spotted a few holes, some ambiguous constructions. I filled and fixed. Myra said she'd move the story along and would call if the national desk had questions. Roxanne, who had been working in the interview room, gathered up her stuff and we left Boston—but not the questions it had raised.

They stayed with us all the way to Maine. But what secret did the Connellys have that an extortionist could use? Was a kid with a bruise enough? A State abuse investigation. Maybe, if the caller didn't know the case was nearly closed.

We clung to that and concocted a theory. What if someone in Roxanne's department had seen the complaint, spotted the Connelly name? What if that person had decided it was worth a try, if the Connellys didn't want the story to come out.

But when Roxanne tried to think of someone in her office who might even consider doing such a thing, she couldn't. She knew them all and trusted them. We felt we knew Maddie and David and trusted them, too.

But were we wrong? Could we still trust our own instincts? What did we do with our secret if we didn't know theirs?

It was unsettling, and when we crossed the Piscataqua Bridge into Maine, the steeples of Portsmouth, New Hampshire, below us, boats streaking up and down the river, there was no relief. Normally when we returned to Maine, a weight lifted from us. This time the problem loomed closer with each passing mile.

"A fine mess we've gotten ourselves into," I said as we drove inexorably north.

Roxanne looked at my splinted finger, cradled on my lap.

"You think they'll come after you up here?" she said.

"I hope so."

"You do?"

"They're the only devil we know," I said.

"And there are others out there."

"Yes," I said. "We know that, too."

36

We stopped in South Portland at Roxanne's condo, but only long enough for her to pick up clothes and mail before we kept on going. It was almost five o'clock when we swung off Route 3 in Waldo County and began to thread our way through the hills to our own sleepy hollow.

We drove in silence as the woods reeled by. After our time in Boston with the Connellys, the trailers seemed shabbier: The ramshackle farmhouses seemed closer to the time when they finally would collapse and their wreckage would be swallowed up by the sumac and poplar that had already claimed the pastures. But the hills seemed wilder, the woods lusher, the place even more filled with the sense of timeless mystery that had drawn me to it and kept me here.

I wondered what David and Maddie Connelly would think, whether they'd understand.

"You think David will still come to cut wood with you and Clair?" Roxanne asked as we clattered onto a gravel road.

"I don't know," I said. "He said he wanted to."

"You think that was just talk?"

"I didn't think so."

"But now you're not sure?"

When we got to the house and brought in our bags, the answering machine was blinking its single red eye. I looked at it, paused and took a breath, not wanting to lift the lid on another Pandora's box. Roxanne was killing a spider on the counter, chasing it with a crumpled napkin as it scurried for its life. Roxanne squashed it and I hoped that wasn't bad karma. I touched the button and bent to listen.

Clair, welcoming us back. He'd collected our mail from the box by the road and would drop it off. Roxanne's supervisor, just checking in. He said he was getting questions from on high about the case in Blue Harbor. Cade, the cop, saying he wanted to get together when I got back so we could compare notes. And David Connelly, his voice buoyant even on the machine. He said he'd bought a new chain saw, hoped my friend and I didn't laugh at him, like he was a kid on the playground with new white sneakers. He said to call him when we were settled in.

"See," Roxanne said. "It wasn't just talk."

"Yeah," I said. "Maybe they're okay, like we thought."

Roxanne went up to the loft with one bag, I took the other to the bathroom to start laundry. When I had, I went up the stairs, too, and she was unpacking things she hadn't used. A silk blouse. A white sweater. A dark green teddy. I looked at it on the bed.

"I've never seen that before," I said.

"You sure?"

"I think I would have remembered."

"I thought we'd have more time in Boston," Roxanne said.

She smiled and picked the teddy up by the straps, which were thin strips of ribbon. I looked at the lace as Roxanne held it up to her chest.

"You like?"

"If's hard to tell, with you all bundled up like an Eskimo."

"Shorts and a T-shirt?"

"It's all relative."

"So you think I should model it for you?"

"You don't have to, if you have other things to do."

"Close your eyes," she said.

I did. Heard the wispy sound of fabric slipping off skin. Then Roxanne said, "'Now you can open them."

She was beautiful, dark hair against the pale skin of her bare shoulders. Brown eyes shining, her breasts nestled under the spider's web of lace. She bent and picked up the clothes from the bed and tossed them to the floor. Drew the covers back and slipped into the bed and slid over.

"You're sure?" I said.

"Do I seem uncertain to you?"

"No."

"Then come to me."

I undressed and got into the bed beside her and looked at her, ran my hand over the curve of her hip. She kissed me gently and I drew in a breath, still as amazed by her touch as I was the very first time.

"You don't seem uncertain at all," I said.

"We can't let anything stop us. Or anyone. Not now."

"No."

"Because this is the most important thing."

"Yes it is."

She kissed me again.

"You know it comes down to just us, Jack McMorrow," she said.

"I know."

Another kiss, this time longer.

"And maybe in a few months, you won't want to see me in this," Roxanne said.

"Sure I will," I said.

I slipped one strap off her shoulder, ran my hand over her, the splint cold against her skin. She flinched, then smiled and put an arm around me and pulled me closer and kissed me long and hard. When she pulled back, she whispered, almost to herself, "They're not going to stop us."

Before I could agree, she drew me to her and we pressed together, melted into each other, and the teddy began to peel away.

"But I just put it on," Roxanne murmured, the gathering of silk around her waist, my arms around her, too.

We'd dozed. I was dreaming there was a woodpecker pounding against the side of the house and then I awoke, Roxanne nestled against me, the dream dissolved but the pounding still going on.

It was someone knocking. Easing into consciousness, I focused on the gray dusk through the skylight. I eased away from Roxanne and swung off the bed, found my shorts and shirt and put them on. Skipped down the stairs and across to the door. I heard footsteps crossing the gravel and I opened the door just as Clair swung up into the cab of his truck.

He swung back down, then reached into the cab and came out with a sheaf of mail. The envelope on top was in a plastic bag.

"You'd better look at that one," Clair said.

I did, holding it up in the headlights of the truck. The address was written in big letters: ROXANNE MASTERSON, PROSPERITY, MAINE. The return address was smaller and I held it closer to read it.

Froze.

"Whoa," I said.

"Yeah," Clair said.

Roxanne's name was in black. The return address was written in dark red marker the color of blood: ANGEL MORETTI, BOSTON, MASS.

37

It was dark when Detective Cade pulled in. He stepped into the kitchen and peered at the envelope, still in the plastic bag, lying on the kitchen table like a sleeping snake.

"Postmark is Boston," he said.

"Friday," I said.

"Weren't you down there?" Cade said.

"Yes," I said. "We both were. Got back today, a little after five."

"Could have just delivered the message to you personally," he said.

"Somebody did," I said, and I held up my splinted finger.

"They don't like your writing style?" Cade said.

"More the subject matter."

He picked up the bag and pivoted it in front of him.

"The red ink is a little much," he said.

"Melodramatic," Roxanne said.

"That, too," he said.

He squeezed the envelope and shook it.

"Don't think it'll explode," Cade said. "Let's see what's inside, if you don't mind us reading your mail, ma'am."

He opened the bag, shook the envelope out, and slipped a pocketknife from his jeans. Holding the envelope by its edges, he sliced the end. He reached in with two fingers and extracted a folded sheet of paper. He unfolded the paper and newspaper clippings fell onto the table. One was my first story in the *Times* about Angel being found. The other was Angel's obituary from the *Globe*.

Angel's name had been crossed out and Roxanne's had been printed above it. Where the obituary listed survivors, the Moretti relatives' names had been crossed out and someone had written "Nobody."

"What's the letter say?" Roxanne said, her voice hard and grim.

Cade laid it on the table and we read it ourselves.

> *Ms. Masterson. Did I get your attention? Good.*
> *Here's the message.*
>
> *Enough is enough. Tell your "friend" to let Angel rest in peace and her parents at least have their memories. She may not have been as perfect a girl as they think, but she tried to be a good person. So tell Jack McMorrow thanks but no thanks. The next story he puts in the paper should be when they catch the person that killed Angel. He will know when that happens.*
>
> *PS: Just because you are a reporter or are shacking up with one doesn't mean bad things can't happen to you. And I mean very bad. That's not a threat. It's a fact. If you're smart, you'll believe me, and so will he. One murder is enough, don't you think? And remember, the last one happened in Maine, right near you. It could happen again, right in your own backyard in Prosperity, Maine. Except this time you could both end up where nobody will ever find you.*
>
> *Tell Jack McMorrow that he might not care about saving himself, but you could die too unless he stops asking questions, because these killers won't leave witnesses.*
>
> *Signed,*
> *A friend of Angel*

"The family," I said.

"Or someone who wants you to think it's the family," Clair said.

"Or Monica," Roxanne said.

"But I just talked to her yesterday. After this was mailed."

"How talkative was she?" Cade said.

"Pretty talkative. I told Sullivan about it."

Cade asked me to tell him what I'd told Sullivan about my conversation with Monica. Sullivan had called him but she was always in a hurry, he said, and he wanted it unedited. We sat at the table, the four of us, and they drank coffee and I had tea as I recounted the stuff about Angel having a sudden influx of cash. Cade took some notes. He asked me if I thought Monica was truthful and I said I thought she was, to a point, but she also was loyal to Angel. Then he asked me if there was another story in the works, and I looked at Roxanne and she said, "Yes."

"Will you write about these threats?"

"I think it's time," I said. "But the *Times* probably will have someone else write the story."

"Really," Cade said. "Then I'd advise you to be cautious, you and Roxanne both. That letter sounds a little goofy, but Angel Moretti, she's very dead. Nothing goofy about that at all."

"I'll be with her," Clair said, and Roxanne didn't decline his services.

Before Cade left, I copied the envelope and the notes and the clippings. He put all of it back in the bag, saying they'd had a case in Maine where they'd gotten DNA from the saliva left when a guy had licked an envelope. "Don't spread that around," he said, "or they'll all start using those little sponges."

I said I'd keep that in mind and I followed him outside.

We stood for a moment by his car, the radio coughing in the still summer night. Moths, drawn from the black fields and woods, pelted the light on the shed like snow and bats swooped out of the darkness.

"So what do you think?" I said.

"I think I meant it about being cautious," Cade said, one hand on the door handle. "It's true what they say about killing getting a lot easier after the first time. Especially if it's to cover up the first one. There may not have been a good reason for the first murder, but there sure is a good reason for the second."

"I'll remember. Anything else?"

"About this? Off the record, that it's going to come down to one or both of two things: money or sex. I think Angel Moretti was handing out one and taking in the other, and she got in too deep. What do you think?"

I watched the moths and bats, and the computer voice ran through my mind. *You're not off the hook.* When I glanced at Cade, I could see him watching me, searching my face for clues.

"I think I'm going to need to talk to you," I said.

"When?"

"Tomorrow. Maybe in the afternoon."

"I thought you were going to say something like that, Jack," Cade said, opening the car door.

"Why's that?" I said.

"Because you have a conscience, my friend."

"I'll call you."

"No," Cade said, showing a glimmer of the hardened cop beneath the facade of the boyish detective. "I'll call you."

38

Clair said he didn't come by the house at all during the night. I didn't believe him but I had to take his word for it, because I wouldn't have heard him if he'd been at the foot of the bed. Most of the time his were useless skills, he said: the ability to move silently through woods or a house or an enemy encampment, to kill somebody before they could kill him.

But there were times when Clair came in handy.

We left at nine, the three of us. Roxanne had called the number Devlin left and this time a man answered and said Devlin couldn't come to the phone, but she wanted to see us. Roxanne said we were on our way; the man, who identified himself as Gary, gave us directions to the town of Castleton, twenty minutes north of Blue Harbor.

With Clair at the wheel, we followed the directions down to the coast, a bank of thunderclouds trailing us as we drove east. It was sunny over the bay, blue sky and blue-green water, the bristled islands and lobster boats plying between them. We wended our way north behind tourists who had come to see this place where all was well and the landscape wasn't despoiled and the people led simple lives that left them content.

I wondered what Devlin had thought of the Maine beyond the Connellys' cloistered and privileged world. Clair said she'd apparently liked it well enough to stay.

The directions took us past the Castleton Quik-Stop, a store at a crossroads with two houses and a sagging chicken barn, the metal roof torn by the wind. We continued on for another five miles, took a right at a junkyard, and drove down a side road. After a mile and two-tenths, we looked for a sign that said R&S and turned down a drive-way through the woods. A hundred yards in was a garage, and next to it, a blue mobile home. There was an old Volkswagen out front, a big lobster skiff on a trailer. The trailer had a flat tire. There were wire lobster traps stacked on one side of the boat.

The trailer's screen door opened and a woman stood in the door-way. She was young, with a round fair face and cropped blonde hair with an inch of dark roots. She was wearing cutoff dungarees and a white T-shirt, the sleeves rolled up. The three of us got out and walked toward the door.

"You're Devlin," Roxanne said.

"Yeah," she said, "and I didn't do anything wrong."

Devlin turned and went back inside and the three of us followed. The trailer was dark beneath the trees, and it was neat, picked up for company. There were men's boots and sneakers lined up by the door, a rifle and a shotgun on a plastic rack that was screwed to the wall. I saw Clair take it in, move to the side, and listen.

"There's enough of you, isn't there," Devlin said. "Must think I'm a very dangerous sort of criminal."

"This is Mr. McMorrow, and this is Mr. Varney," Roxanne said. "We work together."

We said hello and she nodded. The place smelled like cigarettes, and Devlin took a pack off the round dinette table and lighted one with a plastic lighter. The television was on, a talk show, and she walked over in her bare feet and turned it off. She was sturdily built, with muscular legs and sunburned shoulders, and I wondered if she'd been lobstering, too.

"So I heard you were looking for me," Devlin said.

"Yes," Roxanne said. "But I thought you were in Ireland."

"No way," Devlin said. "I didn't come all the way here to turn around and go back with my tail between my bloody legs."

Devlin moved to the counter and leaned. Roxanne took a legal pad and pen from her bag and sat at the table. She laid the pen across the pad.

"So you know what they're saying about you?" she said.

"Why don't you tell me," Devlin said.

Roxanne did. And then she told Devlin that she'd seen the bruises.

"Don't need to be Sherlock Holmes to see them, do you," Devlin said. "I mean, I know they're there. And I know I did them."

Roxanne, used to nursing the truth out of people, looked up at her in surprise.

"Well, you look at the kid, she turns purple. I took her by the shoulder to make her mind, that's all. She's lucky I didn't turn her over my knee as well. When I was a kid, my ma told me to stop doing something, I stopped. I didn't look her in the eye and keep right on doing it just to see what would happen."

"Is that what Maeve did?"

"Sure. Testing me, you know. She says, 'You're not my mother. You can't tell me what to do.' I say to myself, well, nip this one in the bud. I say, 'I'm not your mother but I'm still the boss. And it's time to get out of that wet bathing suit before you ruin the furniture.' Maddie was all into the furniture, all these grand antiques and such. So Maeve starts in with, 'You're not the boss of me,' and I take her by the shoulder and bring her into the bath and she's thrashing and I take the suit off her and put her in the tub."

"Was this a one-time thing?" Roxanne said.

"Well, yeah, when I saw that touching her—it's like she's made out of clay. Leaves these great hand marks. You saw 'em."

"Yes."

Roxanne had picked up the pen and was taking notes.

"So that night, it's like the little kid knows she has me, because of the bruises. I ask her to put her crayons away and she says, 'Why can't you do it?' I say, 'Because you're going to do it.' She says, 'Michaela'— that was the au pair before me—she says, 'Michaela never made me pick up crayons.' I said, 'I'm here now and I do.' She gets up off the floor where she's doing her coloring and she starts to walk away. I stop her, but I know I can't grab her, you know? The bruises. So I take her to the closet and I give her a time-out."

Roxanne wrote. Clair turned to the door and listened as a truck approached out on the main road.

"Was it dark in the closet?" Roxanne said.

"Well, yeah. There's a light but I don't think she could reach it."

"Did she cry?"

"Yeah, for a few minutes. But it was like, if I didn't tell her who was who, I was done. She would've walked all over me the rest of the summer, now wouldn't she?"

"So she cried and then what?"

"And then she stopped. And then I let her out. I figured that was that. I mean, I didn't hit her. If I had talked that way to my mother, I would've been lifting myself up off the floor."

"So then what happened?" Roxanne said, her voice calm and noncommittal.

Devlin turned and snubbed out her cigarette in a scallop shell on the counter.

"Well, Maddie, she called me in the next night as well. Maeve tattled on me, you know. I say, 'I just held her by the shoulder. You know how easy she bruises.' She says, 'Yes, and what about locking her up in the dark? That was very upsetting to her.' I say, 'It was a time-out, like you told me to do.' She says, 'I didn't mean for you to lock her up in the closet. Think of the psychological damage that can cause.' All this kind of shit. I could see there was no talking about it."

"No?"

"Oh, she had an envelope all ready. All the rest of my pay in cash, as well."

"And a ticket home?"

"No, that came the next day. So she gives me the money and she's nice enough about it, you know? I mean, she didn't say I was a child beater. She said we just had different ideas about what is 'appropriate discipline.' I told her this was nothing compared to what I got when I was a kid."

"So it was amicable, your parting?"

"I thought so. Then I hear she's reported me to the government. That's lovely. That you're looking for me in Ireland like I'm a bleedin' murderer."

"Who told you that?"

"My aunt."

"I thought she hadn't seen you in years."

Devlin smiled slyly. "Yeah, well she isn't going to turn in her own family now, is she?"

Roxanne gave her a long look, then said, "That's not exactly how it went. Somebody else saw the bruises and called my agency and I came to check it out. That's when Maddie told me. But I needed your side of it."

"Well, that's what I'm giving you. But you know what? It's not like they're so lily white."

"Oh," Roxanne said.

We listened.

"Yeah, you think they're a bunch of effing angels? I don't think so. Her, I don't think she's all right in the head. I mean, I was there, what, two months? I hear 'em fighting like a coupla cats."

"About what?" Roxanne said.

"I couldn't tell you. Over money, I think. Him saying, 'Just pay it.' Her saying, 'No, it's not right.' That's all I know about that one. Maybe the money supply isn't as endless as people think. You know how much that boat cost?"

"I do," I said. "So what do you mean about Mrs. Connelly not being right?"

"I don't know. She reminded me of one of my cousins at home. She gets depressed, goes down in this black hole of a mood. Maddie was kind of like that. Sometimes she was okay, but sometimes, when she was alone, you'd come in and you'd know something was not right about her."

"Like she was sad?"

"Very. But that's not the worst of it. They report me to the government for being an unfit nanny or whatever, and he's taking some girl for a roll while the wife is away."

Roxanne looked up from her pad. I felt like I'd been punched.

"What makes you say that, Devlin?" Roxanne said, still calm.

Devlin paused, lighted another cigarette, took a drag, and exhaled a blue cloud.

"Because I heard them," she said, delivering her coup de grace.

"You heard them what?"

"I heard them . . . you know . . . doing it."

She smiled slyly.

"You see, Maddie and Maeve, they'd gone home to Boston because Maeve had a doctor's appointment. David was supposed to be going on some boat trip for a couple of days, so I had the weekend off and I was staying here with this guy I met. Gary. I mean, I need to be with some real people once in a while, don't I? This was, what? Six weeks ago? But I forgot something. Something important. So I take Gary's truck and I go back. There's this car out by the garages there, but I didn't think much of it. But then I go in and I'm going to my room and I hear them. I mean, you could hear them all over the house. Him moaning and groaning. Girl was practically screaming. 'Oh God, oh God.' I say to myself, 'Well, that's lovely. Wife's away, the cat's having a good old time. Anyway, she sounded fake to me, if you want to know."

"It wasn't Maddie?"

"No, you could tell she was much younger than Maddie."

"So then what happened?" Roxanne said.

"I left. I was disgusted, really. Mr. Family Man. Mr. Daddy. And he's got some bimbo he probably met at some la-di-da party and he's sneaking her up for a ride when the wife's away, you know? Tucking it right to her, and in his wife's bed as well. Isn't that grand?"

I was sickened, disillusioned. This was the David Connelly of the stereotype, not the one I knew. Or maybe I didn't know him at all.

"And then they run me out of the place for touching their kid too hard? Have you calling my aunt like I was beating their kid with a club?"

"So what did you do?" Roxanne said.

"When?"

"In the house that day."

"Nothing. I said to myself, 'Aren't these people the biggest phonies. Rich, famous phonies.' And I snuck out, very quiet like. They never even knew I was there."

"Which came first?" I said.

"Which what?" she said.

"The argument or walking in on somebody in the house?"

She had to think for a moment.

"Them in the house," Devlin said. "They had fights before, but the one I was telling you about was right before I left."

"And what kind of car was it that day when you went there?" I said.

"Gary's?" she said. "It's a truck. A Chevy. He carries lobster traps with it. He'll be home in a little while, if you don't believe me. I told him when I got back, I said, 'You won't believe—"

"No," I said. "By the garages that day. What kind of car was that?"

"Oh, that," Devlin said. "It was an Audi. Fancy thing. It was from Massachusetts and there was a feather hanging from the mirror. It was white."

"The car?" I asked.

"No," she said. "The feather. The car was silver."

39

We drove out the main road, past the Castleton Quik-Stop, Clair at the wheel, me in front, Roxanne working in back. The clouds had overtaken us from the west and the air was still.

"One case closed," Roxanne said.

"And another blown wide open," I said.

"There are a lot of silver Audis in Massachusetts," Clair said.

"Not with feathers," Roxanne said.

"We may never know for sure," I said.

"Maybe we should just go and ask him," Clair said.

"Maybe we should," I said. "But not today."

I was thinking of the phone message at the house in Back Bay, and what Devlin had said about David and Maddie and their argument. David saying, "Just pay it." Maddie saying, "No, it's not right." The computer voice saying, "You're not off the hook yet."

As it started to rain, the drops spattering the road like something sprayed from a plane, I reached for the phone. I called Myra in Boston. She answered and I asked if she knew the librarian at the *Globe*. She said she did, quite well actually. I said that was good because I needed a favor. I needed everything they had in their file on Maddie

Connelly, and I needed it faxed right away. A LexisNexis search, too. Myra said she'd do a search. She asked if Tuesday's story still held.

"Yeah," I said. "But I think it's the tip of the iceberg."

And I hung up.

"Why Maddie?" Clair said.

"They weren't talking about a light bill," I said.

"And someone knows their secret, has the book," Roxanne said.

"So if they're being squeezed, which one would have a secret?" Clair said.

"Think of David Connelly's life," I said. "Most of it has been spent in and around the spotlight. When he was at Harvard partying, you heard about it. Afterwards he couldn't date somebody without it ending up in the paper somewhere. Kathleen Kind said she was linked to him because they had a breakfast meeting. So how many secrets can he have?"

"At least one," Roxanne said.

"So maybe it was this Devlin with the computer message," Clair said. "Disgruntled former nanny decides to take some Connelly money with her."

"Then why tell Roxanne about it?" I said. "A secret isn't worth anything once it's out. No, I'm thinking that unless he killed somebody, David Connelly isn't going to scare too easily. An affair? It's all been said before."

"And Maddie?" Roxanne said.

"She's more the enigma," I said. "She's the one whose life isn't an open book."

It was a scattering of papers, spat from the fax machine and spilled onto the desk and the floor. I gathered them up and checked e-mail, but the results of the LexisNexis search hadn't been sent. While

Roxanne talked to someone at DHS on the phone in the kitchen, Clair made lunch, and the rain drummed on the deck out back. I sorted through the clippings.

Most were from the *Globe*, and most were Maddie with David. They made the party page a couple of times a year; David in a tux, the big amiable grin fixed on some hapless lesser mortal. Maddie in dresses and gowns and a-soft smile as she greeted someone, an earnest, pensive look in conversation.

She was alone in some stories, mostly announcements of grants, program kickoffs. Finally there was a story from the *Times*, a profile that said Maddie Boswell Connelly was more than an appendage to another handsome Connelly. It talked about her interest in children and foster care, in providing psychological services for troubled youth. There was a reference to her brother Clinton's suicide in Amherst, Mass., her parents' subsequent divorce. Maddie was quoted as saying the ordeal was very difficult, that she did not believe her brother really intended to take his life.

"Clint was a wonderful brother and I worshipped him," she'd said.

Clair brought in tuna sandwiches and pasta salad. Roxanne was off the phone and she came over and we ate, and I handed the clips around as I finished them. Maeve's birth was a short story in the *Globe*, a blurb in *Time* magazine. David and Maddie's wedding was a chunk of the Life and Leisure section front in the *Globe*. They looked young and beautiful, but when I looked more closely at the photo, Maddie's eyes seemed to have an undertone of sadness, even with her smile.

I looked from photo to photo. It seemed that no matter what the story was about, I saw the same hint of melancholy.

"She was a beautiful bride," Roxanne said. "Oh, and look at Maeve. What a cute baby."

I reached over and put my arm around her waist.

"But look at her eyes," I said.

Roxanne looked up from a clipping.

"Yeah," she said. "It's almost like she knows this is all too good to be true."

"That it's somehow built on sand."

"But have you seen that in her, in person?" Roxanne said.

"A little," I said. "It's like she's wistful sometimes."

"Some people," Clair said, "are just philosophically sad."

And Maddie had good reason. Her father, who taught mathematics at Amherst, died in a car accident on Route 2 when Maddie was a sophomore at Harvard. Her mother, who taught anthropology at Amherst, died of liver failure five years later. She was fifty-two. I wondered if she took to alcohol to combat loneliness, whether she ever recovered from the loss of her son.

I handed the clips off and they read them. The rain was heavier and I went to the sliding glass door and closed it to keep the spray from driving in. I stood and looked out at the sky, which was darker now, with billowing clouds like something from a painting. The trees at the edge of the woods were a deep shining green, a dense leafy barrier that hid everything behind it. For a moment I felt an odd twinge of fear, that so much around me was unknown. I shook it off.

"It really is very sad," Roxanne said. "It's like somebody up there decided to give Maddie the whole family's share of good luck."

"I wonder if that bothers her," Clair said. "The brother shoots himself with her in the room. The father drives into a tree. The mother, maybe she just died, maybe she drank herself to death."

"And then she scores one of the most eligible bachelors in New England," I said.

"I don't know," Roxanne said. "It's not like she made those bad things happen."

"No," I said.

"Misplaced guilt," Clair said. "One of the most common symptoms of post-traumatic stress. The soldier who made it when his buddies didn't."

"Maddie Connelly with PTSD?" I said.

Roxanne was leaning over the table, reading the wedding story. I went to the computer and checked e-mail again. This time the LexisNexis search results were in, forwarded from Myra. Her note said, "Happy hunting." I scrolled down.

A lot of it we had. But they'd run Sky Blue Foundation, too, so there was stuff about grants and other Connellys who were only marginally connected to the foundation. And then there were older stories, retrieved from some data bank. Maddie's making the dean's list at Harvard, as reported in the Amherst *Daily Collegian*. Maddie's engagement in the *Berkshire Eagle*. And one last story, in the chronological listing.

It was from the *Collegian*, March 4, 1977. It was short, five paragraphs saying Clinton Archer Boswell's death was ruled a suicide. The last paragraph said the Hampshire County Coroner's Office did not call Madeline "Maddie" Boswell, seven, to testify at the inquest for her brother's death, despite the fact that she was the only eyewitness. *A spokesman for the Coroner's Office cited Miss Boswell's age and that the trauma inflicted upon her had left her a "less than credible" witness. "Her recollection of her brother's death isn't supported by physical evidence," the spokesman said, "and may have been induced by hysteria and medication given her after the incident."*

I read that paragraph to Roxanne.

"That's horrible," she said. "The poor little girl."

"I wonder what she imagined," I said.

"Probably that some mysterious assailant came in and killed the brother and ran away," Clair said. "Anything to keep her from believing her beloved brother would want to leave her."

"But I don't see this as a secret," Roxanne said. "It's in the paper."

"True," I said.

"My vote is the husband screwing around," Clair said. "He's older now. Has a daughter who could hear about it if it comes out somehow. So it would be damaging."

"And I can't believe Devlin has kept this to herself," Roxanne said.

"Maybe Devlin's lobsterman boyfriend decided to shake the Connelly tree, see what falls," Clair said. "Could be a dangerous business."

"I hope not," I said.

"Why?" Roxanne said.

"Because it's our turn to shake next," I said.

40

I called the Connellys in Blue Harbor and told them we were going to be nearby, thought we might stop in. David sounded genuinely pleased, said it was a wild day on the water, that they'd gotten in just before the storm really broke. He said Clair was welcome, too; he needed some tips about the new chain saw. We'd do that, then have a couple of beers, some dinner, and watch the lightning over the bay.

How was that for a plan?

Fine, I said.

Roxanne said we had to call the police soon and I said, that night, as soon as we left. I felt guilty, but then I thought of Angel, dead and barely buried, and the pangs subsided.

We drove all the way east to Blue Harbor, where the rain still was pelting and the shop lights were on and people were scurrying from store to store in green and yellow slickers. The wine shop was busy but we stopped and bought two bottles: one white, one red, both over our usual limit of ten dollars. Clair went into the hardware store and bought bar oil, files, and a sharpening guide. Roxanne bought a bouquet of fresh flowers.

When we got back in the car, I turned to both of them and said, "We haven't given up on them, have we?"

"Last of the cockeyed optimists," Clair said.

Roxanne attempted a smile, and said nothing.

The lights were on at the gate and the carriage house. The wind was whipping off the water so the rain was salty and the woods smelled of the sea. From the drive I could see whitecaps from an onshore wind, the storm swirling and sweeping in from the northeast. We bent as we ran to the door and jangled the bell, which was already tolling from the gusts. After a minute Maddie opened the door, told us to get in before we were drenched. We handed her the 'wine and the flowers and Clair said his gifts were chain-saw-related, and she said David would like that, then held out her hand and I introduced them.

Maddie said she was very pleased to meet Clair and glad to see us. She asked me what I'd done to my finger and I said it was a long story. A few minutes later we were standing in the front room with drinks in our hands, watching *Escape* and the Whaler buck on their moorings. David bounded down the stairs with Maeve a step behind him.

"I won," he said.

"You cheated," Maeve said, tackling him around the legs.

He dragged her giggling across the floor.

"Hi there," he said to Clair. "I'm David. This is Maeve, my daughter and appendage."

"Clair Varney," Clair said.

"Clair's a girl's name," Maeve said from the floor.

"It's an either-or name," Clair said.

"Like Maeve," David said.

"Maeve's just a girl's name," the little girl said.

"You're a girl?" David said. "If I'd known that, I would have called you Lucy."

He asked about my finger, too, and I said I had a bit of a mishap. At that moment Maddie came in with a tray of shrimp and mussels and raw clams. Maeve got up and grabbed a shrimp and David was loose so he gave Roxanne something between a hug and a pat on the back. I thought I saw her stiffen but it may have been my imagination.

"Well, we have a good one going out there, don't we?" David said. "Radio says gusts up to forty knots in the next hour or so. I wanted to take the boat out in the bay but Maddie says she doesn't want to feed the Coast Guard, too. Sandy's off, or we'd have had her outvoted."

Maddie handed him a bottle of some sort of English porter.

"Good thing I'm here, too, or he would be out there," she said. "You can't leave him alone."

So we'd heard.

We watched the storm through the rain-pelted glass, drinking beer and listening to the narration of the weather radio. David pointed out the landmarks on the chart and regaled us with stories of boats that had tried to make the inner harbor and missed, a couple of them running aground right out front.

"Of course, I was out there with a light, luring them in," David said. "Can you imagine? Common as hell in the Maritimes, other places, in the nineteenth century. Lured the sailing ships onto the rocks. It was a cottage industry."

Clair told a story about Vietnamese pirates and that got them started, with David recounting sailing in Indonesia with a guy on deck with an AK-47. The stories went on and then Maddie turned to Roxanne and leaned close to her and whispered something about not drinking. Roxanne, drinking spring water, said something and smiled and Maddie hugged her with one arm, said, "Oh, I'll be so happy for you." And then she turned to the men and said, "Mind your own—"

"Beeswax," Maeve said.

It was pleasant, but our real business loomed like an approaching storm. Finally, Maeve asked Clair if he'd like to see her turtle. She said she'd see if it was awake and she scampered up the stairs just as a young woman, another au pair, this one introduced as Katie, was coming down. She turned and followed Maeve back up. David picked up the tray of shrimp and offered it to me. I said we had something to talk to them about, and the tone of my voice was like a teacher walking into an unruly classroom. They stopped talking and there was a silence and I hesitated and started in.

"When we were at your house last night," I began, "I had a call."

I told them about answering it in the study and inadvertently hitting the button on the answering machine. I said there were several messages, but it was the last one that we needed to talk about. I took out a piece of paper and read aloud.

" 'Hello, Maddie and David: Relaxing? Well, don't. Because you're not off the hook. I know your secret. I have the book.' "

I took a breath. They were both frozen in place. I continued: " 'I won't tell. Not yet. I want to be fair and give you a chance to make an arrangement. We will talk. And don't call the police because I'll know and the secret will be out.' "

The five of us stood there, the Connellys looking away. The wind buffeted the house and rain pelted the windows.

"The person left a number," I said.

David cleared his throat and Maddie said, "Oh," in a small, sad voice. And then she said, "David, I don't think I can take any more. Where will it end?"

"Honey, we'll take care of it," David said, but she pressed her hand to her mouth and stilled a sob and strode from the room into the adjoining study. David turned back to us. He tried to smile, once, then again, but it was like an engine that wouldn't start and finally he gave up.

"What's it all about?" I said.

He looked away. "Oh, it's old news, Jack. Very old. But it keeps popping up, you know? Like something that won't stay buried. It's the damnedest thing, like a ghost. Haunting us, haunting Maddie. Just when you think—"

David turned to us.

"Who have you told, Jack?"

"No one, yet," I said. "I wanted to tell you first. As a courtesy."

"Thanks. That's good of you. Listen, I think I'd better check on her. Just have a seat, okay? Don't run off or anything."

He went to the study door and opened it, stepped inside, and shouted, "Maddie, no!"

Furniture crashed and we broke for the door, Clair first. When we came into the room, Maddie was standing in front of the fireplace. She was pressing a handgun to her temple and David was standing five feet from her, both hands up in front of him, like he was surrendering.

"Nobody move or I'll pull the trigger. I will," Maddie said. "It's easy to do, you know. The finger moves and boom. A little tiny finger does all of that."

Her voice was girlish, almost singsong. Her eyes were both on us and far away. She was smiling, like a sick person who doesn't want someone to worry.

"Maddie, it's okay," David said. "Just put it down. We'll take care of it."

He took a step toward her and she said, "No," and pressed the gun hard against her skull so the end of the barrel made an indentation in her skin. David froze.

"That's the thing, David. It's not okay. It's still out there. We thought it was okay before and now it's not. It's just the same."

"We'll fix it again, honey."

"You didn't fix it last time. It fixed itself. That was our best chance and now it's back, and do you think we'll be that lucky again? It's back, and all of these people know and it'll be in the papers and Maeve will know and oh, my God."

"But they're your friends, Maddie," David said. "You're with friends. They haven't told anyone. They don't even know themselves. So we take care of it and that's the end of it."

"We don't know who it is, David. We don't know what they've done with it or who's reading it. They're probably showing it around. A made-for-TV movie. Maddie Connelly's journal."

My mind raced. Was that what this was about?

Maddie's arm was tiring and the gun barrel was sliding downward, over her cheekbone. It left a pink trail, like chalk on a board. I could see David tensing, but then her arm lifted back up. He stood stock-still. The gun, some sort of antique revolver, was heavy and it began to slip again.

"And Maeve."

"That's right, honey. Think of Maeve. She needs you. You're a wonderful mother."

"I'm not."

"You are. She loves you. I love you. We all love you, and we'll help you."

To my right, I could see Clair inching forward. There was a couch between Maddie and us, and he was moving to his right. David had gone around the couch to the left and stood at its end.

"What can you do?" Maddie was saying. "It's only a matter of—"

Clair lunged and Maddie cried out, "No!" and the gun slipped from her temple and was pointed at Clair and he had it by the barrel, ripped it from Maddie's hands, turned and tossed it onto the couch. I picked the gun up as Maddie collapsed, sobbing and limp, into David's arms and started to fall. David turned with her, like they were dancing, and then laid her on the couch and knelt beside her. Roxanne turned and closed the door, then came around the couch and put her hand on Maddie's arm.

Suddenly Maddie said, "I'm going to be sick," and David and Roxanne helped her up and they crossed the room to a door and David stopped and Roxanne and Maddie went in. Roxanne closed the door behind them and we heard Maddie begin to retch.

David turned away from the door and wiped perspiration from his forehead, focused on us, and said to Clair, "Thanks so much."

"A single-action revolver," Clair said. "You have to cock it."

I still had the revolver in my hand and I handed it to Clair. He popped the cylinder open and dropped out six hefty cartridges, forty-fours, he said. He told David it should be locked up and David said, "Could you just take it? Get it out of here completely?"

Clair asked if there were other guns in the house and David said no, not with ammunition. Clair said he'd put the revolver in the car, and he turned and left the room.

David, without looking at me, said, "I guess you're going to want some sort of explanation."

"Yes," I said. "I want to know whether you know who killed Angel."

He turned to me and, with an expression of both relief and sadness, shook his head.

"No, Jack," he said. "But you know the old saying. Be careful what you wish for. In some ways it was an answer to my prayers."

41

Roxanne and Maddie came out of the bathroom, Roxanne's arm around Maddie's shoulders. Maddie was holding a towel up to her chest and she was pale, her hair damp and disheveled. David went to her and she said she was okay, she wanted to change her clothes.

"I'm fine," she said. "I'm sorry."

They started to leave the room and David followed but Maddie said, "No, I'll be down," and Roxanne went with her. David went to a sideboard and poured brandy in a glass, held it up, then put it down. Maeve poked her head in, holding a small turtle, and asked where Clair was and David said he went outside. She left, feet thumping across the floor.

"Well," David said.

I didn't say anything. He held the glass of brandy out to me and I shook my head. This time he took a sip, then said, "Let's go out on the porch."

It was blustery, the wind punching off the water, and we stood against the wall of the house, out of the rain. David sipped his drink and watched the boats jerk like rearing horses on their tethers, and then he said, "Angel had something of ours. Something of Maddie's."

"A journal?" I said.

"Yeah. It has some personal stuff in it, as you can imagine. Some stuff that would really embarrass Maddie if it came out."

"I got that much."

He looked at me, then back at the water.

"I guess *embarrass* is an understatement. Maybe *devastate* is a better word. I mean, it's not of importance to anybody else, but to her it is. And you know how anything with the Connelly name attached to it seems to have some added value, for some strange reason. I've never been able to figure it out."

"And it's a secret. That's what the caller said."

"Well, yeah. In the sense that it's stuff nobody else has read."

"And Angel got hold of it?"

"Right. I mean, I don't know how. It was in the bedroom, in a drawer underneath a lot of other stuff. She must have gone up there and rummaged around, and somehow came across this. She's only been here twice, the weekend you were here and in the fall, when we had the Sky Blue crew up for sort of a foliage outing from the water. It was a beautiful day."

"And the time you slept with her," I said.

David looked at me, stunned.

"No, I didn't," he stammered.

"Sure you did," I said. "Devlin told me. It was six weeks ago, she said. Maddie and Maeve had gone back to Boston to go to a doctor. You were supposed to be out on the boat, but when Devlin came back, you and Angel were in bed."

"Me and Angel? She said that?"

"Yeah. She said she heard you. You know, in the process. She said a silver Audi was in the drive. Massachusetts plates."

David had looked away, his eyes narrowed.

"I did go on the boat," he said. "I went to Matinicus with Sandy."

I looked at him skeptically.

"Jack, it seems odd that you'd even have to ask. Angel? I had no interest in Angel."

"Who else do you know who drives a silver Audi?"

"Silver? Nobody," David said. "But it wasn't me. It had to be—"

There was a long moment when we both were silent.

"Dalton?" I said.

"I don't know. He has a key. He was, I don't know, pursuing her, I guess. But I didn't think that—"

"That they were in your bed?"

"God almighty. That's pretty low. So he brought her here? And that's how—"

He didn't finish the thought aloud, so I did.

"What did Angel do with this journal, David?"

"She . . . she tried to sell it back to us."

"Blackmail?"

"Yeah, but that's not how she put it. She called it, 'selling it back.' She said she found it and she thought she deserved a finder's fee."

"You gave her one?"

He paused, and turned to me.

"Are we talking as friends?"

"I don't know," I said. "It depends on what you have to say."

David Connelly raised his glass to his lips but the glass was empty.

"Yeah. I mean, I guess we shouldn't have, but it wasn't that much money."

"How much?"

"Twenty thousand, the first time."

"She didn't give it back?"

"No. I imagine she got to thinking about how much money we had. Or maybe we paid too easy. I don't know. But she said she wanted another installment. She said it with this big smile, like she was asking for a new office chair, right to my face. She said she'd made copies of some . . . some of what was in the journal, and had them in envelopes addressed to TV news, newspapers, *Newsweek* magazine. All ready to go, she said."

"Would they print it?" I said.

"Somebody would," David said. "And then everybody else would pile on."

"How much was the second payment?"

"Fifty. A Kenneth Cole tote bag full of cash."

"And still she kept the journal?"

"Yeah. I mean, why give it back? It was like a lottery ticket that just kept on winning."

"And then she was killed," I said.

David hesitated. Turned and put the empty glass on the windowsill behind us. Turned back.

"Yeah. Like I said, it was like the answer to my prayers. Not that I wanted anything like that to happen to her, but I wanted her to go away and leave us alone."

"So you didn't kill her."

David turned to me and our eyes locked.

"I hope that's rhetorical, but no. I couldn't kill anyone. My god."

"You didn't have it done. Somebody like Mick or Vincent?"

"Jesus Christ, no. Then I'd have this person owning a piece of us, too. Some Southie hoodlum or something? That's all we need."

"You didn't do anything?"

"No."

"Did she ask for more money?"

"The day you were here, I avoided her like the plague, the best I could. I didn't want to be near her, and she's 'David this,' and 'David that.' Finally she cornered me on the boat in Bar Harbor. She said she needed another fifty thousand. I said I couldn't get it, that people were going to notice all these withdrawals. She said, 'You're a smart man, David. Figure it out.' And then two days later, she's gone."

"Maybe somebody killed her to get the journal," I said.

"Maybe. Maybe they found out and they wanted the lottery ticket. And now they've got it. And it all starts again. I think that's what pushed Maddie to the edge. That it will just keep up forever."

He turned back to the house and I stopped him with a touch on his shoulder.

"David," I said. "What's in this journal that's worth all of this? Maybe costing a life?"

"It's not up to me to say, Jack," he said. "It's just really been hard on Maddie, all of it."

"Not good enough," I said.

"Sorry, Jack. Sorry you had to get involved."

"It's about her brother, isn't it?"

He went pale for a moment, like it was his turn to be sick.

"It's about what she saw when her brother died and what came out at the inquest. They're two very different things, aren't they? And what's different from a suicide, when somebody's shot to death? Two other possibilities, David. Only two."

"What?"

"It could be an accident. Or it could be—"

"Jesus, Jack," David said. "What are you trying to do here?"

And then he turned away and went through the doors. I followed, saw Maddie come down the stairs and fall into his arms. As I stood on the porch, watching through the glass panes in the door, he was talking. She was listening, and then her face fell into an expression of disbelief. She looked right at me.

Maddie started for the porch and David grabbed her arm but she flung his hand away, pushed the doors open, then stopped for a moment, turned, and pulled them closed. She looked at me, her eyes red-rimmed, her hair blown by the wind.

"How did you know, Jack?" she said, shaking her head. "How did you know?"

"I guessed, Maddie," I said. "I knew about it, your brother. I saw a story saying you weren't going to testify at the inquest. I just couldn't think of anything else that would be bad enough to hurt yourself over."

"Then what now? Is it out, Jack? Is it out?"

She reached out and took my hands in hers, like someone pleading with a doctor to please come help.

"No," I said. "I said it to David, but it was just, I don't know, conjecture. I didn't know it was true. Until now."

"I was seven," she said, twisting my hands in hers like she was trying to warm me. "I loved him. He was my big brother and he doted on me. I didn't mean it. I don't think I did. For twenty-five years I've been asking myself, 'Did you mean to shoot your brother?' He had the gun out. It was my dad's. This little gun, like you'd start a race with. I said, 'Can I hold it?' He said no. And I reached out and grabbed it from him and I pointed it at him and I pulled the trigger. You know what I was going to do?"

"No, Maddie," I said. "I don't."

Her eyes were wide, her mouth turned down in disbelief.

"I was going to say 'Bang.' "

I held her hands and she turned away from me, looked out at the wind-whipped bay like she might fling herself into it.

"So my mom and dad, they took the gun and they wiped it off and they put it in my brother's hand. They said they didn't want to lose both their children. That's what they said, and I was forbidden to talk about it and they never talked about it, either. Not a single word. Not one, until sometimes I thought I'd imagined the whole thing. But I hadn't. And we all kept this terrible secret and it ate away at them like a cancer until it killed them. I kept running. I worked so hard at being perfect that the secret couldn't catch up with me."

"It's not your fault, Maddie," I said. "It was an accident."

"Everyone says that, but it wasn't. I took the gun and I pointed it at him and I pulled the trigger. He told me it was loaded."

"You were a child."

"And I was never punished. I've still never been punished, Jack. Not a punishment that ends. Maybe this will be my punishment. When the whole thing comes out and my daughter will be seven and she'll know her mother did this terrible thing. It'll come full circle."

She turned back to me, with an odd gleeful expression.

"But if we can't stay here, maybe we'll go to Italy, live there. I love Sienna. Or sell these houses and take the sailboat and just wander. But I wonder, do you think they'll put me in jail? You know how they've gone after that Kennedy cousin in that old murder, and he was just a kid."

"Maddie," I said as David opened the door. "I haven't told anyone else."

They both looked at me.

"Just give us a chance to get it back," David said.

"But Angel," I said. "Whoever killed her—"

"Is still out there," David said. "I know. But it isn't fair to Maddie to have all of this made public. It would be evidence, it would be released to the press, don't you think? We'll get it back and then we'll go to the police. We'll tell them . . . we'll tell them her concerns about what happened."

"If Angel was blackmailing you, it'll have to come out."

"Then you can write it, Jack," David said. "We'll sit down with you. But to have this journal get into the hands of some of the awful TV people. Jack, I haven't read it, but—"

I pictured the story, how I would write it. *The gun was loaded. Sitting with her brother Clinton in his bedroom in their home in tree-shaded Amherst, Massachusetts, that September morning, Maddie Boswell knew that. But still, in her seven-year-old mind, she thought if she pulled the trigger, she'd have to say, "Bang."*

"I don't know," I said.

"Jack, this was part of my therapy, so there's stuff about my brother, him dying, about Maeve, about David when our marriage was not so good. And there's all my doubts about myself and being a mom."

"You're a great mother, Maddie," I said.

"This was at a time when I was feeling particularly—what's the word?—damaged. I didn't think I should be bringing a child into the world. I . . . I wrote about giving her up for adoption, I wrote about ending my life when I was pregnant, I wrote about, oh, God, getting an abortion. I actually made an appointment. Oh, for Maeve to see that. Oh, I was not in very good shape then. I wrote terrible things, terrible hurtful things. And about Clinton and what happened and—"

I looked at her, this woman who seemed to have everything but was as fragile as a fading flower. One touch and a petal falls.

"Maybe I can help you get it back,'" I said slowly. "And then we go to the police."

"How can you help?'" David said. He'd moved close to Maddie, arms around her, shielding her from the wind and everything else.

"I've had some experience," I said. "I'll talk to Clair. He's done this sort of thing, in the war and after. He's very good at it."

"And Roxanne?" David said.

"I have to tell her," I said. "We don't keep things from each other."

"So what do we do?" David said.

"I talk to them."

"And if they're okay with it?"

"You call the number, and we go from there."

"You're a good friend, Jack," David said, his wife tucked into him. "There aren't too many people who would do this."

For good reason, I thought, even as he reached across to me and held out his hand and we shook, David staring into my eyes.

He pressed his face against Maddie's.

"You see, honey. I told you it would be okay," he said, and he should have known better, because that was like thinking the storm was over as you sailed into its eye.

42

We went for a ride, the three of us, and we ended up at the turn-off where the Connellys' road reached the tip of a point. We pulled over and sat as the rain pelted the car and gulls rode the gusts, hanging in the sky like kites.

I said we had three options. Go to the cops now, leave David and Maddie to deal with it, or help them end the thing once and for all.

"So you believe them?" Roxanne said.

"Yes," I said. "I believe them completely. No way was she lying. It was like she was baring her soul. And he's trying to protect her."

"Maybe he killed Angel to protect his wife," Clair said. "Maybe he was sleeping with Angel and he wanted to protect his wife and himself."

"No," I said.

"Why not?" Clair said.

"He says he went to Matinicus with Sandy. Easy enough to check."

He handed me the phone. I got the number for the town clerk on the island, called, and got the number of the harbormaster. Dialed and he answered, an old man's voice. I said I was trying to catch up with a friend and thought he'd be staying on a mooring there. His boat was called *Escape*. The harbormaster said *Escape* wasn't there, hadn't been for a week. I asked what day that was, maybe I was a week off. He said it was a Thursday and Friday, a pretty good sea running, that the Hinckley was more rugged than he would have expected, what with its shallow draft.

I asked if he knew if David Connelly was aboard and he said no. "Saw the boat, heard a man on the radio."

I thanked him and hung up.

"Boat was there and he knows a man was on it, but doesn't know who it was."

There was silence as we processed that. It could have been Sandy.

"Sometimes you have faith in your beliefs about someone," I said.

"I was in there with Maddie," Roxanne said. "She said she couldn't believe any of this was happening. She's got nothing to do with it."

"And everything," I said. "She was just a kid. You could see how it could happen. You think it's a toy, pick it up, and bam. Your life is changed forever. One little squeeze of this metal lever."

We looked out as the windshield wipers wagged like someone's scolding fingers. The bay was filled with whitecaps and an odd, confused chop that seemed to come from all directions at once.

"I want to help them," I said. "I really believe them. And I think they need someone. They're like babes in the woods."

"I'm game," Clair said. "If we get the person who killed the girl."

"I don't want anyone hurt," Roxanne said. "Not now."

She looked at me and I knew what she meant.

"We'll be fine," I said. "We'll just try to keep them from botching it up and getting hurt themselves."

"What would I do?" Roxanne said.

"Take care of Maddie. Make sure she hangs together."

"What if it's somebody like this Mick fellow?" Roxanne said.

"So much the better," Clair said.

"That would be black and white," I said. "What you worry about is heading into something like the water out there. A million shades of gray."

It was a pager number. We were in the study, the same room where Maddie had pointed the gun. She was sitting on the couch, wrapped in a down quilt. David had dialed and the message said to punch in his ten-digit number. He did, and we sat there and waited. The phone rang and David picked up the receiver, hit the button to put the fancy phone on speaker.

The robot voice again. It said "Dial this number" and recited one, the area code nothing I recognized. David wrote the number on a pad. He dialed and waited and the phone rang and there was an answering machine, another digital voice. David left a message. He said he wanted to talk to the caller who had left the message at his house.

He hung up.

We sat in silence, all five of us, tense and drawn.

"It's a loop," Clair said. "They listen to the machine, type in their answer, record it off the computer, call, and play it to you. No human contact."

"But we need a human," I said.

"No," Clair said. "They do."

We looked at him.

"First thing you do," he said, "is convince them you're not desperate. You're having second thoughts. You're sick of the whole thing, maybe they can just have it. You convince them that what they're holding has a short shelf life, that it could lose value. That gives you leverage from the outset. That lets you set the parameters; you start to call the shots."

"But we do want it back," David said.

"Very much," Maddie said.

"You don't tell them that," Clair said.

"You've done it this way before?"

Clair hesitated, then nodded.

"With what?" Maddie said.

"It was a kid," he said. "A nineteen-year-old kid. A soldier."

"Did you get him back?" David said.

"Yeah."

"What happened to the people who had him?" Maddie said.

"Nothing good," Clair said.

"Did they go to jail?" David said.

"It wasn't a time or place where jail was an option," Clair said.

No one asked any more.

In the end, that was the plan: Have David seem like he might not pay at all. Then tell them Maddie wouldn't leave the Maine house and David wasn't leaving her alone. Make them come to us, rather than us go to Boston, so that it would be hard for them to slip away. If they balked, buy time.

We waited. Made small talk. Maeve came in to say good night. Her mother kissed her and the phone rang. Maddie shooed her daughter out.

David answered. It was the robot voice again. It said to go to a computer and go online. Go to AOL Instant Messaging. Sign on under the screen name "Fat Cat 33," password the same. Wait for instructions.

"Do any of you know how to do this?" David said after he'd hung up.

"I do," Maddie said softly. "Devlin showed me."

Did Devlin know Angel, I wondered. Could Devlin have gotten the journal?

We went to the computer on the big study desk. Maddie said IM was bookmarked. David went to the site and signed on. Within seconds the first message appeared. The online name was Maddie 666.

She was still on the couch. We didn't tell her.

David typed, waited for an answer, typed some more.

—THE BOOK IS SELLING FOR $250,000.

THAT'S NUTS.

—OK, THEN IT GOES TO THE MEDIA, TV. EVERY PAGE OF IT.

LET ME THINK ABOUT IT.

—NO THINKING. DECIDE NOW.

WHERE DOES THIS END?

—WHEN YOU BUY IT BACK. IT'S A FAIR PRICE.

WE'RE THINKING OF JUST GOING TO THE POLICE OURSELVES.

GET IT OVER WITH.

—YOUR LIFE WILL BE HELL.

David turned to me.

"They're right about that, you know," he said.

"Don't agree yet," Clair said. "Tell them Maddie's had enough of this. She doesn't want to continue."

David typed that. Waited.

—IT'S ALMOST OVER FOR HER. ONE LAST TRANSACTION.

"The balance just tipped," Clair said. "Now get them to come here."

—BE IN BOSTON TOMORROW MORNING.

CAN'T. MADDIE WON'T LEAVE BLUE HARBOR. I'M NOT LEAVING HER ALONE HERE.

—YOU HAVE NO CHOICE.

SURE I DO. I'M STAYING HERE.

—THEN IT GOES.

GO AHEAD. I CAN GET THE MONEY UP HERE, BUT IF YOU DON'T WANT IT

There was a pause. We waited for the response.

—WHEN?

David looked at Clair.
"Say eleven o'clock."
David did.

—SIGN ON AT ELEVEN FOR INSTRUCTIONS. I LIKE THIS PART. COULD BE A BESTSELLER:

I still see the blood, running out of him like some sort of hot syrup. My brother lying there looking up at me in disbelief. He said, "Maddie, what'd you do that for? I'm dying, Maddie. You shot me. Maddie, what did I ever do to you?"

—GREAT STUFF. YOU THERE?

David swallowed, tears welling up. He typed, *Yes.*

—A GOOD BEDTIME STORY FOR LITTLE MAEVE,
DON'T YOU THINK? I LIKE THE SYRUPY BLOOD PART.
BUY IT BACK OR IT'S SWEET DREAMS FOR YOUR LITTLE
GIRL. SHE'LL LIE IN BED AND WONDER IF MOMMY
WILL POP HER NEXT. OK?

David gave a silent gasp and looked at me. I nodded.

OK.

43

We went home that night. Roxanne wrote a report on her interview with Devlin, including the part about her hearing someone she believed to be David Connelly having sex in the house with someone who was not his wife. Also included was the reference to arguments between David and Maddie, and how Devlin said Maddie seemed emotionally unstable at times.

She turned to me.

"I have to include the rest of it," Roxanne said.

"When do you have to turn this report in?" I said.

"Not tomorrow," Roxanne said.

"Then we'll have time," I said.

"I hope so," she said.

"I mean, time to handle this part of it."

"I don't mean that," Roxanne said. "I mean time for us."

"We'll have time for that, too."

"I hope so," she said again. "Sometimes I feel like we're being swept along, that one thing leads to another and we have no control over any of it. You know, like dominoes that they line up."

"It'll be okay," I said and I wondered who I was trying to reassure—Roxanne or myself.

We slept fitfully, both of us awake part of the night. A car passed on the road at a little after three and I heard it stop. I got up and went downstairs and listened at the front window. I could hear men talking. Mick's buddies or a few locals with a twelve-pack? I went to the closet and took out my rifle and loaded it in the kitchen with shells from the box in the back of the silverware drawer. I went back to the window and sat in a chair, the rifle across my lap. A car door closed and the car moved slowly away, no lights showing.

I waited five minutes, listened to a barred owl, millions of crickets, the soft scratching of bats in the eaves of the shed. A tap at the back door.

I walked in my boxer shorts to the door and listened.

"Jack," Clair said.

I opened the door. He was standing there in jeans and a black T-shirt, his Mauser cradled in his arms.

"Just thought I'd let you know they're gone."

"How'd you know I was up?"

"I could hear you breathing."

I hadn't even heard him approach.

"Locals?"

"Maine plates, Budweiser cans."

"Didn't drop anybody off?"

"Just the empties."

"See you at seven, then."

"I think I'll take my truck, follow you down," he said. "It's all ready to go."

I knew what that meant. That Clair meant business, that he was bringing the tools of his trade. I went back to bed and listened to

Roxanne's soft breathing, felt the warm aura around her, put my arms around her and wondered if we were doing the right thing. And then it was six and yellow light was streaming in through the skylights like beams from heaven, and it was time to get rolling.

I still was wondering: Should I protect my own child, assuming there was one, or worry about somebody else's? Did David and Maddie need me, or did I need them and their dangling offer of a story?

And then the time to wonder was over. We were on the road, heading east on a glorious summer day in Maine, where the air was clean, the forests were pure, and the simple values endured. Maine, the way life should be. I wondered how many guns Clair had in his truck.

We led the way, over the Waldo County hills and east along the shore and over the Penobscot River, and east again. When we did see glimpses of the ocean it was blue-green and the sky was clear, puffy clouds hustled westward with the offshore breeze. When we rolled into Blue Harbor, the air was brisk and cool. Summer people in the village had sweaters tied around their necks by their sleeves, like they were being strangled by pastel ghosts.

I thought of Angel and her Hermes scarf. I wondered if the fabric would have cut her. I wondered just how strong you had to be to hold that scarf that tight for that long, And I wondered who among these people would do that, and why. For money? To hide an affair? And then the thoughts crept in. To stop an extortionist and keep a terrible secret? To keep your child from knowing that you weren't perfect, that you'd done a terrible thing?

And then we were there, passing through the gates and down the drive, and Maeve was hurtling across the yard to greet us. Some of my doubts evaporated and Roxanne squeezed my hand.

"That's who this is for," she said, and then we were out of the car, Clair's truck was pulling in behind us, and David and Maddie were coming out the door and the first domino had fallen.

Maddie had coffee on and pastries from the bakery in the village. David had been on the phone to his bank in Boston, had money wired to an account at a branch of a bank in Blue Harbor. At eight o'clock, David had called the local banker and said he was buying a boat and the owner was a bit eccentric and wanted cash on the barrel. The bank manager had said he didn't have two hundred fifty thousand in cash on hand, but he could get it for Mr. Connelly in a couple of hours. It came by courier. It went out the door of the bank in a beat-up duffel with the name *Escape* monogrammed on the top.

We took the Suburban with the blacked-out windows. Clair rode in the back.

At eleven we were back at the house. Katie, the au pair, took Maeve to story hour at the Blue Harbor Library, and from there they were going to lunch. We gathered in the study like we were waiting for the numbers to be called in a weird sort of lottery. David had the computer up and running. He signed on as Maddie 666, wincing as he typed his wife's name and the devil's number.

There was no one there.

We waited ten minutes. Still nothing. Fifteen and nothing. After twenty minutes I could see Maddie becoming more agitated as she speculated what this might mean.

"They've changed their minds," she said. "They've sent the stuff around. . . . How long do you think it will be, Jack, before the press starts calling. . . . This number is unlisted, David; but they'll call the foundation. What will they say to the receptionist? A reporter would have to say something, don't you think? What about when the receptionist says, 'And what is this regarding?' "

After a half-hour, David asked Clair what he thought. Clair said he didn't know, but he wouldn't walk away yet. David said he didn't plan to, but how long should we wait? We couldn't sit in front of this goddamn computer all—

And there it was.

Fat Cat 33.

44

—HELLO, FAMOUS CONNELLYS. YOU STILL THERE?

YES.

—GOOD. WANTED TO MAKE SURE YOU WERE SERIOUS.
IF NOT, I THINK WE'LL START WITH *THE GLOBE* AND
WORK OUR WAY DOWN TO THE REAL BOTTOM FEEDERS.
OR DO YOU STILL WANT TO DO BUSINESS?

YES.

—THEN GET IN THE CAR . . . MADDIE AND DAVID,
IN THE BMW. BRING THE PACKAGE. DRIVE TO THE
MOBIL STATION IN THE VILLAGE AND CALL THIS
NUMBER. DON'T USE YOUR PHONE FOR ANYTHING ELSE.

A number appeared and Fat Cat 33 signed off.

"They're going to lead you around for a while," Clair said. "Make sure you don't have police tailing you."

"We don't," Maddie said.

"You'll have us," I said.

"How?" David said.

"We'll need other cars," I said. "Clair's truck and—whose Toyota is that at the end of the drive?"

It was the au pair's, Maddie said. She'd taken the Suburban because Maddie didn't think the Toyota was safe. I asked if they had keys and they said yes. Clair said we'd better go.

Maddie said, "Does this mean they're actually here?"

Maddie and David left first, and then, after a minute, Clair followed. Roxanne and I waited another minute and headed out in the Toyota. When we reached the village, the BMW was parked at the Mobil station. Clair was parked in front of an art gallery across the street, the big pickup sidled in between a Mercedes convertible and a Lexus, a mastiff between poodles. I drove by and pulled into a restaurant lot just up the street. I adjusted the mirror to watch the Connellys while Roxanne went up to the door and read the menu. When she got back in the car, the BMW was pulling away. I backed out and we followed.

Clair brought up the rear, three cars back.

We drove under the elms, past the library where the Suburban was parked. I could see Maddie turn as though she wanted to go back and get Maeve and run. But David kept driving, out of the village and south down the peninsula. A mile outside of town, he turned right. I turned, too, hanging back.

I watched the mirror to see if anyone else had turned and there was one car, a Volvo wagon, and then Clair. I looked up to see that Maddie and David had pulled into a driveway. I continued past and the Volvo stayed with me. Clair was gone.

I drove a half-mile and stopped at a roadside vegetable stand. Roxanne looked out at the produce, then shook her head, as though the lettuce were wilted. I pulled out and headed back. In the distance

I could see Clair's truck. When we reached the intersection, the BMW was three cars ahead.

And so it went for more than two hours. Through Brookline and Sedgwick and over the Deer Isle Bridge. I called Clair in the truck and he told me he'd passed them, they were doubling back onto the mainland. I pulled into a camp road and turned around and waited. When Maddie and David drove by, they were looking straight ahead, their faces drawn, jaws set.

Back to Blue Harbor and over toward Castine. In Cape Rosier we came to the entrance to a wildlife preserve where we would be the only cars in sight. I figured this had to be it, this deserted place of deep woods and meandering paths. Roxanne dug a map from the glove box of the Toyota and found two places where the road through the preserve came out, and we skirted it and waited on the far side in the driveway of a farmhouse. After forty-five minutes, a woman came out of the house and started toward us.

The phone rang. It was Clair. They'd popped out on the other side of the preserve and were headed back toward Blue Harbor. We left the woman standing on the lawn.

Ten miles from Blue Harbor we passed Clair, pulled over on the side of the road. On the phone he said they were just ahead, and a mile beyond we spotted the BMW driving slowly on the twisting, climbing road. At a scenic turnoff atop a ridge, they pulled over and parked. We continued past and pulled into a yard outside a trailer. Clair called and said he was below them.

"Should we call them?" Roxanne said.

"They said no."

"What are they doing?"

"I don't know," I said.

"Where the hell are these people?"

"I don't know that, either," I said.

We sat. Clair called every half-hour or so, said the BMW was just parked. And after two hours and twenty minutes, four hours since we'd left the Connelly house, David and Maddie suddenly started the car and pulled away.

They passed us and we could see Maddie, weary and grim-faced. Clair passed and we counted to fifty and pulled out. In fifteen minutes we were back in Blue Harbor village. Maddie and David were on the road home. Clair called and said he figured there hadn't been anybody watching us for some time, but there would be when we reached the area of the house. He said he'd pull into another driveway and walk the shoreline until he had the Connellys' house in sight. He said to drive past their entrance and wait.

We did, sitting under a bank of cedars that lined the drive to someone's estate. The bay glistened in the distance, a field of diamonds, but who cared? We were hungry, thirsty, and tired. And then Clair again, saying Maddie and David were getting into the dinghy. They had the bag with the money. They were going out to one of the boats. The smaller one, the Boston Whaler.

"We've lost them," I said to Roxanne.

And then a car passed, a nondescript blue Chevy or something, two people in front.

"Oh, my God," Roxanne said. "Driving that car—"

"What?" I said.

"That was Monica."

45

We pulled out and followed, and in moments the possibilities were clicking into place. Monica and Angel in it together. Monica killing Angel for her share of the extorted money. Somebody else killing Angel, and Monica deciding to finish the job on the Connellys herself.

"Who else was in the car?" I said.

"I couldn't see," Roxanne said.

I sped along under the trees while Roxanne called Clair. He answered and she told him what we'd seen, where we were going. He said he'd be behind us. I sped up to try to catch the car, winding the Toyota through the curves as the road followed the shoreline.

We drove one mile. Two. The car wasn't in sight. I sped up and Roxanne said, "Slow down. There."

She pointed to our left, turned in her seat as we passed the entrance to a drive to an estate.

"They're in there. I could just see them."

"Turned around?"

"Driving in."

I stopped and turned around and Roxanne told Clair. We drove back to the entrance, and as we passed it, we peered in. The gates were stone. The brush was cut between the spruce trees along the road and there was lawn stretching to a big stone and stucco house, the water beyond it. You could drive over the lawn and between the trees, if you had to. There was no way to seal off the driveway.

We parked along the side of the road. Clair rolled up moments later and backed the truck into the trees. He got out and walked to the car and climbed in the back.

"So it's her friend," he said.

"Or someone else killed her and Angel left this thing behind," Roxanne said.

"I don't see Monica as a killer," I said. "I see her as a scavenger."

"Objective's still the same, right?" Clair said. "Get this book back? Hold on to these people?"

"And keep people from getting hurt," I said.

"On our side, you mean," Clair said.

"Whoever that is," Roxanne said, and she looked grim.

"You're having doubts?" I said.

"Yes," she said. "Because what if none of these people are what they seem?"

I didn't have an answer.

We needed somebody at the road, in case Monica drove back out.

Roxanne said she'd stay. We'd walk in and see where Monica was, who she was with, if the Connelly boat was in sight. I asked Roxanne if she'd be okay, and she said she would. I told Roxanne that if Monica came back to just drive off, fast, and go to the village. If there was an emergency, she should lean on the horn.

She squeezed my hand and I squeezed back and then we were out of the car. Clair walked back to the truck and opened the cab door and took binoculars from the glove box. He handed the binoculars to me and reached behind the seat. There were leather rifle scabbards hung from te seat back and he slid a shotgun out of one and closed the door and quickly walked into the trees.

I gave Roxanne a last look and followed.

We moved along the line of spruce and hemlock that marked the boundary with the next property. The sun was behind us, dropping lower behind the ridgetop tree line, and we were in shadow. I stayed in Clair's track, and when we neared the buildings—the house and garages and a small barn—he moved deeper into the trees and I followed. We stepped between the bare inner limbs, staying behind the dense outer boughs. When we drew even with the first outbuildings, we eased to the edge of the trees and watched.

The house was vacant, gray-painted plywood still screwed over the first-floor windows. There was a long private pier, the railings of a ramp barely showing, orange mooring buoys, but no boats. Monica's car wasn't in sight, but then it appeared, backed in alongside one of the garages. The brake lights flashed and the motor turned off. We could see two figures in the front seats. The heads turned as they talked. I focused the binoculars and saw the two silhouettes but couldn't tell who the passenger was.

We needed to get closer before it got dark.

Mosquitoes stirred from the trees as the sun dropped. They buzzed around our heads while the figures in the car bobbed. On the water, a lobster boat passed well offshore, the white hull glowing with the last light of the sunset. A big sailboat motored toward the harbor, a tiny yellow figure at the helm, a dinghy trailing behind like a little dog on a leash. No Boston Whaler in sight. In the car, Monica and her passenger momentarily were still.

"We need to see them," I said.

Clair said he'd circle along the shoreline and come up through the trees on the other side of the house, see if he could get a look at their faces. He began to move away and in a minute had faded into the trees.

I waited. Watched. Tried not to wave at the mosquitoes. I wondered if Roxanne was okay. I smelled smoke and saw a cigarette glow from Monica's side of the car. I looked at my watch. Clair had been gone for nine minutes, but it seemed like an hour.

It was two minutes after seven.

I looked back at the road. Heard a clattering sound.

It was a car moving fast down the drive toward the house, no lights, just a dark shape beyond the trees. And then it was in the open, a minivan, and it slowed in the place where the drive widened before the house. The brake lights went on in Monica's car and the motor started with a roar but the van swerved left, slinging gravel as it slid to a stop in front of the car. The van door whipped open.

A man leapt from the van, a black ski mask covering his face, a gun in his hand. He ran to the car as it started to back up, yanked open the driver's door, and pointed the gun in.

There were two pops, softer than firecrackers, then two more, two more after that. I remembered the binoculars and used them and looked. The guy drew the gun back out, reached in with his left hand, and turned off the motor. Then he shut the front door, opened the back. He leaned in again and I could see his arm moving, as he rummaged. After a moment he backed out of the car, a dark case in his hand. He closed the car door, opened the front door again, and leaned in and seemed to shove.

The bodies. He was pushing them over onto the seat.

And then he closed the door and trotted to the van, leapt in, and yanked the door closed. The driver, also masked, backed the van up, then circled into the drive and backed out, in the direction of the road.

I lurched to my feet, still in a crouch, and started through the trees. Branches slashed at my face and the binoculars swung on their strap. I dodged left and right between the limbs and trunks, and then I heard something.

Someone coming toward me. I eased behind a tree and waited, peering into the shadows. There was a snap, a branch cracked, and I saw a figure moving, the head weaving between the branches. I leaned down and groped for a limb and found one. Held it low along my leg and waited.

46

It was Roxanne. She was panting and there was blood running down her cheek from a long scratch on her temple. She saw me and said, "Oh, thank God," and crouched beside me.

"They killed them," I said softly.

"The men in the van? They killed Monica?"

I nodded

"Did they see you?" I said.

"Yes, as the van turned in, into the gates, the driver looked back and saw me in the car. He put on the brakes like he was going to stop, but I pulled out and drove the other way. And then I thought of you and I came back."

"What did he look like?"

"Big. It looked like his hair was reddish, but he was wearing a black hat, the knitted kind. It was hard to tell."

"Mick Egan," I said.

"I don't know."

"Did you see anybody else?"

"There was somebody in the back but it had those dark windows. I couldn't see anything else, just that there was another person."

"Vincent," I said. "He must've been the shooter."

"Where's Clair?" Roxanne said.

"Right here," came a voice from the trees.

Clair came toward us, the shotgun pointed at the ground.

"Did you see it?" I said.

He nodded.

"A real pro," he said.

"We need police. Did you look?"

"Yes. For a second."

"Who was the other person?"

"A blonde woman. Maybe fifty. Hair short, dark-rimmed glasses."

"Kathleen Kind?" I said.

"Why would she be here?" Roxanne said.

"They must have cooked this up together."

"Why would somebody kill them and leave?" Roxanne said.

"He took something from the car. Must have been the journal," I said.

"They jumped Monica and whoever else is in that car."

"Did you call the police?" I said.

"I tried," Clair said, "It didn't connect."

"Where's your phone?" I asked Roxanne.

"In the car," she said. "I can go get it."

"No, don't," Clair said. "I don't think they're gone. I think they went to check the road, see if you're still around. Where's your car?"

"In the next driveway."

"They'll see your truck, Clair," I said.

"That won't mean anything to them," Roxanne said.

"Prosperity, Maine, will," I said.

"The dump sticker," Clair said.

And then the muffled rattle of a car rolling, coasting, no sound of the motor. The van came rolling back down the drive, lights off, heading for the house. It made the circle then swung around on the far edge of the property, opposite Monica's car. We saw brake lights flash once, then nothing. They were sitting in the growing dusk, watching the water.

"They're waiting for David and Maddie and the money," I said.

"And if they killed these other two . . . ," Clair said.

"They've got to get off this peninsula and out of Maine," I said. "They're going to need time."

"Killing the Connellys buys them some," Clair said.

"Killing us," I said, "buys them more."

"But we can't just leave Maddie and David to be executed," Roxanne said.

"No," I said. "And we don't know if Vincent was dropped off at the road."

"I don't think so," Clair said. "But you never know."

We moved through the woods, very slowly, Clair in front, picking the path. When we were abreast of Monica's car, Roxanne stayed behind, tucked in a hollow beneath the draped boughs of a spruce like a fawn left by its mother. Roxanne was our backup, the one who would run for help. Clair and I wanted to get behind the van, which meant crossing the front of the property at the waterline, just below the rocky embankment at the shoreline. There was thirty feet of open lawn between the woods and shoreline, and we waited at the edge of the woods for a moment, then Clair went first.

He lay on his belly and crossed the grass like a lizard. When he'd slid over the edge of the lawn onto the rocks, I waited. Listened. There was no sound, no car door opening. I counted to ten and then slithered out and rumbled onto the rocks.

We crossed in a crouch, along the rocks, under the pier, stepping from stone to stone, looking for the darker patches of weed and mussels that would be wet and silent. It was slippery and we used our hands, scraping them on the barnacles. The tape was scoured from my splinted finger and I tore the splint off and left it in the rocks. And then we had crabbed along far enough, and were ready to go over the bank and up into the trees. I picked up a baseball-sized rock, big enough to break Mick's thick skull. Put a smaller one in my pocket.

Clair crouched behind me with the shotgun ready.

I turned to tell him I was going up and over—and there it was, coming around the next point. A green light, the starboard bow of a boat, a white light at its stern. It was a quarter-mile offshore, moving close, the outboard purring faintly.

"They're here," I said, as a car door opened above us.

"Too late to get behind them," Clair said. "Get down."

We crouched against the bank as the boat moved closer. I heard the sound of feet brushing through grass and then a figure appeared on the pier to our left. It was Mick. He walked out ten feet and pulled his mask down, adjusted it over his eyes, and flashed a light. One long. Two short. The lights of the boat moved closer, the white hull of the Whaler visible now but not the people on board.

We watched as Mick flashed the light again, and this time the signal was returned from the boat. Mick turned and walked back up the pier, turned back to the water, and spoke into a phone.

"Looking good, my friends," he said. "We had a change of players, but the plan's the same. I'll leave the item on the edge of the dock. You toss me mine. I'm going to stand on the dock and wait. I give it a quick check, you do the same. When both parties are satisfied that the terms have been met, we go home. Just like that. Nice, simple transaction."

We heard him open the van door and close it. There was no sign of Vincent, and I wondered if he was in the backseat, whether he could make that shot with a pistol, whether he had something better. Or maybe this was the deal. Take the money, leave the two bodies, and run.

The boat was fifty yards out now, moving closer. I could see David standing at the helm, a dark baseball hat pulled low. Maddie was beside him, gripping the console in front of the wheel. The motor burbled and the boat approached and soon I could see their expressions, tense and afraid. And then they were closer, and Maddie took the wheel and David bent behind him and picked up the duffel. He moved toward the bow and stood there with the bag in front of him, like he was waiting to get off a train. The motor idled and the boat drifted on the dark water and Mick crossed above us and walked onto the pier, down the ramp, and onto the float. He placed the dark case from Monica's car on the edge of the float and stepped back ten feet. The boat eased alongside and David reached down for the case, the boat still drifting. He unzipped the case and pulled out what looked like a notebook and riffled through it. Then he tossed the duffel toward Mick. It landed short and Mick bent to pick it up. He quickly unzipped the bag and dug through it. David had put the notebook back in the case.

And Mick pulled a gun from his waistband, said, "Sorry, Connelly. I changed my mind." But before he raised the gun, Clair called out, "Drop it, or I'll cut you in half."

Mick didn't drop it. Clair stood and fired one shot above the boat, fire spouting from the shotgun, a clap echoing across the water. He jacked another shell into the chamber.

"Last chance," Clair said.

Mick eased down, the gun in his right hand, held out by the barrel. He laid it on the dock and then he turned slowly.

"Jesus," he said through the mask. "It's fuckin' McMorrow. And he brought some muscle. I like you more all the time, Jack, you know that? You're my kinda people, McMorrow."

"Jack," David said.

"Oh, my God," Maddie said. "Oh, my God."

"What do you want me to do?" David said.

"Just sit tight," Clair said.

"Where's Vincent?" I said.

We'd eased up onto the lawn and were moving toward the pier. Clair had the shotgun at his shoulder and kept it trained on Mick.

"Vincent?" Mick said. "He doesn't like the country, Jack. He doesn't like bugs."

"I saw him kill Monica," I said. "And I think Kathleen Kind."

"Oh, no," Maddie said, and she started to sob.

"Where is he?" I said.

Mick didn't answer. David jumped out of the boat and fixed a bowline to a cleat, then scurried over and picked up Mick's gun. He fiddled with it and then pointed it at Mick.

"You killed her?" he said.

"Easy with that thing," Mick said. "You'll hurt somebody."

"Back away from him, David," I said. "Don't get too close."

We were walking down the ramp, Clair first, me behind him, still carrying my rock. Maddie was sobbing at the helm of the boat, both hands on her mouth, her whole body shaking.

Clair said, "Keep your hands right up there. Way above your head. Now lie down on your belly, hands still up."

Mick shook his head, said, "Just don't let this amateur shoot me. I think he's got the safety off."

"Down," Clair said. "One. Two—"

"You drop it," said a voice behind us. "Or I'll kill her right here."

47

It was Vincent, underneath the mask. He had his arm around Roxanne's neck, a pistol jammed against her throat. He was walking her across the lawn from the trees. They moved stiffly, like it was a three-legged race.

"Drop it, I said," Vincent screamed. "Lay it right down."

Clair lowered the shotgun. David dropped the pistol to his waist. Mick stepped up to Clair, took the shotgun from him, and turned and pointed it from the hip at David.

"You, too, moneybags," he said.

David did a knee bend and left the gun at his feet. Roxanne and Vincent were on the pier now, looking down at us. I could see that Roxanne was crying. I held the rock behind my back.

"It's okay," I said. "Just be calm."

"Sure, it's okay," Mick said. "Keep telling yourself that. Everything's great. Toss the rock in the water, Jack, and it'll be even better."

I did, and it made a deep *ka-plock* and a splash. Mick motioned for Clair and me to stand on the end of the float with David. It rocked gently as we walked. The boat bobbed up and down, the outboard still idling, Maddie trembling now, chewing on her lip.

PRETTY DEAD · 287

"Just like walking the plank," Mick said. "Just like pirate days. When I was a kid, I loved pirates. Read all about 'em. Blackbeard and Captain Kidd. Hey, Jack. We probably won't write my story, will we? Too bad, huh. Well, I gave you your chance. You decided to go with these rich assholes. Shanty Irish underneath, too, no matter how much you dress 'em up. That's what my dear mum used to say."

Vincent eased Roxanne along the ramp and stopped at the end.

"We'll keep her separate," Mick said. "Awful lot of work for two hundred and fifty grand, don't you think? I told Kathy there, I'm not going all the way up to Maine to pick up this merchandise for ten grand. You nuts? And I said, 'Lady, just 'cause you killed some little North End skirt doesn't mean you can push me around.' "

"Angel?" I said.

"My God," David said. "Why would she—"

"Hell if I know. But it's good to know who you're working for, I always say. I had to peel away a couple of layers and there she was. Nice-looking lady, too. Was she Swedish or something? Anyway, from what I can figure, Angel was squeezing you and it worked so good, she decided to squeeze the ice lady there, too. If I were you, I woulda kept a closer eye on the books. I think the ice lady was skimming. But for Angel there, it was a bad idea, this squeeze play number two. So if it had been up to me, the price woulda been half a million, at least. What's it to you, Connelly? You don't even know how much money you got. Worth it to keep the world from knowing you whacked your brother, right, Mrs. Connelly?"

"Shut up," David hissed.

"Hey, I didn't know what this was all about until just now, when I was sitting up in the car there, reading your little diary thing. Killing your brother—now that's gotta be heavy. I mean, me and Vincent, we're no altar boys, but we never killed anybody in our own family. I mean, that takes iron balls, except you ain't got any. Must have an iron—"

"Shut up, you filthy piece of shit," David said.

I reached into my pocket and eased out my rock.

"Sticks and stones, Connelly. I just want to know what it's really worth to you to get that book back. I mean, word gets out that your old lady here, she not only popped her brother, but she made him look like a pussy, too, with this suicide stuff. There goes the kid's rep. I mean, who would shoot himself in front of his baby sister? People musta thought he was a real wingnut, and turns out he wasn't. I mean, who thinks their little sister is gonna—"

"No," Maddie shrieked.

She had a flare gun, bright orange plastic, and pointed at Mick. Vincent said, "No," but she pulled the trigger. A pop and Mick shouted and put his hand to his face and something was hissing and burning on the deck of the float. Clair was on him, and Vincent fired once and the windshield on the boat shattered. Maddie dropped and Roxanne shoved Vincent and he grabbed her by the head and flung her against the railing. She fell hard and Clair fired and Vincent spun backward and crumpled, his gun flying into the water. Mick grabbed the barrel of the shotgun and Clair turned and kicked him in the groin but Mick held on, and I lunged for him but kicked the pistol along the deck and he dropped and grabbed it, still holding the barrel of the shotgun. I had him by the throat and he put the pistol to the side of my head.

Clair hacked at Mick's arm, and the gun turned and Mick fired, and a black hole appeared in Clair's shirt at his shoulder blade and he gasped and fell to his knees and I bulled Mick onto his back. I pounded his face with the rock and blood came from his mouth, his nose, and then he bellowed and got me in a bear hug, his blood on my face, and rolled both of us off the float against the boat.

The water was black and cold, an awful darkness, and I spun with Mick still hanging on to me, dragging me down. We hit bottom head-first and I needed to breathe and he was tearing at my shirt, kicking at me, pushing me down as he tried to claw his way to the surface. He went up first, his knees slamming my belly, my chin, and I spun and he kicked me in the spine and my legs went numb. I came up underneath him and he was thrashing, clawing at me, and then he hit something and went still. I shoved him away and paddled sideways, my lungs bursting.

And I hit something hard just as I was about to explode for breath. It was light and smooth, the bottom of the boat, and I clawed my way along it, fingernails scraping at the hull, and then I was out, into the air, gasping, sucking air in. One breath and back down I went, my legs hanging limply underneath me like sacks of sodden bones.

I clawed my way up and something sharp hit my head, cut it. I pushed away and the motor revved, the propeller churning the water, inches from my belly. I paddled back and hit the boat with my head, felt warm blood running down from my forehead.

I was on the far side of the boat, and couldn't see them. "Pull me up," I said. "Somebody pull me up."

The boat rocked, like somebody had just gotten off of it. Then it rocked again like someone had jumped on. Maddie leaned over and saw me but the boat was moving and I lunged upward, got a hand over the gunwale.

"Stop," I shouted. "Stop!"

And then I was falling away. The motor revved and the wake washed over me, black and cold but scalding at the same time, and I was scrabbling with my arms to keep my head up and the boat was leaving, then circling and coming back and another wake washed over me, into my mouth. And I coughed and gagged and said, "Help," and the bow brushed over me, and I grabbed for a ring on its underside and got a finger through it and held on.

The motor was idling, and I heard them.

"Those two are dead," David said. "The big guy never came up. Clair, he might not make it, and she's just lying there and—"

"David," Maddie said.

"Nobody has to know," David said.

"David, my God. What are you saying?"

"Two people dead over this? Angel, too, and Monica. My God, it'll be everywhere."

"Help," I said. "Get me out."

"Baby, I don't want this to happen to you. We'll go. We'll go to Mexico or Costa Rica or anywhere. I know people who can help us. You don't have to be blamed all over again. Nobody else has seen the journal, or this. Nobody else knows."

"David, I can't stand any more secrets. Mom and Dad, they tried to protect me, and look what—"

"It's going to be a nightmare, Maddie. A nightmare."

"It can't be any worse than the nightmares I've been having all these years, the nightmare I've been living."

"Maddie—"

"David," Maddie said. "You can't stop this. Get the ladder and get Jack out."

There was a pause where neither of them spoke and then I heard a clattering and a ladder appeared over the side of the boat.

"Get on the phone, Maddie," David said. "Call an ambulance. Call the police."

48

Roxanne was okay. Clair, not so good, but going to make it. Mick and Vincent died there on the shore of the bay, paying a price for breaking their own rule: You don't leave your turf. Monica didn't make it, but Kathleen Kind did, though as is the case with so many blessings, this one was mixed.

Her story, told to Cade and Sullivan in a hospital room at Mass General, was that David must have killed Angel—that Angel tried to get Ms. Kind to help her with a scheme to steal from the Connellys' foundation accounts. Angel threatened to have Ms. Kind killed by the Mafia when she refused and pledged to go to the police. Ms. Kind said it was Monica who found the journal in Angel's things. Angel found it in the Connellys' bedroom when she was there in bed with Tim Dalton, Monica said. She decided the best revenge was to bleed more money out of the Connellys and then let the secret out. Ms. Kind said she went to Maine with her hoping to dissuade her at some point along the way.

Ms. Kind didn't expect that Monica's criminal friends would show up, too.

That was the story for about a week. And then the bean counters found that Ms. Kind had been skimming from grant awards for years, a few thousand at a time, for a total of $420,000, and counting. The forensics people matched DNA from skin under one of Angel's fingernails with Ms. Kind's blood. Police went back to Ms. Kind, who by then was in physical rehab, and asked if she'd like to change her story.

She said no.

They said the DNA alone would hang her.

Ms. Kind said people like the Connellys had no respect for her, they used people like they were appliances, they didn't even really see her after all the years she'd worked so hard for them.

She was invisible, she said. And then she said she wanted to talk to her lawyer.

Cade said Ms. Kind was one cool customer, that you could almost see the wheels turning inside her shaved head.

Tim Dalton folded more easily. He admitted to sleeping with Angel at the Connellys' house in Blue Harbor, but said he hadn't hurt anybody. His wife didn't agree, and filed for divorce. Dalton said he didn't know Angel had taken anything from the Connellys' bedroom, but Cade and Sullivan were threatening to charge him with being an accessory.

As for Clair, he couldn't cut wood. The bullet had passed through his shoulder just under his collarbone and had damaged the muscle systems there. He was in physical therapy, working to raise his right arm above his chin. He said it was no big deal, and besides, if we hadn't gone along, the Connellys would certainly have been killed. I hobbled around with a cane for a few days, one leg still numb from the bang to my spine. The whole story came out, but I didn't write any of it.

Instead, with Myra's blessing, I gave three interviews, to reporters from the *Times*, the *Globe*, and the *Portland Press Herald*. I talked about David and Maddie, Mick and Vincent. Roxanne, with a special dispensation from the higher-ups, told the reporter about Maeve and Devlin. The above-the-fold headline in the *Globe* said HOODS, GRIFTERS, AND A TERRIBLE SECRET: SHADOWY FIGURES FROM PAST AND PRESENT HAUNT CONNELLY CAMELOT. In the *Times*, the headline was low on page one, all editions: CONNELLY SECRET TAKES FOUR LIVES, HAUNTS A FAMILY. The *Press Herald*'s choice: WEALTH AND POWER NO MATCH FOR A FAMILY SKELETON.

Maddie and David were interviewed at length. They said they regretted the tragic loss of life, but were glad to have the matter of Maddie's brother's death out in the open. Maddie said it had been a terrible burden to carry, all those years. She was photographed at the Boston house, in the third-floor study where I'd answered the phone that fateful night. Maddie said the lesson to be learned was that the truth is always preferable to a lie, even if the lie is told with the best of intentions. David announced that the Sky Blue Foundation would give $5 million to Boston Children's Hospital for the purpose of founding a center to treat children with psychological trauma.

I wondered if Maeve would be the first patient.

The Hampshire County district attorney said he would not prosecute, and considered the case of Clinton Archer Boswell to be closed. And in the end, I told only two people about the conversation the Connellys had on the boat while I was in the water.

Clair and Roxanne.

Clair said the same thing happened in war. A soldier ran or froze and caused a buddy to get hit. Did the first soldier call for help and admit his failure, or did he just turn and walk away, letting his shameful secret seep into the ground with his comrade's blood?

"In the end, David made the right decision," Clair said, the Zen in him coming to the surface. "The rest of it I'd forgive."

The Connellys asked for that, though not in those words. They wrote a note to us from Boston, said they were terribly sorry for getting us involved in any of this. They asked that we not think less of them, that we'd saved their lives and they were eternally grateful. I said I thought they were trying to do the right thing.

Not Roxanne. She'd just gotten back from the hospital. She was horrified that David would even think of such a thing. That he would consider even for a nanosecond leaving Clair to die, leaving her unconscious on the dock, leaving me in the numbing water to drown. It wasn't just us, she said, as we stood in the kitchen in Prosperity that night. It was our child.

"Are you sure?" said.

"Yes," Roxanne said. "When I went in for my head, I told them maybe I was, and they did the test."

"Oh, boy," I said.

"Or girl," Roxanne said.

I held her and kissed her and she wrapped her arms around me and held me tight for a long time. I could hear crickets and night sounds and I could feel Roxanne's heart beating and it was like the world was teeming with life, and here was one more. Where once there had been none, we had created someone. In the midst of all this death, there was a new life.

"You know what's scary?" I said.

"What?" Roxanne whispered.

"That you can't really protect this person you're bringing into the world. Not all the time, not from everything. And then you're gone and they're on their own."

"That's okay," Roxanne said.

"Think of Maddie's family and all of this mess."

"You just do your very best," she said.

"We'll do that."

"That's right, Jack McMorrow. And the rest we'll just have to take on faith."

"In us," I said.

"And that the world is basically a good place," she said. "It's just some people who aren't."

"Not everybody," I said, "is an angel."

ABOUT THE AUTHOR

Gerry Boyle is the author of a dozen mystery novels, including the acclaimed Jack McMorrow series, and the Brandon Blake series. A former newspaper reporter and columnist, Boyle lives with his wife, Mary, in a historic home in a small village on a lake. He also is working with his daughter, Emily Westbrooks, on a crime series set in her hometown, Dublin, Ireland. Whether it is Maine or Ireland, Boyle remains true to his pledge to send his characters only to places where he has gone before.